CONTENTS

Title Page	3
A Prologue... Of Sorts	7
Chapter 1	9
Chapter 2	18
Chapter 3	34
Chapter 4	48
Chapter 5	69
Chapter 6	89
Chapter 7	105
Chapter 8	118
Chapter 9	128
Chapter 10	138
Chapter 11	151
Chapter 12	165
Chapter 13	182
Chapter 14	205
Chapter 15	217
Chapter 16	236
Chapter 17	250
Chapter 18	261
Chapter 19	269

Chapter 20	282
Chapter 21	296
Chapter 22	306
Chapter 23	317
Chapter 24	330
Chapter 25	340

SALEP AND GINGER

JANE GÜNDOĞAN

Due to strong language and sexual content, this book is
not intended for readers under the age of 18.

Copyright © 2019 Jane Gündoğan

All rights reserved

For Marisa.

You taught me that the importance of a bottle of wine should never be underestimated or overlooked. And cheese. Cheese should never be overlooked either.

And to Hugh John Mungo Grant. Because goddamnit I just love you.

A PROLOGUE...
OF SORTS

I had never really been in love, or even in a serious relationship, for that matter. Still, I remained a hopeless romantic, spending hours daydreaming about the moment when I would finally meet my one true love.

The leading lady of my very own romantic comedies, me and my dream man would both reach for the last pair of pyjamas, or maybe I would break the heel of my Gucci shoe while sauntering down a Manhattan street. All the packages I was holding would fly into the air as my arms flailed and I teetered to the side on my way to slamming into the concrete below, but then strong arms would catch me. Our skin would meet as his grip tightened around my waist and an electric pulse would race through my body even before I looked up into his aqua-blue eyes.

In my fantasies, all senses were heightened. Smells were sweet and potent, sound was laced with a tinkling of crystal, and sight... oh, sight... I would drink in every glittering drop of his sparkling eyes and luscious blonde hair and my breath would hitch as I stared at his pillowy, pink lips. The corner of his mouth would turn up, deepening the dimple in his cheek as he smiled a crooked smile down at me. Then, he would open his mouth. "Hello." That's all it took for my pulse to beat wildly and adrenaline to rush through my veins releasing satisfying endorphins into my blood stream.

Inevitably, the phone would ring or a horn outside would blare, or something equally jarring would rip me from my rom-com leading man. Cold emptiness would replace the space he had filled only moments before and the fantasy would be over. Until next time…

In reality, I didn't actually own a pair of Gucci's, and had honestly never sauntered down any street, let alone in Manhattan. I didn't care though because my daydreams always produced the perfect meet-cute, and they were… electric.

By the time I reached my late 20's my idea of finding true love had become somewhat jaded. I mean, it really should have happened by then, shouldn't it? I dated. A lot. Some nice guys, and a few not so nice, but sadly, none turned out to be the one. And then, when I had just about given up, I finally got to have my very own meet-cute moment, and to quote a rather famous rom-com, he "had me at hello." Until he didn't.

Let me explain.

CHAPTER 1

Cue Dramatic Flashback

It was New Year's Eve, and all I wanted to do was order a pizza and curl up on the sofa with a glass of wine, well, alright, let's call it what it is, a bottle of wine (pfft who was I kidding really), and see in the new year with Mr. Hugh John Mungo Grant tripping awkwardly across my television screen.

And before we go any further, don't think me some kind of dolt for my love of the romantic comedy genre. After a long day, I don't want to come home and watch Bruce Willis beat the bollocks out of someone, and Oh my God have you switched on the news lately? No, thank you.

I want to lie on my sofa and watch a foppish Englishman fumble his way around London in the pursuit of love, or maybe a slick sports agent begin his life again and learn how to love with the help of a cute kid and Bridget Jones (before she was Bridget Jones, that is). I want to see a light-hearted romance all neatly packaged into ninety minutes and know that when the credits roll at the end of the film there is a happily ever after.

But getting back to the story at hand.

New Year's Eve is that one night that always seemed to end

up being a total disaster, full of vomit, tears, and regret — and that was just me! So, no thank you! I'd much prefer to stay home with my dapper Englishman and a pizza.

My best friend, Tash, knew full well my aversion to any New Year's Eve shenanigans and usually left me alone, but that particular New Year's Eve she had other things in mind.

She had spent an hour trying to convince me that all my disappointments of that past year, or should I say, the past twenty-seven years up to that point, as well as all my embarrassing moments, dead plants, burnt dinners, and regrettable encounters, could be cast aside, and I would go forth into a fabulous new phase of my life, if I only attended this one party. According to her, if I made an appearance, all my worries would be over, and at the stroke of midnight, I would magically be transformed into a new me, lose ten kilograms, win the lottery, and meet my dream guy. All in one fantastic evening!

Of course Tash would have this new and bright outlook on life. After telling me how wonderful my life "could" be if I just did this or that, she dropped the best friend bomb. She had met the Man Of Her Dreams — in capitals no less — and said "MOHD" was having a party. Message received. She needed her BFF (sorry for all the acronyms!) by her side for support because supposedly, all his friends were pretentious wankers. She made me promise to come. And I did love her to death. So yeah, I was going to that party whether I wanted to or not. Tash knew she'd owe me big time for this one!

I looked down at my rumpled cotton shirt and sweatpants. My Fairy Godmother was going to need one hell of a powerful wand to spruce me up so I could ring in the New Year right. Ugh! I dragged myself off the sofa to get to work.

And that's how I found myself, along with tens of thousands of others, all making our way harbourside to watch the New

Year's Eve fireworks. Sydney was famous for its fireworks, but I would still have preferred to watch them from the comfort of my sofa, rather than dealing with the crowds converging on Sydney Harbour.

I finally found MOHD's building and rolled my eyes at the throbbing music that was blasting topside. I was tempted, so very tempted, to hail a taxi right then and disappear into the night, but I didn't, mainly because it would be impossible to find a taxi, but also because I had made a promise to Tash. I would do just about anything for her, including drag my ass across Sydney on New Year's Eve.

In the polished metal of the lift doors before me, I took the time to take a little inventory while it slowly made its way to ground level. Even though I threw my style together at the last minute, I looked pretty damn good, despite the swishy bits around my middle.

I channelled a young Jennifer Lopez in skin-tight jeans, a black cami and some chunky jewellery, and I was so very proud of myself for not tripping once, yet, in my new pair of fabulous spiked heels. The cami did the job it was designed for, and drew attention to my best assets, my boobs. Definitely more than a handful, my girls always got their fair share of attention when they were out for the night; meanwhile the jeans gave my butt the lift that it desperately needed. Bonus my corkscrew curls and olive skin, courtesy of my Sicilian grandmother, had actually played nice tonight. No humidified frizz to my usually unruly hair and not a pimple to be found. I checked my teeth, pushed a stray curl back behind my ear, and fixed a smile at my reflection. Go, Ginger, go!

When the lift doors finally opened, a perfectly-proportioned couple appeared before me, wrapped amorously in each other's arms. Only the woman pulled away to see who the new addition was to their joy ride. She gave me a quick once-over, smirked and returned to swapping spit with her man, no doubt miffed that they had to share their next precious minutes travelling to the top floor with some nobody like me. Next to them I suddenly felt distinctly frumpy in my jeans and cami. I tried not to look like I cared as much as I did.

And that's why I should have stayed home with Hugh! Seriously! I would've rather thrown myself into a shark-infested ocean than have stepped into the lift with those two, but I did, because, well, Tash needed me.

I went to press the floor number and realised the couple had pressed every single button! All thirty-four freaking floors!

"Really? You couldn't just get a room, you have to use the public lift as your sexcapade venue?"

The guy lifted his eyes to mine while he kept right on snogging his date and didn't even flinch when I made a gagging sound. Disgusting. But was it, or was I jealous? They were both supermodel gorgeous. I guess I'd bang in a lift too if I looked like either of them.

We began to ascend to the penthouse, his hand snaked down over her ass and disappeared under her impossibly form-fitting minidress. He hitched her leg up around his hip and while he spun them, I caught a glimpse of his raging hard-on. Not even his skin-tight leather pants could conceal it. Floor after floor, the supermodels panted and moaned as they dry-humped beside me. I did my best to pretend I was fixing my hair in the reflection of the polished metal wall, unaffected by them, when really I was fifty-percent mortified and fifty-percent, shall I admit it, turned on.

Ugh — awkward situations. Somehow, I always found myself in awkward situations.

In my head, I did multiplication tables (you know, 1 x 1, 1 x 2) to take my mind off the live sex show happening beside me. By the time we reached the penthouse, I was at 6 x 4 and had unwittingly experienced my first threesome, even though officially I wasn't part of the "some."

Finally, the doors opened to reveal MOHD's penthouse apartment in all its ostentatious glory. My threesome buddies stepped out into the vacuous entry and were immediately welcomed by more beautiful people, while I stepped out — and was promptly ignored, this time by an entire room of people. Invisible. That was me. Too normal to even be noticed, except for when I was having a bad hair day, but of course then I was noticed for the wroooong reason.

I scanned the crowded room for my bestie who was nowhere to be seen. Bugger! Spotting the nearest waiter I grabbed a glass of Prosecco and chugged half of its contents in one mouthful. Liquid courage.

Handing back my glass I wandered out onto the terrace. Wow! The view was pretty spectacular. From the Opera House and Botanical Gardens to the Sydney Harbour Bridge and North Shore beyond, most of the city was lit up and ready to celebrate the new year. There were hundreds of boats on the water, and tens of thousands of Sydney-siders on the foreshore, all jostling for the best vantage point of the fireworks at midnight.

Around me the terrace was jam-packed with groups of people dancing, including my threesome buddies whom, despite still having the slight blush of afterglow about them, had resumed dry-humping against each other, but now they were doing it in time with the deafening music. I still hadn't found Tash, and it was at that moment that I realised I had no idea what MOHD looked like or even his name for that matter, so I found a seat and pretended to check all my critically essential messages on my mobile. Of which, I had none. Naturally.

I guzzled down the rest of my drink and messaged Tash. I told her I had come, then left, and I crossed my fingers that I would find a taxi or even a bus, in the hope that I would make it home before midnight.

Then I saw him.

Any thoughts of leaving the party vanished. He was stunning. Of course he was stunning. He was a Chris Hemsworth clone, all blonde hair and chiselled jawline. Yep, this was one gorgeous specimen of a man, and it wasn't just me who thought so, as half the room was watching him as well. By the amusement in his eyes, and his puffed out chest, he damn well knew it too. For a moment, I wondered if this was Tash's MOHD. If he was, then Tash was the luckiest fucking girl in the world.

Hot Chris Hemsworth clone sipped on his beer, and I found myself wondering what it would be like to have his lips on me rather than on that lucky, lucky bottle of Heineken. I sat back and watched girls circle around Thor, like lions stalking their prey. He smiled at one or two, but you could tell his focus wasn't on them at all. His eyes scanned the crowd searching for that elusive someone. I looked around, wondering who it would be, secretly wishing it was me, when suddenly, his piercing, blue eyes locked with my hazel, but sometimes green depending on my mood, eyes. Wait! Me? Why was he looking at me?

My cheeks turned blazing hot, and my heart literally stopped as we stared at each other from across the room. And then, I forced myself to do the most un-Ginger Knox thing imaginable. I smiled at him. He grinned back at me, cocked his head to the side, and raised the beer in his hand. I nodded, so he grabbed another bottle and, still grinning, crossed the room toward me. And the closer he got, the better he looked.

I was instantly the recipient of nasty girl-glares from half the women in the room, but who cared when the corner of his mouth tipped up into a broad grin. A grin meant for me. His white t-shirt clung to his broad shoulders perfectly and his blue jeans sat below his hips at just the right angle, hugging, what was no doubt, a great ass. He moved through the crowd, dodging people who tried in vain to get his attention until he was standing right in front of me. He handed me the beer and our fingers touched. It wasn't electric, not like in my rom-com styled fantasies, anyway. It was something else. It was as though we were destined to meet each other and, at that moment, I mentally thanked Tash for guilting me into being there, in that room, at that moment.

Neither of us spoke. We just stared at each other, both of us holding onto that bottle of beer, grinning stupidly.

And then, reminiscent of that wretched movie (but doing it so much better than Tom Cruise), he bent down and whispered into my ear, his hot breath on my neck sending a shiver down my body.

"Hello."

I opened my mouth to reply, but before any sound came out, he pulled me out of my seat and crushed his mouth down on mine. Mother of all holiness, Thor was kissing me.

And although I would usually never do anything this bonkers, in public no less, I lifted my arms around his neck just as his tongue met mine. The kiss was demanding and his tongue plundered my mouth. He pulled his mouth away from mine with a loud smack and moved his lips to my neck, then my cheek before finally slipping his tongue in my ear. My lady bits swelled with a hot flush, and I wondered whether I might get to see Thor's hammer before the night was over.

This doesn't ever actually happen in real life, does it?

"I was looking for you." His whisper tickled the hairs on my neck.

I sighed. "Kiss me again, Guy I Don't Know."

Could this be my very own meet-cute of my very own romantic comedy?

He pulled away to look down at me but didn't release me from his arms. "Maybe I should introduce myself then. Hi. I'm Henry, Henry Hennessy."

My brain chose that moment to shut down, and all I could do was stare up at Henry / Thor / Chris Hemsworth clone, and wait for it to re-boot. You see, I'm not the girl who would typically ever kiss a complete stranger. In fact, I'm usually so awkward around the opposite sex that I have been known to stumble into walls and trip over air when trying to make my escape. I'm also uncomfortable around new people, which often impedes my brain from turning thoughts into actual words, like right now.

He stared down at me with the strangest look on his face. I mean, he was still stunning, but he also looked a little apprehensive, undoubtedly wondering if he had chosen a bunny boiler.

Reboot completed, I cleared my throat and found my voice. "I'm Ginger."

"Nice to meet you, Ginger. I'm going to kiss you again, now."

And he did. And it was amazing.

Henry swept me off my feet. Literally. He wrapped me in his arms and whisked me out of the party. We spent that first night together wandering around Sydney Harbour, talking about anything and everything, laughing at the drunken antics of New Year's Eve revellers around us. By dawn, I was well on the way to being head over heels in love with my Nordic god.

And whoever said that they hated New Year's Eve (aka me), well, they just didn't know what the hell they were talking about because it's actually the best night of the whole freaking year!

CHAPTER 2

Life... Interrupted

So I got my happily ever after... fade to black... credits roll...

Hold on, hold on... before you go any further, go grab yourself some popcorn, or pour yourself a glass of your favourite plonk (I know I would), because like any great rom-com, nothing was quite what it seemed.

Fast forward fourteen months and we were still together (my longest ever relationship). Henry had been offered his 'dream job' in London, and so, with the help of Henry's very English and practically perfect in every way personal assistant, Charlotte Poppleton, we were living on the other side of the world, in a very natty one bedder in Bayswater, which was just one tube stop on the Circle line to Notting Hill.

The real Notting Hill!

And for those of you who were wondering there *is* actually a blue door but sadly William Thacker does not live there (I know, I knocked), but I was definitely well on my way to becoming the leading lady of my very own romantic comedy.

Sadly though, London didn't welcome me with open arms. I imagined that I would arrive at nothing short of a street parade, find the most amazing job and become Meghan Markle's bestie. I would spend my free time exploring the market on Portobello Road searching for antiques, some genuine, and some… not so genuine, and live happily ever after with my leading man, or at least my very own (and more often than not these days) grumpy (because he was under so much pressure) man. It didn't quite pan out like that, though. Sure, I found a job, but the commute was a sixty-minute killer. Portobello Road markets weren't quite as, ahem, eclectic as I had imagined. I hadn't become besties with Meghan, in fact my friends were mostly Henry's friends, but none of that mattered, because I still had my guy, and he still had me at hello.

When Henry presented me with his grandmother's engagement ring on Christmas Day, the proposal was an uneventful disappointment. In fact, he didn't ask me to marry him, he just handed me the ring box and said, "This is forever, Gin."

I slipped the ring on my finger, and we went about our day preparing Christmas lunch. Our maybe-not-so-perfect romcom went on as usual. It might not have been the ideal proposal, I mean, could I even call it a proposal at all? But when the credits start rolling at the end of a movie real life goes on, doesn't it?

And then, on a surprisingly sunny February afternoon, my now slightly indifferent romance fell apart because I had decided to play hookey from work.

You see, since Henry handed me his Grandmother's ring, things had been a little strained. It was completely understandable, as Henry's job was incredibly hectic (I think) and his workload was brutal (apparently). We didn't see a lot of each other, thanks to his crazy hours and my long commute.

Weekends away were cancelled, romantic evenings were postponed, and time together had become practically non-existent.

I missed the old Henry, that Nordic god that had swept me off my feet, but he didn't seem to exist anymore. I knew there was something wrong. I wasn't in complete denial, but nothing could have prepared me for the implosion of our relationship on that surprisingly warm, February morning.

Henry wasn't expected home until late. He had been in New York, and caught the red-eye back to London arriving early that morning but, rather than coming home, he went straight to the office.

Meanwhile, I had planned to woo him with dinner followed by a good old-fashion romp in the bedroom. I had just left Tesco loaded down with bags of shopping and crossed over to the park when my mobile rang. Henry's face popped up on my screen and, as always, I grinned at the photo of him staring back at me, all handsome in his William Hunt three piece which cost him more than I spent on my first car, his sandy, blond hair slicked back and his blue eyes smiling back at me.

"Hey babe, are you home yet?"

"No, no. What about you?"

Not wanting to ruin the surprise, I fibbed. "Nope. I'm stuck in the office. I've got a mountain of work ahead of me."

"Oh? Okay. Great, good."

"How was the trip?"

"Fine. Boring. I missed you."

"I missed you too. It's been a dull week of rubbish TV and take-away for me."

"Sounds disgusting. Listen, I'm about to go into a meeting. Can we chat later?"

"Of course. Oh, wait! Before you go, Julia wants to know if we are going to make it to their engagement party next week."

"What? Do we have to talk about this now?"

"I need to let her know. It's in Portsmouth, so probably best if we book a room for the night as well."

"Christ!" he snapped at me. "Not now, Ginger. I'm fucking swamped."

"No need to speak to me like that."

"For God's sake."

It's safe to say our honeymoon period was over before we'd even had the wedding! "It was just a question. Calm down."

"Don't tell me to calm down."

I sighed. I knew full well that Henry was about to impose one of his holier than thou, I am the centre of the world, lectures on me.

"You just don't seem to understand the kind of pressure I'm under, Ginger. I need you to be a little more supportive and help me. That's why I expect —"

"That's why you expect what?" Of course, in that moment, he could have said "that's why I expect my staff to get shit done efficiently," or "that's why I expect you to do everything for me," or "that's why I get to stomp all over you every day" and it would have made complete sense, because that's what he did.

He grunted, and in my mind's eye I could see him at his desk, cracking his knuckles in a manner that I knew full well was his way of dealing with tension or frustration. It was usually caused by me.

"Listen, I've just walked back into the office, and Angus informed me that our current acquisition is below the bar, so I'm back trying to explain my actions to the Board. I'm surrounded by imbeciles, and you want me to tell you if I want to go to Ben and Julia's party? I don't give a damn whether we go or not. Make a decision and deal with it. Sometimes I really wonder whether you care about me at all."

And sometimes I hate you, Henry.

I took a deep breath. "Fine, leave it with me."

There was a knocking sound from Henry's end of the line that almost drowned out his question. "So you're going to be late tonight?"

"Yep."

"Great. Me too."

"Okay, I'll see you later then. Love y-."

He'd already hung up.

Well, at least I didn't have to cook now.

Just then, the phone rang in my hand. Henry? He must have been ringing back to apologise.

"Babe?" I waited for Henry to reply, but there was nothing. "Henry?" He must have butt-dialled me.

I'm not proud to admit it, but I stood there on that walkway in the park, stupidly trying to listen to what was most likely papers shuffling and background noise. I mean, he was at work, but I still stood there with my phone plastered to my ear until —

"...she's going to be..." Henry's voice was muffled by the swish and sway of his phone rubbing against the fabric of his pocket.

"This is getting... I'm not waiting... you said it was over..." A woman's voice faded in and out as Henry's phone bounced around in his pocket, but it sounded an awful lot like his thoroughly perfect PA, Charlotte Poppleton.

And what precisely was over?

"Come here."

Now, that was definitely Henry.

I put down the shopping, plugged my other ear and pressed the phone against the side of my face as hard as I could to try and hear the conversation, but there was just too much distortion. But I didn't hang up. Instead, I stood there eavesdropping on my fiancé until it happened, and I heard the words that changed my life forever. "I'll never finish falling in love with you."

What. The. Very. Real. Fuck???

There I was, standing in the park, surrounded by happy people going about with their happy lives, and I had just discovered that Henry was cheating on me. I mean, I thought Henry might be cheating on me. But of course, Henry would never cheat! Would he? I must have misheard. I mean, there was no way that could be real. Not really real. Despite the telephone call, and the fact that my spidey senses were on high alert, I knew that underneath the power suits and occasional selfish behaviour, Henry was a pretty decent man. There was no way he would really cheat on me. He loved me, and I loved him.

But he wasn't the same Henry, was he? He'd changed. My family did try to warn me about Henry. I wondered whether they might've been right. Was Henry really cheating on me?

Regardless of what my heart told me, that annoying voice in my head that seemed to control most of my actions had gone into overdrive, so by the time I made it back to our flat, I realised it was all true. Of course Henry was cheating on me. It had all made sense. He had been a little "off" the last few weeks. Working late. Agitated. I could even say he was secretive. And lets be honest, our sex life had been pretty much non-existent for months. He was tired. All the time. The clues were there. I was just too blind, or maybe too complacent, to admit the truth.

I opened the front door and dropped the shopping on the kitchen island, which was, before today, was where I would enjoy a glass of wine while watching Henry get his chef on. (I've always had a bit of an masturbatory crush on Gordon Ramsay. He's so foul-mouthed and competent. A lethal combination.) I ignored our bespoke suede sofa that Henry had ordered for our living room that was so cozy we would sink into it and snuggle amongst the pillows that I had painstakingly chosen from that tiny shop on Golborne Road. I glared at the fireplace that Henry would have, at one time, lovingly stoked to keep us warm on a winter's night. And I cursed the sixty-five-inch flat screen that Henry said he bought for me, but really wanted it for himself so he could watch his favourite football matches in ultra high-definition. I did, however, smirk at the half-empty mug that seemed to have left a nasty ring on his coffee table, a reclaimed piece of vintage wood that was custom made. Normally, I would have been frantic about Henry's reaction to the ring on his precious table, but at that moment, I wasn't concerned with cleaning up or even getting yelled at. I was more interested in finding evidence that Henry was cheating.

Now, I'd watched enough episodes of Criminal Minds to know that the smoking gun was always found on the unsub's ("unknown subject" for you non-CM viewers) laptop, so I made my way down the hallway to our bedroom to see if Henry had left his on his desk, but as I reached the dark, panelled door, something made me stop. The hairs on the back of my neck were at full attention. I didn't know what to do. Then I heard it.

Muffled, but very real moans. Sexy moans. The "I'm having the best root of my life" moans.

Henry?

No!

Is he actually screwing her here?

In our bed?

No! He wouldn't!

I knew that whatever happened in the next few moments would be life-altering. For better or for worse. It was either Henry, and we would have it out, or it was a deranged killer who was probably wanking himself over my fleecy pyjamas, and I would be fish food (again way too much Criminal Minds). At that moment, I was hoping for the deranged killer.

I took a deep breath and opened the door.

With the curtains drawn it was pitch black, but the moans didn't stop, in fact now that I was in the room with the moaning. It was infinity louder and, joy of joy, in unison with a female joining in.

"Don't stop baby. Please don't stop."

Long moan.

"Yes, yes, like that, do it like that."

"Oh, God. You taste amazing."

Henry.

I stood there for a moment, dumbfounded, and frankly a little pissed as well, as my eyes tried to focus in the darkness. They were so caught up in their screwing they seriously didn't even realise I was standing there!

I hit the switch, flooding the room with light. There he was. My Henry. Ass in the air, with his head buried between the legs of a very enthusiastic blonde who, I guessed, went by the name of Charlotte-fucking-Poppleton.

And here's the thing, despite my horror at the sight of Henry going down on his PA — who had some seriously gigantic nipples — what upset me the most, was that he was doing it on my brand new white, cotton sheets.

Perhaps I was in the midst of some kind of dissociative break and attempting to block out my shock, because at that moment those damn sheets they were the only thing I gave a hoot about. As white as the purest snow, they were Egyptian cotton eight-hundred thread count sheets, and they cost me a bomb. All I knew was that this woman's no-doubt pert bum was having, what appeared to be, a fabulous time. On my sheets. My perfect sheets. They meant nothing to me now and judging by my apathetic reaction to my fiancé feasting on another woman's muff, it was becoming clear that perhaps Henry didn't mean an awful lot to me either. I mean, this never happened in Jerry-Fucking-Maguire!

I watched as Henry pulled his face out from the blonde's tidy muff and blinked, frantically trying to focus in the light. "Ginger?"

"Hello." The irony of saying "hello" wasn't lost on me, but my deadpan tone echoed in the room as I watched him scurry off the bed, his hard-on deflating rapidly. He grabbed his tighty-whities from the floor missing the leg hole twice while jumping around trying to pull them on. "No need to cover up, dear Henry. I've seen it before."

"You said you were working late."

He didn't even look worried about being caught. Annoyed? Maybe. Embarrassed? Probably. Relieved? Definitely.

"Did I? Well, I lied. Guess that makes us both liars, doesn't it?"

He nodded, his shoulders slumped slightly, finally having had the decency to look the tiniest bit chagrined for his cunty actions. "Right."

"I think we need to have a bit of a chat." I couldn't understand how I managed to stay so calm when I was simultaneously fantasising about grabbing his nine iron and beating the crap out of him with it.

"It's not what it looks like."

"It's not?"

"No."

"Well, it looks like you were going down on this, this..." I turned and looked at the creature that was still spread-eagle on my sheets. "... I'm gonna taking a wild crack at it here. Are you Charlotte?"

Thankfully, she chose that moment to shut her legs, so I no longer had to exam her vulva before she replied. "Yes and I'm truly sorry about all of this unpleasantness."

Charlotte-fucking-Poppins (a slip of the tongue... but this will forevermore be her name). I had never actually met Henry's clearly not so proper but terribly whorish personal assistant (something about the security and privacy of their clients) but I recognised her voice immediately — and now I recognised her vulva as well.

"Wow, what a cliché!"

Henry shrugged, but wisely chose to not open his mouth.

I turned my attention back to Henry's PA / whore, still lolling in my bed, and smiled as brightly as I could. "Charlotte, sweetie, I mean it's lovely to meet you and all but would you mind getting the HELL OUT OF MY HOUSE?"

She scrambled off the bed and wrapped my gorgeous, but forever soiled, eight-hundred thread count top sheet around herself like it was a damn Versace gown, yet she made no effort to leave. Instead, she stood defiantly in front of me, all smudged mascara and chin rash from Henry's five o'clock shadow, showing absolutely no remorse despite having been caught in the throes of passion with her boss — and my fiancé!

"Is she a bit simple? You didn't hire her for her brain did you?" I directed the questions to Henry, but he just stared at me, the shock of the situation apparently rendering him catatonic.

I fought down an overwhelming impulse to slap her smug, and

probably Botox-filled face. "Bitch! What did I just say? LEAVE! And give me back my sheet, you disgusting cow!"

I stepped toward her and grabbed the sheet, leaving her bare-ass naked in front of me. Her nipples were staring at me again, more enraged than ever. Judgmental nipples.

She turned to Henry with her hands on her perfectly-formed hips. "Honey, are you going to let her insult me that way?"

Henry shook his head and stared at me, his mouth agape, so I thought I should field her question. "One, I'm not insulting you, I'm describing you, and two, yes he bloody well will. NOW GET OUT OF MY HOUSE!" My foot stomped on the floor, and my arm flung out to the side with a pointed finger at the end of it, none of my doing, of course, because I had already lost my mind.

Henry hustled Charlotte out of our bedroom, while I tried to recall the last time that Henry had spread my legs and gone to town on me? My neglected muff had no memory of the last time it had been the main course of any meal or even an appetizer for that matter.

As Charlotte collected her things, she yelled at him with ultimatums and demands, but before she left, she screeched back at me. "HENRY SAID YOU WERE A FAT BITCH!"

I snorted and yelled back down the hallway at her. "Maybe, but at least I don't need Botox to PARALYZE MY UGLINESS!"

I threw my befouled sheet to the ground in disgust as I sunk down into my wicker chair, which I actually did purchase on Portobello Road, and the only piece of furniture that officially belonged to me. Henry was cheating on me. The love of my life, the man who had me at hello, the leading man of my very own romantic comedy was cheating on me, and he was doing it in our bed and on my beautiful Egyptian cotton sheets!

Henry finally reappeared at the door, his Thor-like face full of remorse. I would never forgive him for ruining Chris Hemsworth for me forever!

He knew he had screwed up, but before he could say anything, I put my hand up to stop him. "I'll never finish falling in love with you?" It was all very dramatic, very Norma Desmond ("I'm ready for my close up now, Mr DeMille") and Henry was again rendered speechless, knowing that I was repeating the words that he had said to Charlotte and her judgmental nipples only hours earlier.

"What?"

"'I'll never finish falling in love with you.' That's what you said to her today wasn't it? You said those exact same words to me as well, do you remember Henry? The first time you told me you loved me? Shit! Clearly that's what you say to every woman you try and manipulate, isn't it? I was just the fool that fell for it."

"What? How?"

"Oh, did I forget to mention that you butt-dialled me? Sorry, I got sidetracked when I caught you with your head between your PA's legs."

"Ginger, let me explain. Charlotte is... she's... it just ..." He shrugged, unsure of how he should reply, of what would appease me.

My mind raced. Henry had really cheated. What happened now? Did he leave? Did I?

"How long?"

"How long?"

"Come on Henry. How long? How long have you been shagging her?"

"A while."

"Like a few weeks or like this has been going on since we arrived?"

"More than a few weeks, I guess. We bumped into each other that weekend you were in Bath."

I sat in stunned silence. I thought back to my weekend in Bath. We had just gotten engaged, and I had surprised Henry with the weekend away to celebrate our engagement, but he cancelled at the last minute. He had a conference, or a client, or a conference with a client, so rather than waste the booking, I went alone.

We had sex the night I returned. It was good. Now I realised it was a little too good. It was guilt sex. I'd been guilt fucked.

I was torn between the desire to vomit all over Henry and the all-encompassing urge to wrap my hands around his throat and throttle the life out of him. Both choices seemed like a waste of my energy.

"And now?"

"I don't know what to tell you. I know it was wrong. I mean, it is wrong. I'm sorry. And I don't want to hurt you. It just happened, you know? But as wrong as I knew it was, it still felt right, you know, being with her."

"It... felt... right." I hoped my crossed arms and pursed lips made me look tough, because I was really trying as hard as I could not to burst into tears. Not because I was losing Henry. No, that part of my heart closed up pretty quickly. But because I evidently wasn't enough for him. And also because I'd be single again. In a foreign country, no less.

"And let's be honest, you just haven't been working as hard on our relationship as you should have been." He ran his fingers through his mussed hair, and the flex of his naked bicep muscle did nothing for me.

Yup, it was over. Officially.

"Don't you try and blame your infidelity on me. It's not me banging *my* boss."

"I should always be your priority and it had become painfully obvious to me that you would never be able to fulfill the various roles that you needed to as my wife."

"You were right to screw Charlotte because you actually do need a beck and call girl." I laughed at my Pretty Woman reference. "And she even gets paid for the privilege of screwing you!"

Any attempt to shift the blame over to me clearly backfired, so Henry changed tactics. "Alright Ginny, I made a mistake, I admit it. What do you want me to say?"

I rubbed my forehead, willing away a sudden migraine. "Do you love her?"

I didn't really care what his answer was, I just needed Henry to hurt me. "I don't know. Maybe I do. She's happy to be second in the relationship. She doesn't argue with me and she doesn't mind when I lose my temper."

"It's in her job description, you idiot!"

I knew it was over. I mean, of course it was because Henry was clearly a narcissistic prick, but there was that other part of me, the part that grew up believing that I would never be whole unless I had a perfect relationship, that made me feel that I had failed as a woman somehow. I wasn't enough for Henry, and it was apparent that I would never have been able to be the wife that he wanted. But if I wasn't enough for Henry was there something fundamentally wrong with me? Did I actually fail as a woman? I gave all that I had, and it still wasn't enough for him. Was there any more of me to give?

I slipped Henry's Grandmother's engagement ring off my finger, placed it on the bedside table, and walked to the door. Turning back, I looked him dead in the eye, held back a sob, and ended our relationship with one word. "Goodbye."

Again, it was all terribly dramatic, but it was exactly right. Our failed relationship began with a "hello" and it ended with a "goodbye". I walked out of our apartment a little wobbly, but with my head held high.

So that was that. The credits had begun to roll on my relationship with Henry, and there would be no happily ever after.

Within two days I had moved out. My meagre belongings, and my white wicker chair were no longer situated in Notting Hill (adjacent), and I was an Aussie alone in a hostile land (very dramatic). Oh, and in case you're wondering what I did with my gorgeous Egyptian eight hundred thread cotton sheets? I burned them. Yes, I did. And it felt great!

It was time to start my life.

CHAPTER 3

Snow Is A Four Letter Word... and so is fuck!

Love sucked. And my obsessive fixation with romantic comedies sucked even more. This addiction had completely ruined my perception of what love actually (yep, I went there) was. It was time for me to become the leading lady in my own life instead of wasting my time on the couch watching Notting Hill for the seven-hundredth time.

Sure, I might have wanted to run away to Bali to find myself, or maybe renovate a villa in Tuscany, but the truth was I didn't even have enough money to buy myself a pizza, so I ended up moving into a teeny-tiny bedsit in Pimlico, and it became a refuge for my post-Henry apocalyptic pain. I stayed locked inside, a recluse only leaving for work. I missed the English summer completely, not just because I resented the sunshine, but because I found it difficult to not want to scream at every shiny, happy person that I passed when I did venture outside.

My time wasn't completely wasted though, in fact, I think I was processing my grief in a completely normal manner. I had completely by-passed denial because the sight of Henry performing cunnilingus on Charlotte-Fucking-Poppins was pretty hard to ignore so I moved straight onto anger. Yes, I do admit things went downhill slightly during this part of my grieving process. Let me just say I *might* have consumed copious amounts of alcohol during that time and I *may* have drunk dialled Henry more often than perhaps a sane person should. *Perhaps* I would yell into my phone if he stupidly answered or leave totally crazed messages along the lines of, "Hey, Shithead! Yeah, you! You are missing out Henry! MISS-ING-OUT! I just banged my brains out with Rodney from Accounting, and he was AH-MAZE-ING! AMAZING!"

Just so you know there was no Rodney in Accounting.

But as on reflection, and in a moment of clarity, the truth hit me like a thunderbolt, and that truth was that neither of us tried very hard to make the relationship work. Even from our very first kiss, it was a very one-sided relationship. He merely took what he wanted (which was me) and I was too overwhelmed, too blinded by my affection, to see Henry for who he really was. And at that moment, I understood that I was merely broken, not heartbroken. That made a big difference to my recovery. Broken was much easier to fix.

I had fitted into Henry's idea of what he wanted his partner to be, or could be, with a little tweak here or there. He had already offered to pay for a gym membership to help me "shift those kilos" and let's not forget he gave me a hair straightener for my birthday last year. A fucking hair straightener! Basically, I was being molded into the perfect trophy wife. With a pity shag twice a week, two point five kids and bellini's before noon I would be ready to prepare a five course meal at a moment's notice, all the while impressing his friends with my fake smile and sub-servient attitude — but with my real tits because they were still amazing.

Looking back at our shitty relationship, the sex with Henry wasn't even all that great. I thought back to my last orgasm, Henry wasn't even there, but of course he wasn't, he was too busy shagging Charlotte-Fucking-Poppins. Ugh! Shouldn't it be mind-blowing, multiple orgasms with the man you love rather than with your trusty vibrator? And what happens if your hoo-ha spends too much time getting off via two hundred and thirty volts? I mean, no man can compete with multiple speed settings. Can they?

By the time summer ended, I had put the worst of my "broken" behind me and was ready to face the world again. I was finally healthy enough to watch The Notebook without uncontrollable weeping and, despite the fact that I got more than a few unnerving glimpses of a Chris Hemsworth clone as I wandered down High Street or left the office at night, I tried to move on with my life. In fact, I had nothing to remind me of my nearly three years with Henry except a few tagged photos on social media and my white wicker chair that now sat in the corner of my Plimco bedsit next to my new ficus tree. I also had the promise I made to myself that I would never let a man break my heart, or me, again. I didn't quite know how I would make good on that promise but, damn it, I would give it a good hard go!

Along with my new life and new ficus, I also landed a new job as a paralegal at Blanch Wigdor Lanier, one of the more prominent personal injury firms in London. The offices gave all the appearance of old money, with their elegant furniture and panelled walls, but once you got past the old school money and senior partners, it was a frigid, grey environment, full of cubicles and mindless drones like me working their forty-five hour week. It wasn't the most glamorous job, or even remotely interesting for that matter, but it did allow me to eat and pay rent, which is great for, you know, survival.

I didn't even have a desk. I had a cubicle. Eight by ten feet of grey laminate to call my own. And, just like my life, it was a shambles. It was overflowing with files, empty coffee cups, and all that miscellaneous crap that every office worker seemed to accumulate, despite never actually buying anything. A blue stress ball with the name of an office supply company sat next to a Minion figurine I got in a Happy Meal last week. An open bag of sweeties that the receptionist gave me was strewn across the desktop along with a half-eaten apple that I was pretty sure wasn't even mine. There were dozens of pens, paperclips, pencils and staplers but they never seemed to be at my fingertips when I needed them so I always needed more. My filing tray was so full that the papers had developed a very precarious tilt. I called it my Leaning Tower Of Crap, and it was ready to collapse under its weight. I know I should probably made an attempt to file some of those undoubtedly time-sensitive documents, but my motivation had gone the way of the birds — south for the winter.

Under the harsh glare of the fluorescents above, I banged my head on my desk a few times in an attempt to either render myself unconscious or put myself out of my misery completely. No luck at either, in fact all I had accomplished was to dislodge my very precarious Leaning Tower of Crap and it began to disintegrate around me. I jumped up and frantically grabbed what papers I could in an effort to stem its overflow onto the floor. Stupid, stupid, Ginger.

As I stood there holding a month's worth of crumbled filing to my chest I glanced around the office to see if anyone was paying any attention to me. They weren't. I hadn't been working here long enough to become an integral member of the team, and other than a few of the girls in admin, I hadn't really made an effort to befriend any of the staff. In fact, I'd pretty much done the opposite and spent most of my time attempting to blend into the woodwork.

I returned the papers to the tower and opened Messenger (despite their old school views Blanch Wigdor Lanier allowed social media in the office to 'boost morale').

I scrolled down my contacts list until I found my sister 'Sadie Knox-Werrington'. I opened a text box and began typing.

> **Me:** Are you awake? I'm guessing you might be. I'm here to vent – feel free to block me if you must.

Her reply was immediate.

> **Sadie:** I'm awake. I can't remember the last time I slept.

> **Me:** Did you know that London is currently experiencing a storm unlike any in the past hundred years.

> **Sadie:** Fascinating.

> **Me:** I know, right? I'm so lucky – NOT! And even though I love the whole idea of snowflakes falling from the sky, actually living amongst the piles of snowdrifts they create is another thing altogether.

> **Me:** What's worse, I woke this morning to the news that the heating is broken in our building. Icicles are forming on the inside of my window! The inside!!! No joke! No one has seen the hygienically-challenged scumbag of a landlord in weeks (Dev from across the hall thinks he's buggered off to Spain) so I'm probably going to be living in a freezer until spring!

> **Sadie:** Life is tough in old Blighty, is it? It must suck to be you living it up with your friends in London, while I'm back here dealing with babies and a neverending stream of poop and vomit (and not just

by the babies, I might add).

Babies. Plural.

Me: Yuk!

Sadie: They're asleep right now so I don't want to talk babies or it will jinx me and they'll wake up. Talk about something else.

Me: Hahahaha.

Me: Here's what I really don't understand. England should have its act together by now. It snows. Every year. They should be used to it, but at the slightest sign of the temperature dropping the world comes to an end.

Me: I spent 45 minutes today packed in like sardines in a train carriage that didn't move. On the positive side, I did get groped by a lovely chap who smelled like a trucker, and who I may or may not have a date with tonight. Could be a summer wedding. Hahaha!

Sadie: Good to see you're finally out there dating again lol.

Me: So by the time I finally arrived at work, Brienne of Tarth had a hissy fit because: 1. I was late; and 2. I'd forgotten her freaking Espresso Macchiato.

Sadie: How many people get to work with an actual ray of sunshine?

Me: Pfft!! So, back out I went to get her coffee

and I bloody well slipped on some ice and landed on my ass in the middle of the street. I probably broke my coccyx (I know you are laughing right now, but my ass really hurts!).

Sadie: Your coccyx is padded enough to take a slide.

Me: Thanks for that insult.

Sadie: So come home already. Come back for Christmas or come back forever. We miss you, Dad especially. You know he hasn't been too great recently. It would really lift his spirit to see you. The girls are nearly one, and you haven't even met them!

Me: Dunno. Maybe.

Sadie: Go tell your mountain woman of a boss right now that you are coming home for Christmas, book in for a wax and start doing some sit-ups to be bikini ready!

A packet of chocolate biscuits appeared on my desk thanks to my neighbour in the cubicle beside me. I stuffed one in my mouth and giggled at Sadie's 'bikini ready' comment. I hadn't been bikini ready in a good while (can I blame the chocolate biscuits?), and I would probably need a weed whacker to deforest my lady thatch right now!

Me: Maybe.

Sadie: Yes!

Me: Love you.

Sadie: Love you too, little whinger.

I passed the packet of biscuits back to my neighbour as a quiet ding announced another message. Half expecting it to be from Sadie, begging me again to come home, I was surprised when it was from one of my office friends, Meg Martin.

Meg: Pub. 10 minutes. Hope you've got your dancing shoes on!

I glanced down at my fabulous Rag & Bone boots. I'd always loved these boots (nearly as much as I loved decadent sheets). Red leather with a fantastic heel, I had matched them with my favourite dress, a black, Kate Spade Saturday Good Times Dress. Since the Henry debacle I had actually shed quite a bit of weight (so Sadie's comment on my ass wasn't quite warranted in my opinion) which was a complete surprise considering the amount of icecream I had consumed in those first few weeks. And even though I might never look like Rosie Huntington-Whiteley, mostly because I was more a young Mini Driver with my crazy curls and curvy bod, but I knew that I could rock my fabulous dress with its legendary name like I was strutting down a Victoria Secret runway. It not only fitted me in all the right places, but it also flounced when I walked and whooshed when I danced. It did! I swear! All I needed was a little wiggle juice and a couple of band-aids for the inevitable blisters, and I would be ready to dance the night away.

I looked over the top of my dingy, depressing workstation in search for Meg who was easy to spot these days in the drab, grey workplace as her long blonde hair had recently been dyed a very pale shade of violet (much to the horror of the personnel department). Today she had co-ordinated her hair beautifully with a men's purple tuxedo jacket that she had picked up at a street market last weekend.

I gave her a thumbs up and she hooted loudly before giving her cubicle a little bump and grind. Meanwhile, my neighbour, and owner of the chocolate biscuits, Courtney Ryan, slid her chair out and looked around before cupping her hands around her mouth for her whisper to reach me. "She's coming."

She gestured with her chin in the direction of the boss, then disappeared back behind the grey cubicle wall.

"She" was Anne-Louise Onion and Anne-Louise Onion was my boss. Tall and broad-shouldered, her ash blonde hair was forever scraped back from her face á la Brienne of Tarth, and like an onion, she could make you cry with just a look or a sneer. Her razor-sharp tongue and ruthless ambition wasn't the only reason that she made junior partner at the age of thirty-five. She was also something of a legal genius and had developed a reputation as a formidable opponent in the courtroom. Most of the time she scared the shit out of me.

"Ms. Knox?" I coughed and swallowed the last of my biscuit, stood up and gaped at the sheer volume of files that she was holding. Shit! If those were for me, I wasn't going to be going to the pub or anywhere before midnight. Just then, her line rang, so I hit the button. "Anne-Louise Onion's office, how may I assist you?"

I pointed to my ear set and shrugged at Anne-Louise. "Sorry," I mouthed, and slid back down into my seat. I felt my boss's glare in the back of my head and I knew without turning around that she was standing behind me, tapping her foot impatiently. I placed the call on hold and turned to my boss. "Lord Kichen is on the line, ma'am."

Anne-Louise huffed in reply and stomped to her office, slamming the door for good measure. I transferred the call and prayed she didn't come back out before I had escaped for the weekend.

While reading Sadie's message again, I had doodled a tiny Christmas tree. It would be my first Christmas without Henry, and I already knew it would suck. Not because I'd miss him, but any holiday spent alone is depressing.

What I really needed was a Cameron Diaz/Kate Winslet inspired holiday. A trip across the pond (or to the other side of the world) to boink my brains out with Jude Law, or hell to the yeah, even a little Jack Black (I drool over his crazy eyebrows)! I craved beach parties and barbeques. And some sunshine. Yep. I had a plan! I was going home and find me a little thunder from down under! And to spend Christmas with my family, of course.

I popped my head back up over my partition and looked around for Anne-Louise. She was off the phone, and now across the room, breathing down the neck of the new associate, Jeffrey Lund. I cringed and glanced at the digital clock on the wall. 5:59. The clock ticked over to 6:00 and around me the whole room moved as one, standing up, bags in hand, racing for the elevators and freedom. I grabbed my jacket and pulled my woollen hat from its pocket before wrapping a scarf around my neck. Carefully, I ducked amongst the sea of co-workers escaping for the weekend, caught up with Courtney and Meg, and we linked arms as we stepped into the elevator. "Now we dance!" We all waved at Jeffrey as the doors closed. Poor schmuck looked desperate for an out. Sorry, Jeff.

Courtney flicked her short, black fringe out of her eyes. "Tonight is going to be excellent, I can feel it in my tits."

"Surprised you can feel anything in this cold weather."

"Always banging on about our fabulous weather aren't you,

Sheila?" Courtney poked me good-heartedly.

"Better than being a whinging Pom," I shot back at her.

Courtney and Meg grinned at each other. My fair dinkum Aussie accent along with my aversion to warm beer and my genuine, although completely self-diagnosed, disorder known as temperature depression, was often the brunt of their English jokes.

Courtney's mobile buzzed and she pulled it from her bag. "Excellent. Nate's coming, and he's bringing along his new girlfriend as well."

"Another one?" I had to laugh. I had only known Nate Reuben for a short while, but seriously, that man had had more girlfriends than I'd had hot dinners!

"No idea where he keeps finding them." Courtney shook her head. "But he does!"

Meg piped in. "Well, he found you once."

"Yeah, until I realised how much I hated the dick and I was, in fact, a muffer."

I glanced sideways to catch the man beside me stifling his grin. "Courtney!"

"So what?" She looked over at the man. "Do you care that I'm a muffer?"

He shook his head minutely, no doubt wishing he had taken the next elevator.

"See? No one cares."

Meg leaned her head close to ours. "I'll telephone Jeffrey in a minute and tell him he has an emergency at home. We can't leave him to take the bullet."

"You've got his number?" Meg hadn't wasted any time digging her claws into the new associate.

"I have all of the associate's numbers. You never know when you will need a lawyer."

"Sure, when its three AM and you're horny." Courtney rolled her eyes. "Someone's gotta get Onion's work done. Jeffrey's only been here a few weeks, so it should be him. Anyway, you only want him to come to the pub in the hope that you will get him drunk and try your luck."

"Yes please." Meg smacks her lips. "I just want to see what's underneath those sweater vests that he persists in wearing."

Courtney and I both snorted at Meg who shrugged, unashamed. "I honestly don't care what you think."

"Oh, Meg. If a sweater vest isn't enough to put me off sex with a man forever, nothing is!"

"A man who can rock a sweater vest is a man who can rock your world – or at least he will die trying! Anyway, what would you know about it?"

I glanced again at the man beside me who was also wearing a rather fetching blue and grey sweater vest. He stood up a little straighter and smiled in Meg's direction.

To change the subject before my two friends, one living with the belief that her Mr. Right would be found wandering through the hallways at the Law Courts, and the other who recently came out of the closet, ended up in fisticuffs, I decided to drop my holiday bomb. "I'm thinking of getting away for

Christmas."

"Don't do that." Meg looked horrified. "Come home with me to Manchester. We always do the full Christmas shindig. So many will be there, me mum won't mind one more. Honestly."

"Or come stay with me at *Chez Courts*. I'm not really going to do anything much, but we can make our own festivities with a bottle of rum and a fruit cake."

"It's the weather, isn't it?" Meg slipped her gloves on. "You know, this storm is well mingin'. It never snows this early in December."

I rolled my eyes in reply.

Courtney turned to me. "It's not the weather. It's the fact that you will be alone. This is your first Christmas without Henry."

"UGH!" These two could read me like an open book. I certainly wasn't about to admit to them that the thought of spending Christmas alone in my tiny flat had me contemplating jumping out its third story window. "It's not because of Henry. I just need some vitamin D. This miserable weather is truly making me crazy. Anyway, I won't be alone. Sadie wants me to come home for Christmas. Australian sunshine and my Dad. I'm going to tell Anne-Louise on Monday morning."

"Shit, you can't go all that way! It's too far for just a week."

"It'll be fine. A week with my family will be worth the trip."

"Well, Anne-Louise will get into a right strop about it, I bet. Listen, make your request by email," advised Meg. "And send it straight to Personnel rather than Anne-Louise, then she can't possibly say no."

Sound advice because the wrath of Anne-Louise was terrifying, indeed. We crossed the foyer towards the exit, and I could already feel the biting London cold seeping in through the cracks in the revolving door. I took a deep breath and braced myself for the onslaught as we stepped outside. "Oh. My. God!"

We spilled out onto the street and the frigid wind whipped around my face. Any attempt to put up my umbrella was foiled, so I ran across the street behind my friends, as the now rain / hail / sleet / snow (hell if I know) pelted down on us relentlessly. When we finally made it to the sanctuary of the pub a few minutes away, I was soaked through, probably bruised and feeling damn miserable.

"I am seriously not designed for this shit!" I shook out my hair already knowing that the awful London weather would have had a catastrophic effect my curls as well as my makeup. I glanced in the mirror behind the bar and spotted the waterlogged Alice Cooper glaring back at me. That was enough to make up my mind. "And I'm *definitely* going home for Christmas!"

CHAPTER 4

Molly, You In Danger, Girl

After a quick trip to the bathroom to remove Alice Cooper from my life and to reapply my lipstick I squeezed through the crowd of like-minded business types, all desperate for a drink or three after what had no doubt being a long, crappy week, to the bar where Courtney had already caught the barman's eye.

"First round's on me, ladies," Courtney shouted over the music and winked at the barman. "Tequila cruda, and line 'em up, gorgeous."

He immediately set to work with a grin. The poor bartender had no chance against the lure of Courtney's wild beauty. The girl was a knockout and, like a Siren's song, her smile alone had wooed many a lover. They only needed one glance at her olive skin, thick black hair, stunning blue eyes and totally rocking body, and they were doomed. Men, and I guessed now women, gravitated to her. She's always loved the attention, regardless of their sex, and encouraged all with her flirtatious behaviour.

"Here you go!" Courtney handed me the first one and, after I licked the salted rim, I threw it straight back before grabbing a piece of lemon, pulling a face the entire time.

Salep and Ginger

"Now, about you running off down under for Christmas. I've got to be honest, I'm not loving this idea." Courtney's interrogation began. "Will you stay with your sister?"

"I think so."

"What if you love it there? What if you realise you miss your family too much and you want to stay? What if she asks you to stay?"

I shrugged. Courtney, used to getting her own way, slammed her glass down on the bar. "Your sister is trying to steal you away from us, isn't she? Well, I won't give you up without a fight!"

"Oh, please! My sister and I under the one roof have a limited "use by" date. We'd kill each other if left alone together for too long, but it's the holidays, and I haven't seen my Dad in forever. Plus I've never even met my nieces, and they're almost one!"

"I think I might hate your sister." Meg grabbed another shot from the bar.

"Most people do. Perfect husband, perfect babies, perfect life. If she weren't my only sibling, I'd probably hate her as well."

"I think I prefer you any day!"

"Yep." Courtney teased. "Frankly, your sister sounds high maintenance!"

How awesome were these two?

"I love you guys."

Courtney snorted, before grabbing another shot. "You drunk already, Knox?"

"No but I want you to know that you guys are my soulmates and I love you both."

And I meant it. Despite having only known Courtney and Meg for a few short months, they immediately accepted me as one of their own, and thanks to their friendship, and our bonding over a mutual love of anything alcoholic, I had finally started to feel like London really was my home.

"Don't get soppy now." Meg threw her arms around me and squeezed me tightly. "We love you too. Don't we, Courts?"

My darling Meg was the complete opposite of Courtney. Don't get me wrong, she was still gorgeous, but in a completely different way. She was soft and sweet and she really believed with all her heart that there is one true love for each of us out there. Every decision that she had ever made is based on bringing her one step closer to meeting her soulmate and living her happily ever after. With her long, violet hair and her thrift shop style, she looked like a tipsy lavender faerie but with huge boobs — so when she gave you a hug you copped a feel whether you want to or not.

Courtney nodded before motioning for another round to the bartender. "Course we do."

"And it's only a week." Meg tossed back another shot. "It's not like it's forever."

Passing yet another shot to me, Courtney rose her drink in a toast. "Well, alright then. Cheers ladies. Live it up while you're down under, Ginny! Enjoy all that Vitamin D you keep banging on about and maybe find yourself a hunky Aussie surfer boy to while away the hours." She leaned in suggestively. "Unless you decide to cross over and take a dip in the lady pond. I think you might be pleasantly surprised."

"And be a muffer?" I pushed Courtney away and laughed. "Nah, anyway, you'd be too much woman for me Courts."

From behind us, a booming male voice announced his presence. "Courtney you let Ginny be. She's not going to be your lipstick lover!"

It was Nate Reuben, who had arrived with a beautiful brunette in tow. "Nina, be careful of that one." He pointed to Courtney, who turned and mockingly punched him in the arm. Nate grabbed her and gave her a kiss while his date stood by with a baffled look on her thin face.

"Eew! Thanks for that." Courtney wiped her mouth. "And people wonder why I prefer girls."

"You miss me. I know you do."

Nate was, once upon a time, Courtney's boyfriend and their love for each other survived even when she dropped him like a hot potato when she realised that she was gay.

"Only when I can't open a jar."

I glanced around the room searching for a free table and rounded up the gang as a group of Accountant-types stood up to leave. Nate commandeered it while we all grabbed seats squeezing in together. Although his arm was casually slung over his date's shoulder, Nate and Courtney immediately fell into deep conversation ignoring the rest of us.

Nate's date turned to me. "Should I be jealous?"

"No. Trust me, he's definitely not her type. I say you leave them to it."

She eyed Courtney curiously before realisation set in, then a confident grin spread across her face.

"Come on," I smiled at Nate's next conquest. "Let's go get a drink. What would you like?"

"Whatever you're having, I guess. I'm Nina."

"Hi. I'm Ginger, but my friends call me Ginny." We made our way through the crowd to the bar. "So, what do you do, Nina?"

"I'm a first-year resident at Royal Brompton Hospital."

"Wow!" I was shocked that Nate could pull someone as serious as a doctor. "And you're with Nate?"

She smiled, with a dreamy look in her eyes. "He's lovely."

I raised a brow. Lovely is the one thing Nate Reuben is not. Rich as hell playboy would be a better description with his ridiculously good looks, six foot four with a rock hard bod and the newest trendy accessory — a man bun. No relationship of his has ever lasted more than two months, and every girl left with a trinket and a smile.

"So, how does a first-year resident meet Nate then?"

"If you must know, he came in with a girl who had a delicate situation, you know, down there." She pointed "below the equator" and smiled.

"Oh my God!"

"Easy extraction. Didn't take any time at all."

"Oh my God!"

I did a mental Google search trying to decide what Nate's friend had stuck up her hoo-ha that she couldn't get out herself. Eek!

"He came back to thank me with flowers. Apparently, she was his neighbour and was calling out for help. He saved her, you know. Climbed through her bathroom window and everything. I imagine it would have been quite painful if it was left there for too long. He's just so sweet."

"Hmmm. Sure he is." Yes, indeed Nate can weave a web beautifully.

"What about you? How do you know Nate?"

"We met through Courtney and Meg." I point out Meg, now in the corner on her mobile. "We all work together."

"Oh?"

"At Blanch Wigdor Lanier."

"Personal injury, right?"

"How did you know?"

"You wouldn't believe how some people get injured. A lot of lawsuits."

"I believe it." I leaned in toward Nina and wrinkled my nose. "But can I just say that right now, I wish I was anywhere but here. This weather is absolute hell."

"I expect it's not quite what you're used to."

"Been here two years now. Hate it. Will never get used to it. In fact, I've just decided to go home for Christmas."

"All that sunshine should fix you."

"Well, you're the doctor, so here's hoping."

We returned to the table to find that Jeffrey Lund had successfully escaped from Anne-Louise Onion's clutches and had joined us. He grabbed Meg and lustfully kissed her. "You saved me!"

Courtney screwed her face into a grimace. "Bleurgh! That is definitely not appropriate workplace behaviour!"

"We're not at work right now, silly." Meg giggled, and sat down on Jeffrey's lap. "And I did save him, you know."

"Nate, I heard you did a good deed recently as well, helping your poor neighbour. You're a bit of a hero, I think."

He gave me his most cheesy grin in return. "Just call me Superman."

"Super Shmuck is more like it." Courtney poked out her tongue at him.

Changing the subject, Nate gave me the once-over. "Can I just say you're looking particularly tasty this evening, Ginny. In fact, you look hot. Approachable hot, not bitch in a thong hot." He scanned the room. "I think it's time that you dip your toes back into the dating waters."

"First, thanks — I think. And second, nope. Not tonight. Not gonna happen."

"I'm just trying to compliment you, here."

"Well, don't do that anymore, okay?" The conversation was making me decidedly grumpy. "It's unnerving."

"Come on, Ginny. Nate's just trying to help." Meg reached over and grabbed my hand. "You're alone all the time."

"Alone is not the same as lonely."

"Well, I think you're gonna end up being both."

"And better for it. I'll be that old lady with all those stray cats up at Marble Arch that flashes her boobs when you go past!"

"A noble ambition!" Jeffrey guffawed.

"Those cats will end up eating you." Meg played with Jeffrey's hair, as she warned me that I was going to die alone. "Is that how you want to end up? As cat food?"

"I'm not going to end up as cat food!"

"You know, come to think of it, Nate is right." I glared at Courtney for chiming in. "I don't believe you've been on a date since we met you."

"She doesn't need a date. She just needs a hot beef injection!" Nate grinned.

"Oh, Nate. Classy. What a way to impress your new girl." Courtney rolled her eyes at him.

"I saw that!" Nate threw a serviette at Courtney's head.

"I meant you too!"

"I'm just trying to get Ginger a bit of tail. Bumping uglies and all that."

"Knocking boots," Jeffrey hooted.

"Wait! I know." Meg joined in giggling like a drunk toddler. "A little slap and tickle."

"Feed the kitty?" Courtney whooped.

"Or coitus." We all turned to Doctor Nina who blushed at the attention now focused on her. "I mean, if we're going to be technical, it's called coitus."

Nate chuckled and leaned over to kiss her on the cheek. "See? Even the doc agrees with us."

"Shut up, all of you! I bump more than enough uglies, knock all sorts of boots and even get my fair share of coitus." I scowled and looked over at Courtney and Meg for support. They shook their heads in reply. "I do!"

"Course you do, Ginny." Meg patted me on the back. "Just not in this fiscal year."

And with that an entire table of seemingly literate adults were reduced to laughter at my expense. I shook my head in faux disgust. "I hate you guys right now."

"Happy to help with your little problem if you like." Jeffrey raised his eyebrows suggestively as he straightened his tie.

"Good on you, mate." Nate gave Jeffrey a high five. "Way to take one for the team."

"Hey!" Meg screeched looking decidedly dejected. "Get your own, Ginny!"

"Thanks, but no thanks."

"It's cool. You're not my type anyway." Jeffrey turned his attention back to Meg, who had begun to pout beside me. "I was just trying to help. Besides she doesn't come close to you."

"I'm right here, you know." I had no love for the new associate at that moment. "Come on guys, just let it be. You know, after Henry, well, let's just say, I have really crappy taste in men, so I just want to wait until it's right. I'm certainly not going to sleep with some random guy just for the sake of it."

"Ah Henry, the man with the golden tongue."

"No, what you should have said was, 'Ah Henry, the man who treated our Ginny like dirt and deserves to contract a severe STD.'"

"He probably already has." Nate shivered at the thought.

And you know the old saying 'once a cheater, always a cheater'."

Nate pointed his finger at Meg and nodded. "Meg is right darl, I know guys like that."

I snorted in reply. "You *are* guys like that!"

"That's fair."

Courtney nodded at me in agreement before continuing, "Let's all just agree that Henry was a total bastard, and you're well rid of him. Plus, he was the one that fucked it up, not you. Well him and his dirty penis that he was sticking into his dirty PA slut!"

Nina's mouth gaped at Courtney's language, which made Nate laugh. "Nina, babe, if you're going to hang with us you mustn't let such things bother you. While Courtney is a tad crass in her wording, she is right. He's the one that's missing out." He turned to me. "All that matters right now is you, and you are looking sexy as hell. You just need to get out there and own it."

"Whatever Nate, but it's not easy to find a guy that's relatively normal."

"You're overthinking it."

"I'm really not. Finding a guy that isn't married, a drug addict, a total perve or a complete tosser isn't exactly easy. If such a man existed, he's bloody not gonna be in this meat market on a Friday night."

"If you spent more time out meeting people rather than sitting at home watching those ridiculous movies on repeat, then you might actually meet a real guy."

Even Nate was aware of my twisted addiction to romantic-comedies.

"It's not real life. You know that, right?"

"I like to think of it more like a hobby."

"It's given you ridiculously high expectations. Not every man is Hugh Grant."

"Shouldn't I have high expectations?"

"I'm not sure whether Hugh Grant falls into the category of 'high expectation'."

Courtney sighed and took the imaginary baton from Nate. She knew that I was an uphill battle. "Look, are you over Henry, or not?"

"I am, except when I choose not to be. Like now."

"Then Nate's right. It's time."

I was being totally bullied by my so-called friends, but thanks to the excessive number of tequilas already consumed, I gave in rather easily. Maybe I really did need a little slap and tickle.

A blow and go. Ah, hell, I just needed someone to throw me a boner! "Fine. You win. I'll give you five minutes to find me the perfect man, Nate. And, if you do happen to succeed, which I very much doubt, I'll owe you a big ass bottle of single malt."

"Hmm, no, I need something more."

"How about skinny dipping in the Thames!" Jeffrey suggested.

"Now that," Nate gave Jeffrey the second high five of the evening, "is a challenge I could get behind."

"Sometimes I don't know why I'm friends with you."

"It's my great personality."

"Bullshit." I deadpanned. "It's desperation."

Nate laughed loudly while Courtney leaned over and high fived me. "Now that's a high five *I* can get behind, Ginny!"

Nina wrinkled her nose at me. "I wouldn't suggest swimming in the Thames. It would be as appealing as swimming in sewage."

"Nina, I can safely say that I will not be skinny dipping any time soon."

"Well, if you're sure."

"Yep. Go on then, Nate. Find me a perfect man."

"I really want that whiskey, plus the idea of seeing you naked is interesting, so challenge accepted." Nate scanned the room. It didn't take long for him to find what he was looking for and promptly played out a drum roll on the table that sent Jeffrey's beer flying before disappearing into the crowd.

I found myself trying to spot Nate in the crowd. "Does anyone see him?"

"He's near the bar, isn't he?"

Courtney stood up to have a better look at Nate's prey. "Who knows what type of Barney he'll bring back with him."

Before long, we forgot Nate and his quest, until I heard Meg's sharp intake of breath. "Jesus, Mary and Joseph!"

We all stopped talking and followed Meg's gaze across the room. "I think Nate might just have found your future husband."

"Or at least tonight's shag."

"Oh Gawd, Ginny, he's like, a twelve!"

I could feel my face redden instantly. "I don't need a twelve ladies, I just need to be left alone."

Courtney nudged me. "Smile, Ginny."

I plastered a smile on my face, but Courtney nudged me again. "Christ, Ginny. You look demented. Stop smiling!"

I wiped the smile off my face and took a long sip of my drink as I turned around. I was totally chill, nonchalant even, as Nate crossed the room with what I could only assume was his idea of my perfect man.

Tall, definitely. Strong jawline with some totally hot stubble and a perfectly straight nose. Check and mate. Olive skin and eyes the colour of ground coffee, fringed with heavy lashes. He was no Chris Hemsworth but he was definitely hitting some buttons.

As he grew closer I realized I just might be in trouble. He was smiling, but I saw a moment of indecision, nerves, flit across his face. I watched in awe as he raked his fingers through his deliciously thick, dark brown, almost black hair that curled when it reached his neck. He had great hands. I inhaled sharply.

It had been quite some time since my girlie parts sat up and took notice, in fact, they had been rather quiet of late, but this gorgeous, dark, hunk of man was just the thing to awaken my comatose "V".

He was wearing skinny, black jeans and a thick, black jacket with a grey t-shirt underneath. I had the sudden drunken desire to peek under the shirt and see what we were dealing with. I would wager that whatever was under there would be sensational.

"Guys? Meet Aydin. I haven't seen him since university. Imagine that? Running into him today of all days." He slapped Aydin on the back. "How have you been buddy?"

Nate's perfect man and my future husband smiled nervously, his delicious brown eyes, locked with mine. "Very well, thank you."

"You know Aydin, Ginger here was just saying she felt like having a quick dip in the Thames. What are your thoughts on that?"

"Sorry Nate, not tonight!" I made a mental note to kick Nate's ass next time I got him alone. This was going to backfire spectacularly. I looked at Courtney in desperation, and she nudged Meg. They both began talking to cover up my embarrassment.

"Aydin is it?" Courtney asked. "Fabulous name. Very exotic."

Meg panted next to me. "You're so pretty!"

"Idiot." Courtney rolled her eyes at Meg and shrugged. "I tried." She dragged Nina and Nate off to dance while Meg resumed snogging Jeffrey, leaving Nate's idea of a perfect man standing beside me. Awkward.

The silence made me uneasy. He just stood there, watching me. Why didn't he say something?

Why don't you say something, Ginger?

"I guess I could sit." He indicated the empty seat next to me. His coffee-coloured eyes looked even darker as his gaze burned into mine. Wow, they were intense. For a moment, I wondered if he could see what was under my dress. It made me feel, well, a little dirty, and a lot horny! Maybe it was time to get back on the horse, or maybe I needed to get on this tall, dark stallion...

I took a sip of my drink and did my best to smile up at him. "I guess."

... or maybe it was time to quit drinking!

He moved the chair next to mine a little closer and sat down, nervously playing with his drink. I smelled a faint hint of cologne. It was masculine but subtle and, as he leaned in, I found myself taking a deep breath. He smelled good. He looked at me and grinned. "Did you just smell me?"

Faarrrkkk!

"What?" I blinked and shook my head as sweat began to bead on my top lip. "No!"

"I think you did, but that's okay."

He chuckled and leaned forward, taking a deep breath at the nape of my neck. "You smell pretty great. Like orange blossom and something else... maybe cinnamon?"

"Well, that's not creepy at all."

He caught my eye and grinned sheepishly. "You know, I didn't really go to university with your friend."

If I tilted my head back just enough, I could kiss those lips.

"I didn't think so."

"But I was happy when he suggested he introduce me."

"Sure."

"Please believe me. I saw you across the room. You are very beautiful but are also a little lost. Maybe sad?"

Who talks like this?

"Er, you know you sound like a total creeper, right?"

He tilted his head. "A creeper?"

"Watching me from across the room?" I shrugged. "Seems fitting."

"But it was you who sniffed me first."

"So you say. We'll have to let the jury decide."

He looked over at the "jury", which consisted of Meg and Jeffrey, who were happily snogging away, oblivious to our banter, then shot me a cocky grin. "I think your jury has other things on their mind."

"Bugger."

He laughed, and ran his hand through his dark curls again.

Damn, he was hot! He could be Salma Hayek and Orlando Bloom's love child... Oh God! Imagine if those two had a love child.

I shook my head to clear away my pervy thoughts and returned to the matter at hand. "So Aiden—"

"Ay-din."

"Right Aydin. Let's get down to brass tacks. What promises did Nate make to you? My first born? My soul? Both? Because I've got to tell you, I've already sold my soul, and I made a good profit for it."

"You're a little funny."

"Just a little?"

He chuckled. "So, who was the lucky buyer of your soul?"

"Confidentiality clause. Sorry."

"Okay then, *meleğim*." I looked at him curiously. "My angel."

"We've just established that I'm no angel."

"I think you might be an angel. But, just for the record, Nate didn't make me any promises. He didn't need to."

I arched an eyebrow at him. Sense of humour on point. Flirting on point. Hotness off the chart. Right. I was sooo prepared to run away with this man.

"I thought I might ask you to dance."

Clearly, he had never seen me on the dance floor.

"Would you like to? Dance?" He smiled at me, just enough that the corner of his mouth that needed to be kissed tilted up. "With me?"

My brain tried frantically to find the right word. What was it? Oh, right. "Yes."

I stood up, and he took my hand to lead me through the crowd. Sparks of electricity crackled and popped in the air between us and a bolt of lightning raced down my fingers where his skin held mine. I mean, it might have been static from the carpet, but either way, it was an honest-to-God spark. He must have felt it too, as his eyes shot up to meet mine. We were both breathing heavily as we stared at each other. And we hadn't even started to dance.

Once we reached the dance floor, Aydin dropped my hand, and we began swaying to the music. He must have also had a few too many bevies, and I laughed as he threw his arms out and spun around whooping loudly. He grinned a wide, lopsided grin. Adorable. With tequila buzzing in my head, and some chilled-out Ed Sheeran song playing, my self-consciousness faded away, and I moved in closer. He slipped his arm around me and pulled me to his chest. My heart skipped more than one beat as his hand slowly ran down my back, leaving tiny sparks along my spine as he settled in the curve just above my ass. The heat of his hand scorched through my dress as his thumb moved in circles in time to the music.

He leaned in to whisper in my ear. "I am enjoying you very much."

This all seemed to be moving a little too fast. I pushed myself away from him as Shape of You mixed into the more upbeat tempo of Billie Eilish explaining why she was, in fact, the bad guy — duh!

Feeling more in control of myself, and with an appropriate amount of space between us, I danced wildly to the beat of the music. Aydin laughed and joined in, dancing with abandon. This guy was one crazy dancer. We threw ourselves into it, both of us trying to outdo each other. All was going well, until, as first feared back in the office, my Rag & Bone boots did not agree with my dance skills, and I ended up face down on the dancefloor, the skirt of my flouncy, whooshy dress around my head and my safe, black, cotton knickers on view to the world.

Oh, for fuck's sake!

Aydin pulled me back to my feet. Embarrassed, I limped to the table where Meg was jumping up and down. "Excellent dance skills, Ginny. I got it all on video! Well done!"

"We should upload it." Jeffrey tried to get the phone from Meg's grip. "It was so good, it might go viral!"

"Shut up, you two." I turned to Aydin, but he appeared to have taken flight and disappeared into the crowd. "Well, that was utterly mortifying."

Meg moved into the empty chair next to me. "I don't think he was your type anyway Ginny, although you did look hot and heavy out there for a minute. Steamy, in fact."

She stopped talking and slid out of the chair as Aydin re-appeared with a glass of ice water. "Perhaps this might help."

My cheeks flamed with embarrassment, but I shot him a weak smile and took the offered glass. "Thank you."

He sat down beside me, and I watched with interest as he

chatted with the rest of the table. His totally sexy-as-hell, unplaceable accent was smooth, rich and sensual. Like melted chocolate. Drizzled. On his chest. Oh God! He was my very own Molten Chocolate Latte. Heat burned through my body and caused havoc between my legs as my imagination kicked into overdrive.

He laughed easily with Nate, chatted with Nina about her job, and even managed to have a conversation with Meg and Jeffrey before they resumed their snogging. He seemed entirely at ease with the group, and the fact that he hadn't done a runner when I went ass over tit, well, let's just say that's more than a lot of men would've done for a complete stranger — unless they expected to get laid — which wasn't going to happen. Well, maybe.

I clutched at my glass of water and gulped it down, trying desperately to maintain my composure when, what I really wanted to do, was to bang him right there on the table. I wriggled in my seat, pressing my thighs together to help relieve the swelling tension between them, and my leg inadvertently, or advertently, touched his. He didn't pull it away, but instead pushed his leg hard against mine. Then he slipped his hand under the table, found my free hand, and slowly stroked his thumb across my palm. He leaned over and whispered in my ear. "I think you might be mine."

I couldn't take anymore, so I did precisely what Ginny Knox always did when nerves kicked in. I panicked.

"I'm going to go get some air," I announced, and jumped up from the table, pulling my hand away and knocking over my chair.

Aydin jumped up beside me. "I'll come with you."

"Okay."

"Have fun you two." Courtney grinned at me before turning to the rest of the table. "Thank God they're leaving. The sexual tension between those two is enough to set fire to the table!"

I gave Courtney the finger before I flounced away. Yep. It was an intentional flounce because I was drunk enough to know damn well that my ass looked amazing in my Kate Spade Saturday Good Times dress, which was totally worth the rather large sum I paid for it. I wiggled my hips just a little more than I usually would... for effect of course. When I turned back, I could see that Aydin was enjoying the flounce as well. I fluttered my eyelashes at him. "Hurry up, Creeper. We haven't got all night."

I had a feeling that Ginger was about to get her groove back.

CHAPTER 5

The One-Night Stand... That Wasn't

We walked through the streets with no particular destination in mind. The tequila shots had the positive effect of warming me up, which enabled me to handle the bitter cold, and the bitter cold had the even more positive effect of sobering me up.

Winning.

After about fifteen minutes of strolling, my nemesis named Embarrassment raised its ugly head again as my stomach growled, loudly enough to make Aydin chuckle.

"Hungry?"

My cheeks burned. Surely, between my embarrassment and the cold wind whipping around, my face must have been as red as a tomato by now. "Yes... well... honestly, I'm hungry all the time."

"So am I." He leaned in closely. "That's the main reason I became a chef so I could eat all day."

Jane Gundogan

"You're a chef?"

My long-time masturbatory fantasy featuring Gordon Ramsay was no more. I'd rather have Chef Aydin squeeze my melons any day — and finger's crossed, hopefully tonight.

Passing a tiny Indian restaurant, I smiled when he motioned toward the door. We found a table in the back and settled in as the waiter arrived with menus. We placed our order, commenting that we both liked what the other chose, then fell into an uncomfortable silence waiting for the other to speak first.

I clasped my hands together to prevent myself from fidgeting nervously as he smiled at me expectantly.

Come on girl. Make an effort!

"So," I said, forcing myself to smile across the table. "I didn't ask you. What are you doing in London? Your accent tells me you're not from around here."

"No. I'm from Istanbul, but I have been here for the past six months."

"What do you do?"

"I've been working with Alain Ducasse at the Dorchester. Have you heard of him?"

I nodded as I grabbed a pappadum. "Of course. You're working in the restaurant there? I hear wonderful things about the food, although I've never been."

"I trained in Istanbul and then was lucky to have been offered an apprenticeship there as a sous chef. It's been an amazing experience for me. A lot of pressure, but I got to work with some extraordinary chefs. I learned so much."

"And now what?"

"And now I must go home. For a while, anyway. Some decisions must be made."

He's leaving. Just my luck.

"What about you?"

I shrugged. "I'm a paralegal at a law firm a few blocks from here. It's not a life ambition or anything, but I get to hang out with Courtney and Meg all day, which is cool."

"What is your life ambition?"

"Honestly? I'm not sure. I'm not even sure what I'll be doing tomorrow let alone for the rest of my life."

"And your accent tells me that you are not from around here either. Australian?"

"What gave it away?" I laughed. "The accent isn't hard to guess. Yes, Sydney born and bred."

"Isn't it summer in Australia now?"

I nodded. "I'm definitely missing home a lot at the moment. Just today, I decided to go back for Christmas."

"You can thaw out a bit."

"I'm feeling pretty toasty right now." Our eyes met and I held his gaze.

"*Aman Tanrım*." He coughed, smiling into his water glass.

"Sorry?" My voice was teasing, and he shrugged in reply.

"Nothing."

"I'm pretty sure I heard something."

Innuendos aside, once we had both relaxed, the conversation flowed quite smoothly, and I found myself happily chatting to Aydin about his home and my home and how we spent our time here in London.

"How did you end up here in London?"

"Oh. Well, that's a slightly longer story and very, very dull."

"I don't mind dull."

I pushed a stray curl behind my ear and tried to forget that my hair had probably transformed into a frizzy mop about now. Instead I took a deep breath and concentrated on his mouth. Oh man. My heart did a little flip. His lips. They made me dizzy. They were thick, especially his bottom one and I wanted to lean in and suck on that bottom lip forever. It had been so long since I had kissed anyone and right now I wanted nothing more than to feel his lips on mine, our tongues twisting and twirling together, with his facial hair scratching my chin.

I tried to focus on the conversation, but I was utterly lost.

"What were we talking about?"

A lopsided grin spread across his face. "How you came to be here."

"It's kind of embarrassing."

"What? More embarrassing than showing your... er... panties to everyone on the dancefloor?"

Panties! He actually said panties!

"Oh God! I'm so clumsy. You know, it's been said before that I can make a tit of myself in just about any situation!" I laughed, holding my face in my hands and peeking at him through my fingers. I would never be able to erase the word "panties" from my mind. "Alright then. I'll give you the edited version, shall I?"

He nodded as he filled my wine glass and raised his glass to me. "Şerefe. That means 'cheers' in Turkish."

I clinked my glass to his. "Panties."

Oh shit!

Heat rushed to my face, and I groaned in embarrassment.

"What?"

"Shit!"

"Did you just say panties?" He grinned wickedly at me, leaned forward and looked me straight in the eye. "You are completely crazy."

"Takes one to know one." I nudged him under the table with my foot. "Okay, okay. So how did I end up here? Alright, I came to London with a guy. Caught him in bed with his secretary. Wait, no, she preferred to be called a PA." I rolled my eyes. "So I burned the sheets. Left our apartment. Quit my job. Began a new life. And now here I am sitting with you."

"None of that seems embarrassing, although I am a little concerned that you just might be a pyromaniac."

I was burning pretty damn hot at that moment!

He lifted his glass again and clinked it against mine. "Your ex-boyfriend must have been embarrassed by his behaviour."

"Actually, he was my ex-fiancé, and I honestly wouldn't know. I haven't spoken to him since that day."

"Oh?"

"Whatever. I really did love those sheets though." I snuck a look at him only to catch his gaze. We stared at each other for a moment, his sexy, melted chocolate but with a hint of caramel eyes on my hazel (sometimes green) ones and I closed mine, trying to regain control of my lady bits that were currently preparing themselves for a big night. "And you?"

"Me?"

"What's your big secret?"

"I don't have one."

"Really? Everyone has at least one big secret. Obviously, mine is that I might possibly be, or probably am, a pyromaniac." I caught his eye, and we both grinned. "But what's yours, because I'm sitting here trying to figure you out and it's proving difficult."

"Lots of things. Too many things, in fact." He rolled his eyes at me. "I have a lot of baggage."

Dibs on being Aydin's baggage handler!

I laughed out loud at my inner voice. I've always been way funnier when I'm tipsy. Or drunk. Call it what it was. I was drunk. "We'll see, I guess."

"You know Ginger, I'm having a really good time, not that I

thought I wouldn't." He passed me the plate of Baingan Bharta. "Well, maybe I thought I wouldn't."

I spooned a small amount of the spicy eggplant dish onto my plate and nodded with him. "I get it. I've been on some crappy dates as well."

"You have?"

"Sure. I mean hasn't everyone?"

The grin that crept across Aydin's face was hotter than an Aussie summer. I just wanted to climb into his lap. "So how am I faring? As a date?"

Heat rose to my face again, most likely due to my dirty thoughts than his blazing gaze. "So this is a date then?" I smiled shyly.

"I think this could be classified as a date, unofficially anyway. And a pretty good one." He tapped my wine glass to his. "And as it's a pretty good, albeit unofficial, date, perhaps you should give me your number."

I was on possibly the best unofficial date I'd ever had, and I didn't even know Aydin's surname! We swapped mobiles, and I added my contact details before handing it back. He read it intently as though he had just been given the answer to the meaning of life. "It has been very nice to meet you, Miss Ginger Knox."

I glanced down at the new contact he'd entered in my mobile. Kaya. His last name was Kaya. "And you as well, Mr. Aydin Kaya."

"You know, I've never met anyone called Ginger before. Ginger is a root vegetable in Turkey. It's called *zencefil*. I like to put it on my *salep*."

"I don't know what *salep* is, but I do love pumpkin soup with ginger."

"When I was a boy, *salep* was my favourite drink in winter. My grandmother would make it and her whole kitchen smelled incredible." He closed his eyes for a moment before he leaned across the table and sniffed me. Again. "In fact, I have just realised *salep* reminds me of you."

"Stop smelling me, Creeper!"

"Stop calling me Creeper!"

I grinned at him. "Then stop smelling me!"

"It's your scent. Orange blossom and cinnamon. Just like my grandmother's *salep*."

"You keep saying '*salep*'. What is it?"

"*Salep* is a drink made from ground orchid tubers. Everyone has their own recipe, but my grandmother's recipe was the best. She would mix the ground powder with hot milk, orange blossom water, mastic and either cinnamon, pistachio or, in my case, ginger."

"That sounds, er, interesting."

"Well, you know, I'm a chef, so recipes are my life." He leaned forward and sniffed me again. "It's delicious."

He pulled back and fixed his gorgeous, brown eyes on me so intensely that I began to giggle like a twelve-year-old with a crush. He smiled at my reaction. "Anyway, Ginger really is an unusual name."

"My friends call me Ginny."

His brown eyes crinkled when he smiled at me. Oh man, he had the most ridiculously long lashes. "No, I don't think so. Ginger suits you."

"No one's ever said that to me before." I grimaced and rolled my eyes a little. "Normally I get reminded that I don't have red hair. Like I don't already know that."

Aydin reached across and tucked a stray curl behind my ear. "It's a beautiful name for a beautiful woman."

I'd always been uncomfortable with compliments and I wrinkled my nose at him. "God, that was corny."

"You do not see what I see."

My stomach flipped and I tried to think of a witty comeback. Something flirty but funny. A little humour to cover up my embarrassment but I had nothing. Nada. I stared at him, my mouth opened and closed wordlessly, like a dying fish.

After an eternity of gaping I finally broke his gaze and looked around the restaurant. The waitstaff were clearing tables, a sure sign that they were getting to the end of their shift and a not so subtle hint for us to get the bill. So… what to do now?

We left the restaurant and walked past the long-closed shops toward the Thames. It began to snow lightly, and Aydin smirked when I groaned as the first flakes started to fall. We walked side by side, not quite touching, but close enough to make me feel the slow burn that seemed to be building between us. Finally, he took my hand, and my heart stopped, just for a moment, before it jump-started again. There is was. That crazy electricity that pulsed from him to me and back. I forgot where I was, where we were and gazed up at him with the biggest smile on my face. I wondered if Nate might just have picked a winner.

"What are you thinking about?"

"Nothing really." I turned away and looked down at the murky water below. I couldn't imagine what Aydin would say if he knew Nate had gone out hunting some dick for me. "Just something Nate said earlier."

"About going for a swim in the Thames, maybe?"

I rolled my eyes and nudged him in the side. "If we are to be friends Aydin, you will learn to never listen to a word Nate says."

"No?"

I snorted. "Basically, he's full of shit."

"So did you lose your bet?"

I pushed Aydin away and bent over, laughing so hard the hot tears seeping out of my eyes cooled by the time they reached my cheeks. "Oh God! You knew?"

He gave me a floppy nod, and his mouth pulled up into his lopsided, goofy smile that released his... wait for it... dimples. Oh, swoon.

"Bloody Nate." I managed in between gasps of air. "I'm going to kill him."

"Your friends are —"

"Dickheads!" I finished for him, and a new round of laughter tightened my abs and stole my breath.

"I wasn't going to say that, but alright." My roars had finally rubbed off on Aydin, and he joined in, tipping his head back with a deep chuckle.

I grabbed his coat lapel and rested my forehead against his chest in an attempt to distract myself. This belly laugh was every bit Ginger and every bit unladylike. I had to stop myself before a pig snort slipped out because that would have been mortifying.

Aydin put his long arms around my shoulders and we chuckled together until I was finally able to catch my breath and start walking again.

"Your friends really look out for you. That's nice."

"True." I smiled up at him. What about you?"

"What? At home?"

"Yeah."

He shrugged. "It's different in Turkey. I work. A lot. And any free time is usually spent with my family. Family is very important."

"I've always wanted to go to Turkey. Gallipoli and all that."

"Ah, Gallipoli is very popular with Australians, although right now it is too cold. There is a powerful wind that comes down from the north. It will be snowing soon."

"Pffftt, so what? It's snowing here now!"

He laughed. "And you hate it right?"

"I grew up on the Northern Beaches of Sydney, so I always

loved the fantasy of snow but now that I'm living through the Ice Age, not so much."

"One day I would like to go to Sydney. Is it true there are kangaroos on every street and bears fall from the sky to kill you?"

"There sure are but what about Turkey? Is it true that Turkish men want to have sex with every woman they meet?"

"Well, not every woman."

Our eyes locked at his inference and we stopped walking. We were close, so very close. I only had to lift my chin, and we would be kissing.

In the distance, Big Ben chimed and Aydin broke eye contact and checked his watch. "It is very late."

My heart quickened, and my voice croaked in reply. "I guess."

"So Ginger, we met, we danced, we ate, and we even exchanged numbers. I think this was a successful night."

"Yes, it was." It was now or never, and some extra air in my lungs gave me the courage I needed. "It doesn't have to end though, does it?"

I can late night flirt with the best of them, and I shifted my weight onto one hip and looked up at him from under my lashes. He made no move toward me, but his eyes were filled with desire as they travelled the length of my body and back up again. I knew that this shift in body language was having a very positive effect on him and when a slight breeze blew my loose, black skirt up, just the right amount of my inner thigh was exposed. Damn, I could see the very positive effect growing before my very eyes.

He moaned slightly before turning it into a cough. "I... I'm not sure."

It was clear that the meal we had just eaten hadn't soaked up the last remnants of alcohol in my system, because I found myself with the overpowering need to touch him. I reached up and threaded my fingers through his luscious, thick hair.

He grabbed my hand and pressed his lips to my palm. The heat of his open mouth against my skin made my whole body tingle. He reached for me, wrapping his arm tightly around my back, pulling me into his chest. There was nothing else in the world except Aydin's lips on my palm, then on my wrist and then, oh my God, his lips on my neck. I lifted my head as he trailed kisses across my collarbone and up to my ear. The heat of his lips on my skin sent bolts down to my now, open for business farfallina, (thank you, Nonnina, for teaching me Italian swear words) and I wanted nothing more than for him to put his hot lips pretty much anywhere he damn well desired.

Aydin lifted his head from my neck and looked at me. "You're eyes are so green."

My face burned. "Nah, they're just hazel."

"No, they're not. They're green." He moved in closer to stare into my eyes. "You are my Green Eyes."

I smiled shyly at him. "And you can be my Creeper."

He wrinkled his nose and chuckled. "Can't you think of a better nickname than that?"

He was so close now, our lips were almost touching. "Let's just see how tonight goes shall we?"

"Have I told you how beautiful you are, Green Eyes?"

Unable to find the right words, I shook my head in reply.

Jane Gundogan

"You are so beautiful."

Dear God!

"I should also tell you that I have thought about kissing you all night."

"You have?"

His hot breath puffed out against the icy air, but still, it was warm against my face.

"I am going to kiss you now... if that's okay?"

Aydin tilted up my chin until our mouths were perfectly aligned. Hell yes I wanted him to kiss me. "It's okay."

This was the moment — the first kiss. Of course, in the movies, the first kiss was everything. The orchestra builds in momentum as the camera tightens the shot to capture the moment. Think Jack and Rose's iconic kiss on the bow of the Titanic. Or Jacob and Hannah's pash in the bar from Crazy, Stupid, Love (bonus points for that oh so hot Dirty Dancing scene). Yep, the first kiss was everything, and I sensed before we were even in each other's arms, that this kiss would be the one that I'd remember for the rest of my life.

His hands moved across my back and he pulled me against his chest. I whispered his name, just once, and then his lips crashed down on mine. It was frenzied. It was uncontrollable. It was just sooo damn sexy. His tongue pushed, I opened my mouth, and then we were tasting, swirling, probing each other with greed.

We broke away and stared at each other, both of us panting, our white puffs of breath mingling together and I knew at that moment that I was ruined. Ruined for all other men, all other lips, all other kisses, forever.

I also knew that I wanted nothing more than his lips on mine again.

Aydin was already way ahead of me and pulled me back against his chest. As he bent down to kiss me again I opened my mouth and let out the tiniest of moans as his lips found mine. My hands came up to the nape of his neck. I grabbed at his hair, my fingers frantic as I combed through his luscious locks while his hands moved down to my hips, pulling me even closer to him.

I knew that he wanted more, mostly because I could feel it pulsating against my hip. Somewhat reluctantly, I abandoned Aydin's curls and slipped my hands under his shirt. I traced his ridged muscles as I explored his torso. His hard, sculptured pecs felt impressive, and his abs ripped. My hands moved even lower, intuitively following his muscles to discover his perfect V-line, before they reached their desired destination. I cupped the front of his jeans and Aydin growled lightly. Oh yes, this was going to be fun.

A car passed by and honked, snapping us both out of our embrace. Aydin pulled away. His head twisted as he searched for somewhere with a little more privacy. He grabbed my hand, and we ran back towards Monument and snuck down a deserted alleyway. As soon as we were enveloped in darkness, Aydin pushed me against a brick wall and kissed me hard. We explored each other's mouths with our tongues, the desire for more overpowering my senses. At that moment, I didn't give a toss about how my hair looked or the light that had flicked on from the window above. All I cared about, all that mattered in my world was Aydin's mouth on mine and the way that he made me feel.

My coat was tossed aside in seconds. He turned me around,

and unzipped my dress and slipped it down my shoulders to my hips. Hypothermia momentarily popped into my head but that was quickly forgotten, replaced by the mortifying realisation that I was wearing my safe, pink, boring, Primark bra. Total bollocks! I swore at that moment I would never leave the house again unless I was attired in perfectly sexy (and matching) underwear.

As I turned back, Aydin caught his breath as he gazed at me. He kissed my neck while he wrapped his hands around my back and unhooked my bra releasing my breasts to fall against my chest. He took half a step back and admired my girls. *"Aman Tanrım."*

There was that saying again. I had no idea what it meant, but it must have been positive because as Aydin admired my breasts, he growled his approval. I arched my back, an invitation for him to take what he wanted. I craved his mouth on me. I ached for his lips to taste my skin. This desire was so overpowering that when he finally lowered his head, and his tongue flicked over my rosy bud, biting and tugging on my nipple, the shockwave of longing that swept through my whole body was so strong that it elicited my own growl of approval. I squirmed against the molten heat between my legs as Aydin alternated between my breasts, sucking and tonguing, biting each nipple softly or rolling them between his perfect fingers.

He lifted his head away from my nipple and I whimpered at the loss. His eyes locked with mine as his hand moved lower. "I want you, Ginger," he whispered in my ear. "I want to make love to you."

My body shook in anticipation because I knew what was to come. Me!

I nodded, and he slipped his hand under the hem of my bunched up dress. I held my breath as his fingers trailed slowly, so slowly, up my thigh until they brushed my 'panties'. He pulled the cotton material aside and began to slowly stroke me, his fingers running along my opening. I could feel my arousal practically running down my leg and he slowly, ever so slowly, slipped first one and then another finger inside.

I began to kiss him again, biting his lip as he explored me, moving my hips in time with his hand, his thumb circling my nub, my pink pearl, my... oooh! I moaned loudly into his mouth as I rocked back and forth in time with his thrusting fingers. I can't remember the last time I was this turned on. Within seconds, wave after wave of pleasure crashed over me as I came and I found myself moaning Aydin's name over and over as I floated away on my magical orgasm cloud.

Three years with Henry and it had never been this good. I mean I had just come — in an alleyway, no less! Like the harlot that I was, or maybe the harlot that I secretly longed to be.

I recovered slowly, mostly because Aydin's thumb kept circling around and around, which never really allowed the waves of pleasure to stop. I reached for his jeans, fiddling with his buttons in a desperate need to free the hardness that pushed against my hip. Right now, I wanted nothing more than to feel that hardness thrusting inside me. I willed him to take me, to fill me and I heard myself groan in his ear begging, "Now. I want you now."

I grabbed his shaft, and it pulsated and thickened in my hand. I stroked him slowly, my grip tightening on his hardness and navigated him towards me when he suddenly pulled away, his eyes glazed over with indecision. "Wait!"

Of course. Condom.

I bent down and searched in the darkness for my handbag. Once I found it, I pulled out a condom that had been living there for a lot longer than I would care to admit. Do condoms have a "best before" date?

I reached out to grab him again, but he backed away, pushing himself hard against the wall opposite. "I can't," he muttered, his body absolutely rigid.

What the holy hell? "Are you joking?"

Aydin exhaled slowly. "I think this might be a mistake."

"Excuse me?"

"Please understand. I absolutely want you. Do not doubt that for one moment. But we cannot start something. Not now, and certainly not here. You deserve much more than this." His voice cracked as he tucked himself away and buttoned up his jeans. "I don't want you to think of me as a regret."

I stared up at him in absolute shock. Was this some kind of joke? "I think I can make up my own mind, thank you very much."

"You know I am right."

Shame and embarrassment bubbled up inside me. I didn't want Aydin to see the tears that I knew were about to fall, so I laughed lightly and busied myself with my dress. "Hey, it's cool. I understand."

I didn't understand.

He opened his mouth to reply but wisely chose to say nothing. He shuffled his feet nervously as I gathered my coat and handbag. "Let me wait with you... for your train at least." His voice was shaky and uncertain. "And I will call you... soon."

"Sure. Whatever."

I stomped off towards the tube entrance with Aydin following closely behind. We stood awkwardly on the platform in silence, both of us lost in our own thoughts, me trying to understand why I was so harshly rejected and him no doubt thinking of bullshit excuses to disappear into the night.

At that moment his mobile pinged and I smiled to myself. One bullshit excuse coming right up.

Aydin pulled his phone from his coat pocket, read the message, sighed and closed the screen, but not before I saw a photo of Aydin with his arms around a gorgeous, and no doubt Turkish, woman.

"She's stunning."

"Yes, she is."

"Your girlfriend?"

Jealous much?

"Um, no. Not really."

"Oh?"

"She is my wife."

He's married?

I was furious. The tears that I had tried so hard to hide now escaped down my cheeks. "Are you fucking serious?"

"Please, Ginger. Let me explain."

"I don't think there is anything at all to explain Aydin. You —," I poked him in the chest, "are an asshole, and I need you to leave!"

"Ginger!" He reached out to grab my arm.

"Don't touch me!" I shrieked, bringing our argument to the attention of nearby commuters.

"You 'right lady?" asked a beefy guy a few metres away.

I nodded, feeling the bile rise in my throat as the train approached and I immediately ran to the doors as they opened. I needed to get as far away from Aydin as I could.

Wife?

Aydin tapped on the glass. "I'm sorry," he mouthed. I turned my back on him as the train pulled away, and my throat began to close as I choked back a sob.

I was going to KILL Nate!

CHAPTER 6

A Hugh Grant Hangover

Despite any rumours that you may have heard, I swear to you that I did not spend the next three weeks thinking about my drunken almost-sex with Mr. Aydin Kaya. I also did not check my mobile every five minutes wondering whether he would actually call or spent hours analysing why the hell he hadn't; which was way worse, because I bloody well didn't want to hear from that married asshole, anyway.

What I did do, however, was arrange my escape from miserable old London to sun-shiny Sydney. Taking Meg's advice, I by-passed Ann-Louise Onion entirely and went straight to Personnel. They approved my leave with a smile, most likely because my mountain woman of a boss seemed to go through staff like toilet paper and the fact that I'd lasted this long meant I was long overdue for a well-earned break. Ann-Louise was most put out about what she considered "underhanded behaviour" by my going behind her back. She made it her mission to ensure that my life was miserable for what little time I had left in the office. That included, but was not limited to, hours of unappreciated overtime, sourcing almost impossible to find Christmas gifts for her family and friends, and some rather shabby Christmas presents for her staff, including me.

Jane Gundogan

I got a candle which I wrapped myself. The icing on the cake of crappy jobs I had to complete for Ms Onion was to take her yappy little pomeranian Byron to his doggy day spa and sit with him while he received his acupuncture (I'm not even joking). I completed all of her tedious tasks with a smile because it meant I was one step closer to Christmas in Sydney for some much needed Vitamin D courtesy the sun, which hadn't seen here in London for weeks now.

There was also some significant retail spending done by me that caused one of my credit cards to max out and, worse still, the very real ordeal of a bikini wax in the middle of winter. But, as I said, there was so much to look forward to. A week with Dad and Sadie. A week getting to know my gorgeous nieces. A week of Aussie sunshine, of vitamin D, of Vegemite and of Tim Tams. I literally got dizzy at the thought of being back on Australian shores.

It also gave me a week to weigh up my options, and there were options to be weighed. If I sourced a job back in Australia, would I stay? My UK work visa wouldn't expire for another few months. It would be a shame to waste it, although if I was honest with myself, I didn't exactly have a lot to keep me in London other than Courtney and Meg. Nate as well, even though I had not yet forgiven him for fixing me up with Aydin the asshole / married man.

Nothing could ruin my excitement, and by 22 December I was happily sloshed and listening to Courtney and Meg's recap of last night's epic work Christmas Party, while I turned my attention to the empty suitcase that lay on the floor beside me.

The four "S's" necessary for a trip Down Under: shorts, sundresses, singlets, and swimwear. I doubted I would need much more than that because I could raid my sister's wardrobe if desperate. I guess the real question was how many sundresses (two), what type of shorts (denim or cotton?) and exactly how many bikinis, I would need for seven days on the beach? (The answer was three, at least.) Oh, and one fabulously skimpy (but not slutty — okay maybe a little slutty) dress for dinner. Wait! Maybe two because, well, there would definitely be more than one invitation to dinner. Which meant, of course, matching shoes (say hello to my Christmas present to myself a brand new pair of Miu Miu pumps). I tossed in a handful of accessories and carefully stuffed in all the brightly-wrapped Christmas presents for the family.

I finished up and admired my work. "You know guys, I have some stellar packing skills. I wonder if I could turn this into a career?"

"Didn't Kimmy Kardashian-West start her career tidying up wardrobes?"

I snorted. "I don't think that's how she became famous, Meg."

"Well duh, I mean, I know how she became famous. That Ray J though. Boy he is hung!"

To move the topic away from Ray J's penis, Courtney brought up a very touchy subject knowing she would get an extreme reaction. "So Meg, did Jeffrey speak to you last night?"

"No!" Meg blew her now freshly dyed pink fringe out of her eyes. "He's a bit of a shit, that one. Hasn't spoken to me since that night at the pub, has he? I mean, other than work stuff he hasn't uttered more than two words to me."

"Really?"

"I thought he was mad for me, but all he wanted was sex. He Jedi mind-fucked me into boinking him."

Courtney and I glanced at each other. Meg rarely swore, so when she did we paid attention. "They all do, Meg."

"And did you see him last night? He was snogging Cassie Mathews from Property."

"We saw."

"Property? Pfftt!"

Property Law was for losers.

"I mean, seriously, she's like fourteen or something!"

"Well, if she were, then Jeffrey would have a whole new set of problems, wouldn't he?"

Meg poo-pooed me. "Do you realise that I will be twenty-eight next month? Twenty-eight!"

"And?"

"Me mum had already been married for five years and had had three kids by my age! I can't even get a guy to go on a second date!"

"Your vagina certainly thanks you."

"But my ticking clock doesn't."

"What? You want to have a baby?"

"Not really. Well, not right now. I just want to know that it's out there. Somewhere."

"What is?"

"Life. Love. All of it."

"Of course it is."

"Is it? I mean, look at tonight for example."

"Tonight?"

"If we weren't here right now watching you pack, what would we be doing?"

"I'll have you know that I have a very active social life." Courtney sat on the end of my bed and trimmed the split ends off the ends of her ebony hair with my nail scissors. Social life, indeed. "I certainly wouldn't be at home."

"Yeah, but you've got a whole new pool to paddle in." Courtney snorted at my reply and made an "L" with her fingers. "Whatever, Courts. Anyway, I was going to catch up on Outlander."

"Oh my God! Sam Heughan, right?" Meg wiped pretend drool from her chin. "Other than my Sam Heughan fantasies, the rest of my life seems to have become a revolving door of paying bills, saving for a house which I'll probably never be able to afford, and searching for the best health insurance. This is not what I thought my life would be!"

Courtney grabbed a book off my side table and tossed it to Meg. "Read this then. Might help."

Meg turned it over. "Seriously? 'He's Just Not That Into You'? Am I a social pariah?"

"I'm not saying that but I think the book might say it though."

"Cow."

Courtney poked her tongue out at Meg. "Sorry, I just suck at empathizing with your hetero problems."

"Don't you complain, Meg. At least you got laid. I didn't even get that. And I'm pretty sure I have a depressed vagina."

Meg looked up at me curiously. "Is that a thing?"

"I read somewhere that it was a thing." I nodded vehemently. "What if my depressed vagina was the actual reason why Henry left me for Charlotte-Fucking-Poppins and her ginormous nipples? What if my depressed vagina is holding me hostage?"

This time Courtney laughed. "Darl, your vag isn't doing any such thing. It's your addiction to Jude Law that's holding you back."

"Hugh Grant."

"I'm pretty sure they're the same person."

I rolled my eyes at her. "And I hate my job, and the weather, and I'm beginning to really hate London as well."

"You're just homesick."

"Of course I am." I spread my arms wide to illustrate my point. "I mean look where I live!"

We all paused to appreciate the hellhole that was my current place of abode. Despite my best efforts my teeny-tiny flat really was quite repulsive. It was always damp, summer or winter, and frankly, I was surprised that I hadn't died of some kind of respiratory-related illness. The yellowing floral wallpaper, which had probably been hung in the 1970's, was peeling, the floorboards warped and creaked with every step, and the carpet was so threadbare that it couldn't even mask the wafting smell of Chinese food being eaten by the couple downstairs. But all those transgressions could be forgiven because the worst part of living in my teeny-tiny bed-sit in Plimco with my white, wicker chair and ficus was that right now there was still no fecking heating!

Now it wasn't just my vagina that was depressed.

"Would you like some cheese with that whine?"

I threw one of my Golborne Road pillows (potentially one of the nicest things in my whole flat) at Courtney's head. "Pom!"

"Convict!"

"Come on, it's Christmas. We should be out having the time of our wasted lives, not sitting 'ere like dafties, freezing our tits off." Meg sat on my sofa still wearing her puffer jacket for warmth. "I just don't like all this adulting. It doesn't suit me."

"When I get back, we shall have to play the 'Let's find Meg the Perfect Guy' game."

"I should have let Nate play match-maker with me instead of you that night."

"Yeah like it worked out so well." I scoffed, thinking of Aydin ... and his tongue ... and his thumb. Oh, God! His thumb!

"True." Meg sulked. "And Jeffrey can just fuck off."

"I guess Aydin should fuck off too eh, Ginny?" Courtney wiggled her eyebrows at me.

"Come on Courts, enough!" My face burned as the memory of Aydin's rejection washed over me again. "That was weeks ago."

"So?"

"So nothing. He's married, and frankly, I don't give a shit either way. I haven't given him a second thought."

A lie.

Maybe I had given him a second thought when Meg and I *accidentally* found ourselves outside The Dorchester the other night, but that was solely because I heard of a fabulous Thai restaurant nearby.

I swear!

I had only thought about him that one time.

Alright, that was a lie too, because despite my depressed vagina I seemed to be in a constant state of horny. I would wake most nights covered in sweat, my heart racing, having experienced some of the most erotic dreams of my life with Aydin as my leading man. Which meant I had thought about him daily, well, nightly, actually.

Fantasy Aydin was precisely the man that I wanted in real life. He was the perfect blend of raunchy and romantic and, even on one occasion, was joined by Channing Tatum who satisfied me firstly with a bumpy, grindy show before we all got bumpy, grindy and downright dirty together. It was awesome. Fantasy Aydin (with or without Channing Tatum) knew what he was doing, and he did it well. He was a man with exceptional lovemaking skills that alternated between giving me the raunchiest and hottest shag that my mind could conjure, to idolising every inch of my body, before filling me with his perfect proportioned penis until I woke up screaming his name, "Aydin! Aydin! Aydin!"

I was bloody surprised the neighbours hadn't complained.

Salep and Ginger

I flapped my hand in front of my face to cool down. Even there, sitting beside my two friends, my skin prickled and heat rushed between my legs as my mind wandered back to last night's mind-blowing orgasm, brought on by Fantasy Aydin. He had bound me to my bedhead while he slowly ran his tongue over my body. He worshipped my breasts as he sucked, bit and kissed them while I writhed and bucked, begging him to move his tongue lower. Finally, his mouth drifted between my legs, and he parted my silky folds. I was so wet, so juicy and I just couldn't wait anymore. I screamed his name, desperate for him to enter me, to screw me hard. And he did. Over and over.

"Is that right?" Courtney snapped her fingers in my face to get my attention. It was clear that she didn't believe a word I'd said. "I mean, of course, he was hardly Mr. Perfect."

"That's right, he was so not Mr. Perfect. In fact, he was Mr. Asshole."

"Mr. Waste of Time."

"Mr. Married Man!"

Mr. Take Me Now And Do Whatever You Damn Well Wanted!

"Right, right, right!" Courtney laughed. "I'm going to sum this up real quick. You hate him, but you're obsessed with him."

"Obsessed? I'm so not obsessing. Hell, you brought him up!"

"Come on Ginny." Courtney wasn't going to let this go. "So, you didn't catch two trains to walk past a particular hotel with Meg the other night after work?"

Ugh! Caught red-handed. "And here you are saying we never go anywhere!"

"Sorry darl, she got it out of me." Meg piped up, but sunk lower onto the couch when I scowled at her.

It seemed appropriate to throw my next pillow at Meg's head. "Really?"

"Alright, so let's say you're not exactly obsessed, but he definitely did get under your skin."

"But sadly, not into your pants!"

Courtney grabbed my mobile off the table. "And what if we looked at your search history?"

"Get off!" My yell sounded much louder than necessary in the tiny space. "You'll find zip."

"Are you sure?"

Courtney opened my Facebook and started typing. "A-Y-D- oh wait, there he is." She clicked on his name while grinning at me. "Aydin Kaya. So glad you hadn't stalked him."

"I was merely curious." Not true. I completely was obsessed, just like they said!

Courtney and Meg scrolled down his feed. "Doesn't a dude know to have his shit on private?"

"I know, right?"

Courtney stopped scrolling for a beat, examined a photo closely, before starting again. "Yeah, he's definitely not here."

"Here?"

"In London. Where did you say he was from anyway?"

She tossed the phone to me, and I also scrolled through his photos. Again. Hot, sexy Creeper with his fiery, sexy eyes and thick, sexy... lips.

"That's probably Turkey somewhere." I pointed at the photo of him and an older man standing on a bridge with people fishing in the background. "Wait, the photo's tagged. Yep. Istanbul. He's in Istanbul."

"There are no photos of the supposed wife though." Meg watched from over my shoulder as I scrolled down his feed.

"It's not 'the supposed wife' Meg. It's the wife-wife. He told me. Straight out told me when I practically had my hand down his pants. And anyway, he probably has more than one Facebook account. Most of these two-timing creeper assholes do, don't they?"

Didn't matter to me anyway. Aydin was married. Married! I still couldn't believe that he led me on. Did he lead me on?

Hell yeah, he did!

"He's terribly good looking, though." Meg grabbed the phone out of my hand and continued scrolling down the page. "What's with all the followers?"

"Yeah, I noticed that."

"A couple of followers, sure but 60,465 followers? I mean, that's a LOT of followers for a chef."

"Probably 60,465 women that's he's boinked."

"Let's see if we can find the wife."

"Come on guys, give me the phone."

Courtney and Meg tossed the phone to each other while I made a half-assed attempt to grab it. Courtney jumped out of the way and threw the phone to Meg who reached out to catch it, but it slipped from her fingers and landed on the ground with a crash. "Oops!"

"Sorry, Ginny." She picked it up, dusted it off and handed it back to me. "You know we love you. We just don't want to see you pining away."

"I am not pining! I am indignant." I looked down at my phone for a moment before – "Hey? What? What did you guys do?"

"Nothing. Why?" Meg was back looking over my shoulder. "Oh bollocks!"

"Bollocks is right!"

Holy freaking hell.

"You sent him a friend request?"

"No, I didn't!"

"Well, one of you did." I turned my screen to face them. "A FRIEND REQUEST!"

"Oh shit." Courtney was reading my screen and looked up at me with a big grin spread across her face. "It truly was an accident. We're sorry."

"It's too late to say sorry." I dropped the phone on the coffee table, and it beeped in reply.

Courtney picked it up and read the message. "Oh shit."

"What?"

"Like I said, I'm really sorry."

Meg looked at the phone. "This is not good!"

"I know!" Courtney nodded in agreement. "Do we tell her?"

"Tell me!"

"Tell her."

"She's gonna to lose it."

"I'm gonna to lose it?" I leaned over and yanked the phone away from Courtney. "For fuck's sake, just give it to me!"

"Bugger." I read the notification on my phone and sighed. "He accepted."

"Yep."

"I'll need to block him now. How embarrassing."

"You can't do that."

"Why not?"

"Because you just sent him the request. It'd be weird."

"You guys suck. Why would I friend someone who is a two-timing asshole? I've been through this once already, no way I'm going to be the whore that ruins someone else's life."

"And the hot, never to be repeated kiss?"

I shook my head, and tried to sway any sexy thoughts out of it. Oh man, I was horny. Someone needed to lock up my Alter of Venus and throw away the key. I took a deep breath in an effort to hold onto what was left of my sanity. "Ugh! Whatever that kiss might have been doesn't mean it's going to be anything more."

"Or so says Confucius." Courtney's handbag beeped, and she rummaged through it to search for her phone. "Oh! He just friend requested me! I'll accept; after all, I have never seen his peen."

"I never actually saw his penis," I mumbled to no-one in particular. "It was too dark."

Meg gave me a hug. "I'm so sorry, darl."

"S'okay."

I dropped my phone on the couch, resigned to the fact that I had spent way too much time thinking about a married man, and instead grabbed the remote, turned my attention to the channels until — "YEAH!" The three of us screamed and jumped around the room. "LOVE ACTUALLY!" My evening improved dramatically with the ultimate Christmas movie, and my absolute favourite rom-com just starting.

"Drinking game!" Courtney danced over to my itsy-bitsy fridge, returning with a bottle of vodka that was conveniently located in the freezer, while Meg scrounged together three mismatched shot glasses. We pushed the bottle of wine aside and settled down to watch the movie with a mountain of popcorn, a family-sized Cadbury's Dairy Milk Chocolate and what was no doubt going to be way too much alcohol thanks to Colin Firth's constant fuck up of the Portuguese language and Hugh Grant making ridiculously cringe-worthy statements at every opportunity! Oh, and anyone saying the word "bollocks", "wank" or "piss". Man, I was going to feel like shit for that flight tomorrow!

And when my alarm sounded at the crack of ass, I knew that

last night's premonition had come true. I had a stonking hangover. I mumbled at Courtney as she attempted to drag me into an upright position.

My tongue felt like sandpaper, so much so I could hardly speak. "Oowww! How did I end up sleeping on the floor?"

"Fucking Hugh Grant!" Courtney moaned. "Now get up. You need to move. I've just seen on the news, it's madness at Heathrow. There's some massive storm over Europe. Are you sure your flight's still leaving?"

Flight?

I looked at the time. Bollocks! I only had twenty minutes! I swore in that moment that I would never let an alcoholic drink pass my lips again. Okay, that was a lie. How about I would never drink vodka again, and that's a promise!

"What happened last night?"

"Well, there was drinking and dancing and singing and Hugh Grant."

Fucking Hugh Grant.

"Why did you let me drink so much?"

"Me? Don't even think about blaming me for last night! I was the one throwing up in your sink."

"Where the hell is Meg?"

We both looked around the room and laughed. I mean, my bedsit was so small there really weren't many options where she could have been hiding.

"Okay." I attempted to stand, but my head had other ideas

and I sunk down onto my couch pulling a blanket around my shoulders. I turned to Courtney. "I'm officially dying."

She waved her hand in front of her face. "Actually, you might already be dead 'cause you smell like a corpse!"

I sniffed my pits and I dragged myself up, hugging the wall for support, before taking the three monumental steps across my bed-sit to my bathroom door. "I'm showering. Back in a bit."

And that's where I found Meg fast asleep in the bath. "I guess I'll shower when I land." I rummaged through the vanity drawer for deodorant.

Pulling my out of control curls into a messy knot, I whacked on a little lip gloss and mascara before I grabbed my red leggings off the bed. I topped them with my ripped jeans (after all it was a ridiculously cold minus two in London) and slipped on an oversized football jersey that at one time belonged to that other two-timing asshole that was Henry. What was it with me? I must have had a neon sign over my head that only dickheads could see that flashed "Asshole Wanted. Apply Within."

I groaned, safe in the knowledge that I had the worst taste in men. I also had an even worst taste in my mouth, so I ran back into the bathroom for some much-needed mouthwash. After I gargled and had one final look in the mirror, I grabbed my black jacket and my black converse, perfect for the flight, and just the right amount of cute. I slipped on my sunglasses to cover my red, raw eyes, grabbed my suitcase, double checked that I had my passport and walked to the door just as my mobile beeped to announce my Uber's arrival.

I was just too organised — even with a stonking hangover!

CHAPTER 7

Kismet In All Its Glorious Splendour

Courtney was right. I walked into what was nothing short of a war zone at Heathrow. T'was the morning before the morning before Christmas (or something like that) and every man, woman and child were desperate to get to where they needed to be. I checked the departure board. A scary number of flights had been delayed and even more than a few cancelled, although thankfully, the long haul to Sydney was still leaving on time. I pushed through the surly crowd to check in, and by the time I had my boarding pass in hand and made my way to my flight I was feeling quite exhausted. And hungover. Still.

I fell asleep before we had even begun to taxi, having taken a couple of headache tablets before I boarded, so when I was jostled awake, I wasn't prepared for the onslaught of turbulence that tossed the plane around the sky.

"Ladies and Gentlemen, this is the Captain speaking. We're experiencing quite a lot of turbulence due to the near-blizzard conditions outside. We tried to dodge the weather, but we've been informed that we will need to ground quickly as this system is worsening. I do apologise for any inconvenience, but right now your safety is paramount. In the meantime the fasten seatbelt sign has been switched on. Please return to your seats and keep your seatbelts fastened."

What the actual fuck?

I looked out the window but could see nothing other than thick cloud cover. It honestly felt like I was on a rollercoaster. I pulled at my seatbelt. Where the bloody hell were we?

"Ladies and Gentlemen, this is the Captain again. We have just been given clearance to land at Istanbul International Airport in Istanbul, Turkey. Once we have you all safely back on the ground, you will be given further details on onward flights and alternative arrangements."

Turkey? Bloody hell! They've GOT to be kidding!

I could feel the week in Sydney disappearing from my grasp.

"It might not be so bad." The man in the seat beside me piped up. "They will put us in a hotel and feed us. Five-star service."

"Fuck!" I grabbed his hand as an air pocket dropped us a couple of thousand metres, which made me want to vomit. "I just want to get on the ground in one piece."

An hour later, my wish came true, and I found myself standing alongside the rest of my flight all waiting for our luggage and wondering just what the hell to do having been informed that we were grounded until weather conditions improved. The airport hotel had no vacancies, and the ground service staff told us to go and find our own hotel and claim it on our insurance.

That definitely seemed easier than waiting with the hundreds of other stranded passengers, and so, decision made, I purchased a visa (a drama in itself, "Why didn't you purchase the visa online?" Why the hell do you think, asshole?), collected my luggage and walked through to the exit where I was confronted with a sea of faces, at least four people deep, and mostly men. There was a lot of yelling going on as I stepped through the doors. I was utterly overwhelmed, unsure of exactly what to do next, and still very much hungover.

"Lady? Lady? Taxi? Hotel?" A small, Turkish man with a very thick Turkish moustache which, under normal circumstances would have earned him a massive grin from me, pulled at my suitcase as I tried to push my way through to the taxi rank. "You come with me."

I wrenched my suitcase out of his hand and told him where to go ("fuck off" is universal language, isn't it?) before turning around and darting back into the terminal. I made my way to the Information Counter only to find it surrounded by an even larger group of irate passengers, including my neighbour from the plane, who waved at me to join him. I shook my head and resignedly found a chair to collapse into. I crossed my arms and mumbled to myself. "I think it's probably easier to stay right here."

Closing my eyes to the chaos around me, I took a deep breath and tried to decide just where to start with this calamity.

I pulled my phone out and hit Courtney on speed dial mentally thanking her for her sage advice to turn on my International Roaming before I left London. "Ginny? Is something wrong? Did you miss your plane?"

I pictured Courtney looking at the clock above her kitchen bench.

"No. You won't believe this."

"I will believe anything. Try me. Wait a sec! Let me put you on speaker. Nate and Nina are here. We're about to go for drinks."

I tried to muster some enthusiasm in my tone. "Hey, guys!"

"Hiiii Ginny."

"We miss youuuu!"

"Have a fabulous time!"

"There will be no fabulous time. The flight was grounded."

"Mile High Club! Tell me it was the Mile High Club!" Nate screamed down the phone so loudly I had to pull it away from my ear.

"No, and for fuck's sake Nate, get your mind out of the gutter! This is serious. We got caught in a blizzard. I'm stuck in Istanbul."

"Istanbul?"

"Shit!"

"Yeah. And there are no hotels to be found. I'm like Mary trying to find a freaking room at the inn or something."

"Aydin!" Courtney and Nate both shouted out at once. Nate must have also accepted his friend request.

I hated them both!

"Uh-uh!"

"What?" Nina piped up. "The amazing kiss, married guy?"

"Yep." Courtney squealed down the phone. "He's in Istanbul. Ring him. Facebook him. This is some serious kismet."

"No. Not after what happened!"

"You should talk to him, Ginger." Nate's tone had thankfully dulled to a yell. "Trust me. I have ever really lead you wrong?"

"Do you really expect me to reply that, Nate?"

"Just call him. He'd be right chuffed to talk to you."

"And you know this how exactly?"

"Believe me when I say you are going to love his story."

"Wait a minute, how do you know his story?"

"Oh Ginny, I've got to agree. There's a lot more to it." Nina's dulcet tone came down the line. "And now you are there. It's very serendipitous."

"You are so brainy. Come 'ere beautiful." Nina squealed as Nate no doubt wrapped himself around her.

"Nate! I'm in the middle of a crisis here. Focus!"

"Okay. Right. I've got a plan. Where are you right now?"

"At this second? I'm sitting at the exit. I'm going to sit here until my flight is ready to leave whether it's a day or a week, and in the meantime, I will spend my time watching the crazy locals outside trying to get my attention and the crazy stranded passengers inside trying to get a room. It's actually quite entertaining!"

"We'll call you back."

They hung up. I stared at my mobile. They bloody well hung up? So much for calling them. My friends. My posse. My helpful buds.

I grabbed my suitcase, passed by the chaotic information counter again and straight into the coffee shop next door. I reckoned I could stay there for at least the next twenty-four hours before security realised that I had set up camp and tossed me out.

I ordered a cappucino and settled onto the last free stool at the counter. I opened my Facebook and clicked on Aydin's name. As his photo smiled back at me, I wondered what to do with his account. I didn't delete him last night. I guess that meant I wanted to see him again, even if it was only to stalk him on social media. I mean, sensibly there was no option. I knew it would be disastrous. He was freaking married! But the chemistry between us? When he touched me — well let's just say that my punani was very impressed.

Asshole!

Instead of becoming lost in yet another fantasy featuring Aydin I sent an email to Sadie to warn her that I wasn't going to make it to Sydney anytime soon. My second email was to Dad. Seeing as I was stuck in airport prison, I thought I would send him a novel-sized email giving him a complete, albeit rated PG, update of my life. When he read it, it would be like I was right there with him on Christmas morning.

I spent the next two hours tapping away when my mobile rang. "Nate?"

"Where are you right this second?"

"Where am I? At the — "

"Coffee shop."

"Wha —?" I gasped, turned and found myself gazing straight into Aydin's mocha eyes. In a state of shock, I fell straight off my stool and landed at his feet. Again!

"Are you alright?" He bent down to help me back up, and flashed me a full grin as he laughed loudly. "This is the second time I've had to pick you up off the floor."

"Aydin?" Was I hallucinating? Did I hit my head when I fell off my chair? Damn, he was gorgeous. "What? How did you know I was here?"

"Nate and Courtney… don't forget your phone." He pointed at my phone which had fallen under the table. "They messaged me on Facebook. They are incredibly annoying."

I retrieved my mobile from the floor and put it to my ear. "Guys?"

"Yeah?"

"Firstly, I hate you, and secondly, I'll call you back."

As I hung up, shrieks and hooting echoed from the earpiece of my ex-friends back in London.

"Is it really you, Creeper?"

He shook his head and grinned at the nickname. "You're persisting with Creeper, are you?"

"It seems more fitting than ever." I didn't need a mirror to know I was the colour of a ripe tomato at that moment. "Why are you here?"

"This is certainly one way of getting a second date, isn't it?"

"Oh? Do you really want to bring up our last night in London? And anyway, I don't date married men, thank you very much!"

He grinned sheepishly. "Right. Well, we can talk about that later but right now —" he looked around the terminal, "— I think we need to find out exactly what is going on."

He turned to the barista behind the counter who was watching our banter curiously. "*Iki tane kapuçino istiyorum.*"

While Aydin spoke to the barista, I took the opportunity to ogle him. Just for a moment. Alright, maybe more than a moment because despite the fact that he was a bonafide asshole he was also one gorgeous looking man. He was also still married, so his dark eyes and thick, glorious hair were entirely off limits. I gazed at his lips as he spoke. I guessed they were speaking Turkish which, aside from the fact that it was Aydin speaking so I may have been slightly biased, Turkish was one ridiculously sexy language. I mean, I don't know what these two were blathering on about, but I could have sat there all day and let their dulcet tones wash over me. Like a warm shower. Or even better like me naked under a warm shower with Fantasy Aydin. Or maybe Real Aydin.

He turned to catch me off guard and in mid-ogle. "What are you doing?"

"Nothing." Perving on your hotness.

He knew exactly what I was doing, and his cocky grin confirmed just that. "Like what you see?"

"Don't flatter yourself, Creeper!"

"Sure." He chuckled and changed the subject. "I just ordered some coffee."

"Oh, okay. I pointed earlier." I couldn't help but laugh. "But he knew what I wanted."

He took a sip of his coffee before he stood back up. "Can I leave you here for a few minutes while I go and find out what is happening?"

"Of course."

Aydin disappeared into the crowd at the Information counter so I opened my Messenger and started a new group chat which I named 'Burn In Hell' which seemed entirely appropriate under the circumstances. I added Nate, Courtney, Nina and Meg (even though Meg wasn't guilty of this particular treacherous act).

Me: I hate you.

Me: And I'm unfriending you all as soon as I can! I swear I will never speak to any of you again.

Courtney: Nah, you love us really.

Me: I bloody well do not.

Meg: What's happening?

Courtney: Ginny's gonna get her stocking stuffed.

Meg: ???

Nate: Yep, with a Turkish kebab.

Meg: No idea what yr talking about.

Nina: Ginny's flight was grounded and she's stuck in Istanbul.

Meg: Isn't Aydin in Istanbul?

Nate: He's the one who's going to stuff her stocking Megster.

Meg: OMG!

Ginger: And damn it! He's still hot!

Meg: I bet he is.

Courtney: What happens in Istanbul and all that!

Nate: Think of this as a free pass. Just get your leg over and thank us later HA HA HA or maybe it should be HO HO HO!

Ginger: Just so you know I'm giving you the finger so hard right now Nate.

Laughing loudly, I slammed my phone face down on the table as Aydin re-appeared beside me. "It looks like you really are stuck here."

"So it seems."

"You are coming with me then."

"To where, exactly?"

"Well, I certainly don't want to put you in an uncomfortable position so —"

(You can put me in any position you like!)

"—I will arrange for you to stay at my Aunt's *pansion* in *Sultanahmet*."

"Alright, more words I just don't know."

"A *pansion* is a small hotel. Like bed and breakfast."

"Really? And she has a spare room?"

"Of course." He grabbed my suitcase and wrapped an arm around my shoulders, guiding me out of the bar. "And it's in the area known as Sultanahmet. It's a very touristic area. You will feel very comfortable, and my Aunt will look after you."

As much as I hated the way we finished things back in London, I did appreciate what he was doing for me now, plus having his arm wrapped around me was making me feel all hot and tingly and hot. And yes, I know I said hot twice! "Thank you, Aydin."

"You're welcome. It's definitely nice to see you again, Ginger."

He smiled as we moved towards the crowded exit. I spotted my neighbour from the plane, and he called over to me as we passed. "Hey? Hey? Did you find a room? Where are you going?"

I shrugged out of Aydin's arm. "Staying with my friend."

He scratched his head and looked at me like I was about to be kidnapped into the slave trade. "A friend you know, right?"

I smiled at him. Sweet. He was worried about me. "Thanks. Yes, I know him from London."

"Oh? Okay. Well, good luck!" He waved me off as he returned

to the masses at the information counter. "And Merry Christmas."

"You too."

I trailed behind Aydin as we made our way towards the exit. Can I just say that the view from behind is as good as the view in front. His ass looked great in those jeans but coupled with his leather jacket, and the hot as hell Ray Bans he had just slipped on, made him look like a goddamn Turkish Johnny Castle (from Dirty Dancing, not the porn star). Patrick Swayze always looked great in jeans as well.

Although I was about to walk into what looked like a mountain of snow outside, I had to fan my hand in front of my face to cool down my hot blush.

Gotta stop thinking about sex, Ginger!

Gotta stop thinking about sex with Aydin!

Gotta stop staring at his ass!

"Aydin."

"Yes, Ginger?"

"Ginny."

"I like Ginger."

"Can we stop for just a second?"

I tried to ignore the heat rising in my cheeks — and in my lady bits — and keep my mind centred on what I needed to say. And, as we stopped in the middle of the arrivals hall, surrounded by the hustle and bustle of stranded passengers, Aydin's eyes met mine and everything and everyone else around us disappeared. Those pesky sparks of electricity between us returned. I instinctively stepped closer to him, the desire to be by his side too overpowering to resist. As soon as I realised what I had done, I forced myself to back up.

Step away from the hot man, Ginger Knox!

"Let me just say this before I lose my nerve. Just don't alright. Don't touch me, and definitely don't smile at me." The corners of his mouth began to twitch as he tried to keep his dazzling smile at bay. He failed dismally and grinned at me as I squirmed. "That! Don't do that! I mean, thank you for coming to my rescue and everything, but please don't think that there is something here. There's not. And there never will be. You're married, and with my shitty taste in men, well frankly, I just don't need the complication."

There. Done.

Sensible Ginger Knox thinking with her brain instead of her twat!

He reached for me, but I dodged him, rather clumsily. "Ginger, you must let me explain."

"Can we just forget what happened? Let's just get through the next few days and then I'll be back on a plane and out of your life forever."

"Yes, of course. You are right." His tone was a little bitter and I knew he was frustrated, or maybe he was a little angry, I wasn't sure. He grabbed my luggage and walked toward the exit, leaving me to trail behind. "Traffic will be bad. We should leave now, Ginger."

The way he said my name though. Jeen-jar. I was a horny trainwreck!

CHAPTER 8

It's Istanbul Not Constantinople

As we stepped out into the blizzard I was reminded that I was actually stranded in a country that I knew very little about, with a married man who happened to be a two-timing asshole with an excessively large number of Facebook followers, and with a suitcase containing nothing more than some itsy-bitsy bikinis and Christmas presents for the family. My poor credit cards were surely ready to self-combust, but I hoped I had enough left on them as I needed to go shopping. Badly. I knew this because as we walked in awkward silence to a tiny, white car my Converse became soaked and squelched loud enough to make me grimace.

Aydin opened the passenger door for me while stuffing my suitcase into the back seat. Moments later he was seated beside me. The engine started with a few pops of the exhaust and we were off. Aydin weaved our way out of the airport — and straight onto the wrong side of the road! Well it was the *right* side of the road to Aydin, but to me? WE WERE ALL GOING TO DIE! Plus he appeared to be hell-bent on depositing me with his Aunt at the earliest opportunity because he drove at break-neck speed past honking cars, swerving taxis and overcrowded buses, as he weaved in and out of traffic.

"Aydin?"

"Hmmm?"

"You drive like a maniac."

My comment seemed to break the awkwardness between us and he threw his head back and laughed. "No Ginger, I drive like a *Türk*."

While Aydin drove, I went back to what was clearly going to become my new favourite past time. Ogling him. It was ridiculous just how magnificent he was.

Hubba hubba.

Let's start at the top, shall we? His hair was still tousled and gorgeous, maybe more so as it was a little damp. I had an overpowering desire to run my fingers through the curls at the base of his neck. Then there were his lips. Was it possible for a man's lips to be too beautiful? I had to pinch my thigh to stop myself from leaning over and licking them as we came to a screeching stop at a set of lights. His chiselled jaw had just the right amount of stubble, darkening the cleft in his chin. And lets not forget those dimples that made an occasional appearance — just so we don't forget they're there.

I was then distracted by Aydin's right hand which was, at that moment, changing gears. And when he grabbed that gearstick I imagined him wrapping his hand around his... Ginger!

For feck's sake! He's still married and therefore still entirely off limits.

But a girl can dream, can't she?

I cleared my throat. "I just want to thank you again, Aydin, for helping me."

"Of course. We are friends."

Friends?

Friends with Benefits.

"I guess we're friends."

But we could be fuck buddies.

He removed his sunglasses and turned the full force of his gaze, the colour of a freshly brewed espresso, on me. "I wonder what you are thinking right now?"

If the burning feeling in my face was any indication then it was probable that I was about to spontaneously combust. "No, I don't think you do."

"Maybe we are thinking the same thoughts." Aydin winked, slipped his totally unnecessary sunglasses back on and returned his attention to the road.

Thankfully I somehow managed to not self combust at his double entendre so I followed Aydin's lead and turned my attention to the view out the passenger-side window rather than the view in the seat beside me. I was a little curious (and more than a little bit nervous) about being in Istanbul. I knew that they had had their fair share of terrorist attacks over the years but I was also excited to explore this city that I found myself stranded in.

And so far Istanbul did not disappoint.

When we left the airport there wasn't really a lot to see. Freeway mostly. Snowy / sludgy / rainy hills. The occasional building. But then Aydin pulled off the freeway and merged into the chaos of Istanbul, turning his car into the tangle of impossibly narrow backstreets and narrow alleyways which I guessed would make Istanbul an incredibly easy city to find yourself lost in.

The tiny car zipped in and out of lanes, past honking cars, swerving taxis and packed buses until finally we were driving along the waterfront. I gasped in astonishment. I leaned forward in my seat so I could take in the view. Snow-topped domed mosques topped with fairytale minarets were to my right, crumbling arches and half collapsed stone walls to my left. Boats of every size navigated slowly through the waterway and under large bridges that were probably filled with crazy commuters fighting their way through the awful traffic to get to where they needed to be.

In fact, the traffic was so heavy that we eventually came to a complete stop and I pressed my face against the coolness of the car window. It had been a pretty eventful day up until this point, and every part of me was exhausted, still hungover, and all the stopping and starting as Aydin's navigated through the traffic had made me feel a little queasy. Oh, and I was pretty sure I smelled. I tried to sniff my armpit, without looking like I was sniffing my armpit. Yup, I need a shower. Pronto!

Aydin played tour guide and pointed out features of interest. "Right now we are in Europe. The water here is the Bosphorus river and past it —" he indicated to the land mass in the distance, "— is Asia. You can catch a ferry across to *Kadiköy* from just up there."

I nestled comfortably into the passenger seat, and my eyes grew heavy. It really had been a long day, and Aydin's thick accented English washed over me like a warm fantasy shower (which as I had already ascertained was desperately needed). I closed my eyes, for just a moment, but when I opened them again, the tiny car had pulled into an alleyway and was coming to a bumpy stop in front of an ancient stone wall with an intricate wooden gate. I sat upright and took in my new surroundings. A small plaque to the right of the entrance declared its name, 'Saklı Bahçe.'

Aydin jumped out of the car and walked around to open the passenger side door for me. Not wanting to inconvenience him any further, I stepped out of the car, only to fall flat on my ass, (for the third freaking time) and straight into a puddle of mud and snow.

Fuck my life!

"*Hoşgeldin* and... oh, my, what are you doing on the ground, *aşkım?*"

From my vantage point in the gutter, I looked up to find the owner of the very thick accent; an older lady, who had popped her head through the gates to greet me. A fat tabby cat meowed at her feet, no doubt wanting to return to the warmth indoors. Sprawled out in the snow, I moaned at my clumsiness. The lady yelled at Aydin in Turkish, then helped me up, took me by my elbow and directed me towards the gate. "Silly boy." The woman patted my cheek. "Let me get you inside to dry off before you catch a... what is it called... you know the word I am thinking of... the *grip.*"

Aydin grabbed my suitcase off the back seat. "The flu, *Teyze.*"

"Yes, yes. The flu." Aydin's aunt wiped the snow from my backside.

"She is incredibly clumsy, *Teyze*. It happens all the time." Aydin laughed loudly as he pushed the gate wide open. "Better to leave her, or you will spend all your free time picking her up off the ground."

I poked my tongue out at him and giggled when he poked his tongue back at me and wiggled it for good measure. Maybe we could be friends after all.

I stepped through the entrance and found myself in a large courtyard, a time-chiselled tree with its long, reaching branches naked, but for a thin layer of snow, in the centre. Holy crap, I had arrived in Narnia. Was Edmund Pevensie going to suddenly appear and offer me a piece of Turkish Delight? I was kind of hungry.

Across the courtyard was a set of intricately carved, wooden doors leading to what was I guessed the main two-storey stone and wood house. To my left were three smaller doors that possibly were rooms that Aydin's aunt rented out to tourists and stranded Australians. Walking through the nearly ankle-deep snow was difficult in my already-soaked shoes. I stumbled backwards, nearly losing my footing yet again, but was caught by Aydin's aunt who merely patted my hand as she walked beside me, helping me shuffle through the snow.

Once inside she dropped my hand and stepped behind a small reception desk beside the door. She began clicking away on a keyboard before she looked up with a smile. "Now that we have you safely inside let me start again. *Hoşgeldiniz* which means welcome in Turkish. My name is Refika, and I am Aydin's aunt. My nephew —," she reached across the desk and grabbed Aydin's cheeks, pinching them until they were red, "— tells me that you are a very, *very*, good friend of his and asks that I take care of you while you are here."

I glanced at Aydin whose cheeks remained red, although I wasn't sure if it was because his Aunt squeezed them or if it was because he was blushing. I returned my attention to Refika who still hadn't taken a breath. "My home has been in my husband's family for many generations, all the way back to the period of rule by the great Ottoman, Selim III. Our family began as merchants, and we were held in great esteem by the Ottoman and his consorts."

I smiled politely while she continued with her history lesson. "Now we rent out rooms for income. I have visitors from all over the world, which is why I speak such good English. It is important to speak many languages."

Aydin looked up at the ceiling before he smiled at his aunt. "Yes *Teyze*, your English is excellent."

She wiggled her finger at him. "You are being a little smart, my nephew. You watch your manners." She turned to me conspiringly. "You be careful of this one, Miss Ginger. He was big... Aydin, what were you when you were a boy?"

He sighed. It was easy to see that he enjoyed indulging his aunt. "A trouble-maker, *Teyze*. I was a big trouble-maker."

"I believe you, Refika." I raised my eyebrows at Aydin, and he twitched his lips slightly before shooing me away while he sorted out my accommodation with his aunt.

I took the opportunity to look around. The building itself was kind of old and perhaps a little rundown, but I imagined that it would have been splendid in its heyday of the great Ottoman, something or other. I gave myself a small grin. The room was inviting however and carefully furnished with rustic-looking leather armchairs and overstuffed sofas scattered around for its residents and guests to enjoy. An enormous wooden table that could have comfortably seated an army dominated the centre of the room. I wondered how many happy dinners Aydin had spent here with his family — and his wife.

A stone fireplace dominated the back wall, and a fire blazed which made the whole room toasty warm. I moved toward it to dry my soggy bottom. Soon, Aydin and his aunt returned with a key and directed me back outside and across to the three wooden doors opposite the main house.

Refika beamed mischievously. "You will be staying in one of my best rooms. I think you will be very comfortable."

I smiled at her gratefully as Aydin whispered in my ear. "It's where they used to keep the animals."

"I heard that, nephew." Refika opened the door with an old-fashioned key which she handed to me. "I will leave you here. Aydin will help you get settled." She poked Aydin in his side. "You build a fire for our beautiful guest."

He nodded dutifully. "I will."

"Thank you."

"Oh, and tonight you will join our family for dinner. *Tamam*? Okay?"

"Er —" I looked to Aydin for some direction who nodded. "Yes?"

"*Süper!*" She threw her arms around me and pulled me into her chest and kissed me on both cheeks. "I will see you this evening, my girl."

I stepped through the doorway, but immediately stopped in my tracks, which forced Aydin to side-step to avoid hitting me with the suitcase. "Oh my goodness."

Our eyes were both drawn to the centre of the room, and to the massive wooden bed that stood there. It was extraordinarily large, and at that moment it seemed to taunt me, its incredibly plump pillows and thick, decadent duvet called to me and dared me to climb in (and to bring along the hot, hunky man standing beside me). I immediately speculated what the thread count was of the thick, white sheets that peeked out from the side of the bed.

Aydin dropped my suitcase, his eyes never leaving the bed. "It's big."

"That's what he said."

"You're still funny."

I tapped on the side of my head. "In here I'm still eleven."

"I was talking about the bed. It's very big."

"It sure is."

He chuckled and looked at me incredulously. "How did I go my whole life and not know anything about this bed?"

"I'm going to need a ladder to climb into it."

"And we'd have to tie a rope to you in case you get lost."

YES PLEASE!

"Maybe a Saint Bernard will have to come and rescue me."

"Don't worry, I'd come to your rescue."

"You would?"

"Of course." Our eyes locked and we grinned at each other's jokes. He reached up and tucked a curl that had escaped from my bun behind my ear and sighed. "Green Eyes…"

"Don't." I crossed the room to put a little distance between us. "Anyway, the bed looks very comfortable."

He leant forward and pressed down on the mattress. "Feels like it would be."

My nerves were already shot, and I was dangerously close to some sort of breakdown as I watched the headliner of my fantasy sex romps test the mattress of my freakishly large bed. All I could think of was getting naked and having my dirty, dirty way with him. On my mammoth bed and decadent sheets.

I glanced down at his jeans. It was apparent that he had the same idea. He caught my look and took another step toward me, but I dodged him again and pointed at the door. I swear he only had to say the word and I just might've said yes!

"Time to go."

Married man. Married man. Married man.

That would be my new mantra.

He didn't make any effort to leave. Instead, he just stood there and gazed down at me with his melted chocolate, sexy, throw-me-on-the-bed-and-bang-me eyes. "We need to talk and we will tonight — whether you want to or not."

"We'll see."

"But now I'm going to have a word to my aunt about how she came into ownership of that bed!" He pointed at the bed and laughed. "I am sure it will be very entertaining because my aunt is known to tell a great tale when she puts her mind to it."

I chased him out the door, closing it behind him and threw myself face first onto my gargantuan-sized-but-oh-so-soft bed, and covered my face to muffle my scream.

What a beautiful mess I was in!

CHAPTER 9

Audrey Hepburn

I showered, a necessity after my lingering hangover and less than stellar flight, and I wrapped myself in a bathrobe while I perused my limited clothing options of bikinis, shorts and sundresses. And not much else. I definitely needed to go shopping. I would downright freeze otherwise. Oh, and that other little thing. What was it? Oh yeah, I was having dinner with Aydin, and his family — and possibly his wife — tonight.

No big deal.

Bullshit.

The problem at hand was my ability to go shopping alone in Istanbul. In my stinky clothes and squelchy shoes. In a freaking snowstorm no less and in a country that spoke a language that I didn't understand.

Totally doable.

Re-dressing in my smelly clothes, I opened the door to face the snow that was now coming down quite heavily. A little mountain of the white stuff had built up against my door, and

Salep and Ginger

I had to push through to get across the courtyard to the main wooden gates. My already wet Converse had soaked through again, and I wondered how long it would take for my toes to freeze and fall off.

Despite my lingering hangover and the very real possibility of frostbite in my future, I was feeling pretty excited about this unexpected adventure I had found myself in. I was in Istanbul. And it was precisely what I had expected — fecking amazing!

I stood at the gate and tried to decide which way to go. To my left was an old stone wall that ran all the way up the hill, no doubt built a couple of eons ago to keep out some marauding army. To my right was a plethora of tiny shops and restaurants ready to be explored.

Although I was on a mission for warm boots and maybe a jacket, I found myself mesmerized by the sights, sounds and smells of this busy street in Sultanahmet. Around me, noisy tourists with their expensive cameras and North Face jackets, laughed and chatted in their various languages as they trudged through the snow, while exasperated locals darted past the meandering tourists in a desperate effort to get to their destination. Cars zipped by making a huge racket as they sped over the icy cobblestones, and the occasional tram whooshed by so precariously close to the walkway that I half expected it would take out a tourist or two on its journey.

Tiny shops that sold everything you could imagine ran along that main road and down all the narrow alleys and my eyes were drawn to each shop window curiously but I quickly learned to not dwell too long at a window as their owner would magically appear at the door in an attempt to coax me inside.

"*Gel, gel*. We have beautiful lamp for a beautiful lady."

I waved off the first shopowner politely and kept my eyes to the ground, but that didn't seem to deter the next shopowner from doing the same.

"Welcome to my shop. We have the most famous Turkish Delight."

Or the next.

"Come inside and look at my genuine Ottoman rugs. I have *çay*."

I didn't know what '*çay*' was, but I was in desperate need of another coffee right about then.

My jet lag, mixed with lack of food, Aydin's crazy driving and last night's boozy overindulgence, had made me seriously queasy. I needed my standard hangover cure. A beef kebab smothered with barbeque sauce. I knew that I was in the right city for the kebab, but maybe not the sauce, either way, a kebab would definitely fix what ailed me.

I stopped in front of a small clothing store with Turkish music blaring out its glass door. Looking inside, I wasn't really sure whether or not to enter, but the heat emanating from within helped make up my mind. It was way too cold, and my shoes were way too wet, to stand outside any longer.

A young woman behind the counter smiled at me. "*Hoşgeldiniz.*"

"Hi." I stepped through the door, more for the sake of warmth than for her welcome.

"English?" she asked. I nodded. "Welcome. How may I help you?"

Maybe I was delirious from the lack of food, maybe it was the residual hangover, or even my desperate need for a friend in this strange land, but I found myself blurting out my whole pathetic story to the shop assistant, whose name was Leyla. From my first encounter with Aydin — well a PG version of that night anyway — to finding out he was married, and finally being delivered by Aydin to his aunt's hotel for refuge through the storm.

"So tonight you will dine with this... this *eşek* and his family?"

I looked at her confused. Leyla tried to find the right word. "This donkey and his family?"

I smiled. I already liked this girl.

"This is not an ideal situation to be in."

"Definitely not."

"You must make of it what you will," she leaned in covertly, "but one thing I can say is sure, you must look sensational."

"Absolutely."

"And with my help, you will because as you can see that I am very good with style." She struck a pose to show off the outfit that she was wearing as proof of her flair for fashion. The geometric print pantsuit in a myriad of colours matched with a pair of purple-heeled boots. While I admit it was very Dolce and Gabbana and no doubt very fashion forward, it was definitely not something that Ginger Knox would usually wear. I peered around the store with its bright clothing and wondered whether I could sneak out while Leyla was in the storeroom.

She reappeared with a small glass of hot liquid before I could make up my mind. "Drink, it is *çay*."

I sniffed at the rim of the delicate tulip glass, and Leyla giggled at my apprehension. "It is tea, silly. I am not going poison you. You are my most welcome guest!"

It was delicious and very sweet, and I sunk into a small chair to sip on the hot brew while Leyla rushed around grabbing clothes off racks for me to try on. There didn't appear to be any escape for me, so I decided to throw myself into it and let Leyla have her way with me.

Satisfied that she had every piece of clothing in her store for me to try on, she stared at me objectively. "Now let's discuss your style."

"I'll just need a few things."

"No!" she insisted. "You need to look fabulous. Let me help you find a few things to tide you over, but these few things will be stylish and will make you feel beautiful."

We walked around the shop looking at pieces, mixing and matching until Leyla clapped her hands with glee. "You are Audrey Hepburn."

I laughed, looking at my full figure in the mirror. "Yeah, not really."

"No, not Audrey Hepburn the woman. Audrey Hepburn the style. You want classic. You need black. You are elegant but with a little pizzaz. Yes?"

Leyla kitted me out with a pair of skin-tight Mavi jeans ("the tighter, the better. Trust me"). I could mix and match them with the two turtleneck sweaters I had already chosen. We then decided on a gorgeous black woollen ankle skirt that flicked out at the bottom which she coordinated with a crisp, white men's shirt. Sure, I had no idea when I'd wear it, but I had to admit it looked fabulous on me.

"Wear your hair up. Can you braid?" Her style suggestions kept coming.

Next was a black, knit mini-dress by AllSaints.

"Stop pulling the skirt down, Ginger!"

"It's too short."

Leyla shook her head dismissively. "You have perfect proportions and the short skirt will make your legs look much longer."

I looked at myself in the mirror. Perfect proportions? I was a size twelve or maybe a fourteen on a really bad day and I would never, ever normally wear a dress this short. Or this tight. My boobs were busting to escape and I prayed that the dress had the gumption to keep me under wraps for the whole evening. But despite my misgivings the dress *did* seem to possess certain magical powers. My stomach definitely looked flatter than it usually did, in fact it looked like I had miraculously lost a few centimetres off my waist and gained a few centimetres in height. I turned around and looked at my butt in the mirror. It was still there but perhaps not quite as bootylicious as before. Yep, I was definitely warming up to this dress.

Finally, after spotting my red leggings, she squealed loudly before disappearing into the back, returning a moment later flourishing a red, woollen overcoat that was to die for.

"Audrey Hepburn once said that there is a shade of red for every woman."

I had to agree with Ms. Hepburn because the overcoat looked terrific on me. Stopping at the hips, it hid my squishy bits which seemed (well to me anyway) accentuated by the skin-tight jeans, but also made my often-overlooked bum (because my tata's are usually the centre of attention) look fabulous. I twisted left and right. Yep, my bum looked smoking hot!

Once we began, it was hard for either of us to stop. Before I knew it, we had added a couple more pairs of leggings, a cute t-shirt dress, which Leyla rightly said was entirely inappropriate for this weather, but commented on how great my legs looked in it, gloves, a scarf, and finally, a pair of waterproof boots, to my stash on the counter. I took one final look around the small store and spotted the most beautiful pashmina with an intricate design woven in gold and red. I slipped the pashmina on top of the ever-growing pile of clothes and cringed. I would probably need to buy a new suitcase to take this all home with me, but to hell with it!

"Tonight you will wear the mini-dress, and you will look amazing. A black dress is always classic. One is never over or underdressed in a little black dress. Just remember, you are Audrey Hepburn."

"Breakfast at Tiffany's Audrey Hepburn or Roman Holiday's Audrey Hepburn?"

"Why not a little of both?"

"Then I'm going to need pearls or a big-ass tiara!"

"Yes!" She then looked at me with pity in her eyes. "I don't suppose you have any bling, do you?"

I shook my head, and Leyla reached under the counter and pulled out a grey, velvet box which she immediately handed over. Opening the box, a four-tiered diamante necklace which, without a doubt, would look perfect with the dress, gleamed back at me.

"Bling!"

For the first time since I stepped into Leyla's store I looked at the price tag. "Oh my God Leyla! It's beautiful, but I can't afford that. I'm sure I've got something back in my suitcase that will pass as 'bling.'"

She stared at me for a moment longer before snapping her fingers and pulled her diamante rosette headband out of her hair. "This might not be a tiara, but I think it will do just fine."

I tried to say no but it seemed that arguing was with Leyla was a losing battle.

"*Sus ya!*" she tsked at me. Reading her body language, I took that to mean 'be quiet.' "It is my gift to you."

We sealed our friendship with another glass of sweet tea and a *simit*, which looked a little like a bagel, and I waited patiently for Leyla's assistant to tally up the total and fill bag after bag with my fabulous, new purchases.

"It has been lovely to meet you, Ginger. You must come back tomorrow and tell me all about what happens tonight. But remember —" she said, brandishing her finger in my direction before she pulled me in for a hug, "— this man is not the man for you. If he tries to seduce you again, you tell his family. I cannot imagine they will stand for his disgraceful behaviour."

"I will."

She kissed me on both cheeks. "I will definitely see you tomorrow."

It was amazing what an hour, a few glasses of *çay*, and a new Turkish bestie did for me. By the time I left the store, I was confident enough to survive dinner with Aydin's family and not to make a complete fool of myself in the process. Well, not too much of a fool, anyway.

Laden down with shopping bags of all sizes, I wandered back along the street toward the pansion, but not before I stopped in at one of the many tiny shops that I had passed by earlier. The shop was a literal cornucopia of sounds, colours and heavenly smells and my eyes darted around in an attempt to take it all in. Like Leyla's shop, it had Turkish music blasting out the door, but instead of clothes, this shop was packed with souvenirs. Shelves were filled to the brim with colourful ceramic bowls of various sizes, hand-painted tiles, leather purses, every imaginable spice available, Turkish teas and even a wall of postcards depicting Istanbul life, mostly photos of bridges, mosques, or cats. Do people still send postcards in the era of instant gratification? I shrugged and turned my attention to the racks of Turkish Delight near the door. Still feeling peckish after my *simit*, I successfully purchased a big bag of Turkish Delight, and juggled my shopping bags so I could nibble on the soft sweet, made all the more precarious by yet another layer of fresh snow that had fallen onto the cobblestone street.

Along with Leyla's *çay*, the Turkish Delight gave me a desperately needed sugar rush, and I made it back to *Refika*'s pansion without injury to either myself or anyone who passed me on the slippery cobblestones.

As desperate as I was to crawl under the covers and sleep away the rest of my stay in Istanbul, I emptied the many bags onto my enormous bed and rummaged through the contents for the folded invoice that Leyla's assistant had slipped in. Sensibly, I chose not to look at the total before I tapped in my pin number at the store, but now there was no excuse. It was time to see the damage. Nestled in between my new boots and scarf was Leyla's receipt. I glanced at the total which resembled a telephone number, momentarily hyperventilated, then shrugged. Buyer's remorse be damned!

I was now officially broke — stylishly broke — but broke nevertheless, having spent more than two weeks income in two hours. To hell with it.

I was Audrey-Fucking-Hepburn! Well, except for the swearing. And my tits and bum.

CHAPTER 10

I Crave Awkward Situations, Don't You?

The lingering hangover coupled with the aborted flight and being kidnapped (I don't care, I'm calling it a kidnapping instigated by my so-called friends) by Aydin, had left me feeling totally knackered. The idea of crossing the courtyard to Refika's wooden door was about as appealing as playing leapfrog with a unicorn, but as I still hadn't eaten more than the half bag of Turkish Delight and a simit, I dragged myself back into the bathroom and began the transformation.

I slipped into the black, woollen mini-dress which, I had to admit, made me look all kinds fabulous. I pulled on my high-heeled boots and mentally hugged Meg for convincing me to pack them. I stared at myself critically in the mirror. What to do with my out-of-control curls? Always a problem, I finally pinned my hair into a high bun and added Leyla's bling to complete the look. Although I didn't want to overdo my makeup, I did vamp up my eyes with black kohl before finally adding a little red lipstick. To finish, I grabbed the pashmina and wrapped it tightly around my shoulders.

I stopped in front of the mirror and stared at my reflection one final time.

Hair? Under control.

Tits? Always amazing.

Bum? Still huge but looking fine.

Yep, I was very presentable — and ready to see Aydin.

Bugger!

I know I shouldn't care what Aydin thought, but I did. I also wondered if the wife would be there.

Holy moly, what would I do if the wife was there?

Bollocks to this! I'd tell her about her philandering husband, that's what I'd do!

Nooo. I shouldn't go. I should just sneak out, grab a kebab and hide away in my room.

I rolled my eyes at my reflection in the mirror. How many conflicting thoughts could one person have in the space of a minute?

"Pull yourself together, Ginger!"

And now I'm talking to myself. Great!

My fearless walk across the courtyard came to a screeching halt as I peered through the window of the main house. The room was at full capacity with Aydin's family, and dear Lord, there seemed to be a lot of them.

I stepped backward, wondering if I should run back to my

room and wait for someone to come and get me or, better yet, slip out the front gate and not come back until all the lights were off. Refika appeared in the room with an armload of plates and set them up along the huge table all the while yelling instructions at two young women who followed her. A group of older men with distinctive, positively Turkish moustaches, stood smoking by the door while an equally large group of older (and a few younger) women sat near the fireplace chatting animatedly. Children squealed as they climbed over chairs and ran around, while even more people congregated at the bar. Thankfully, Aydin was nowhere to be seen, and that gave me the confidence that I needed to open the door.

I was Ginger The Brave!

I stepped into the large room and all eyes momentarily fell on me.

"Miss Ginger!" Refika crossed the room to me with open arms. "*Hoşgeldin*! Welcome!" She kissed me on both cheeks and swept me around the room introducing me to her husband (who pulled me into his chest and kissed me on both cheeks, all the while yelling "*çok güzel, çok güzel*"), her sisters, their husbands, their children, her cousins, her cousin's children, their aunt, their neighbours — Oh.My.God. — before she left me to fend for myself. I forgot all their names immediately but a young couple from Texas (the only other people who seemed to *not* be related to the family in some way) waved at me from the bar, and I gratefully join them.

"She's a bit overwhelming, isn't she?" whispered the woman whose name she reminded me was Cel.

"A little. Honestly, I'm happy to be here. This will definitely be an experience."

"Well, we could hardly say no." Cel laughed loudly.

"Only because we couldn't get a word in," her husband Jack added as he passed me a glass of red wine. "So, which one are you?"

"Me?"

"How do you fit into the family?"

"Oh!" I laughed and shook my head. "No, no. I'm just staying for a couple of days. My flight was grounded."

"So, you're not family?"

"No. I mean, I am a friend of Refika's nephew, but no, I'm definitely not part of the family."

I excused myself from the couple and followed Refika out the back to offer help as she set up. She chased me away with a flick of her tea towel and a 'tsk', so I returned to the living room and sat in a chair by the window. Beside me, a young girl with tight, black curls and a chubby, little face was patting the tabby cat. I smiled at her and gave the cat a small scratch behind his ears. She spoke to me in Turkish, then giggled when I replied that I didn't understand her.

"That is okay. I am learning English since I was a baby."

"Oh?" I smiled at her. "And how long ago was that?"

"I am five." She held up her hand to show five fingers.

"You are very old now."

"Not as old as you are."

Ouch! I just got burned by a five-year-old!

"I've got you, Emine." Now *that* was a voice that I recognised. I looked up and straight into Aydin's chestnuts-roasting-over-an-open-fire eyes. He smiled at me before scooping the little girl off the floor and kissing her tiny face. "*Merhaba, aşkım.*"

"*Baba!*" she squealed loudly, her face beaming when Aydin scooped her into his arms.

Fuck. Fuckity. Fuck.

"*Baba?*" I scowled at him.

"Down. Put me down, *Baba.*"

Aydin looked embarrassed as the little girl squirmed out of his arms and back onto the floor where she ran off chasing the fleeing cat. "Bye, *Baba.*"

Aydin waved her off before sitting down across from me. "Good evening, Ginger."

Damn, for a creeper he's totally gorgeous.

"I guess that *Baba* means father?"

Aydin nodded.

"So, the little girl is your daughter?"

"Yes. Her name is Emine."

"Seriously?" My head immediately pounded reminding me that I still had a residue hangover thanks to Hugh Grant. "You don't think you should have told me this? What the hell is wrong with you? I'll tell you one thing though, you might be a father and a husband, but you're also a fucking asshole!"

Heads turned, mouths gaped and several older ladies looked like they were about to faint at my foul language, but I didn't care. Screw all of them!

"Ginger, let me explain."

"I don't need an explanation. I've heard just about all I need to hear." I was so stupid. What was I doing here? I stood up and headed for the door. "I'm going to leave. Please apologise to your aunt for me."

He followed me through the wooden doors and out into the freezing courtyard. How could it be so cold?

"Just give me three minutes to explain and then if you want to leave, you can."

I shivered, and my teeth rattled as I spoke. "And n-n-n-now you want me to catch pneumonia! Great, just great!"

"I can keep you warm," he growled while helping me stay upright when I slipped on the doorstep. "I'm not going to bite, you know."

I stomped behind him across the courtyard and when he indicated to my door I shook my head vehemently — hell no — so we walked to the old tree. Aydin leaned against it before pulling me into his chest. I admit that I didn't exactly push him away this time, but that was more out of the fact that I was freezing, than the fact that I hated his two-timing guts. "I will give you three minutes to explain yourself and then I'm going inside to tell your entire family exactly what type of asshole you are."

"Apparently, I am a fucking asshole."

"Right. Fucking asshole. Oh, and you're an *eşek* as well. I learned a new word today."

"A donkey! You are picking up Turkish quickly, aren't you?"

"Are you mocking me?"

"No, not at all. You are practically bilingual."

Wrapped in my Aydin cocoon, my frozen nose against his chest, I took a deep breath. His heady scent filled my nostrils. The simple mix of soap, wool softener and his natural musk made me crazy. Who was I kidding? It made me horny. "It's t-t-too cold to be out here. J-just get on with it."

"The truth is that I was married. I am not married now."

"You're divorced?"

"Yes. We were married very young." He looked back to the main house and I followed his gaze to his daughter visible in the window. "We were, perhaps, too young but —" he shrugged, "— now I have my daughter."

I nodded, not trusting my words at that moment.

"Simge, my wife, well, my ex-wife —" He stopped speaking and shook his head before he sighed. "Can I just say, that perhaps I did not fit in with what she expected her life to be. I was only a cook, but she wanted much more from me than I had to give."

As his words sunk in, my relief was instant. "So you're not married?"

"No."

"But you just called her your wife. Again!"

"Would you believe it was lost in translation?"

I rolled my eyes at him.

"I think it is more, er, habit, yes, habit more than anything. That, and she is the mother of my daughter." His mouth twitched into a smile. "I did say I had baggage."

"This seems to be a little more than baggage. This is a cargo ship full of drama."

Several curly strands had escaped my bun and Aydin tucked one behind my ear. "That night in London I tried to explain, but you did not want to listen. And I did not think I would see you again, so in the end, it was not to really matter. But now it matters because I don't want to be your friend."

"Excuse me?"

"I need to amend what I said earlier. Please understand that I do not want to be your friend."

"Oh?"

"Do you remember that first moment that we met, that we touched?"

I nodded but didn't trust myself to say anything.

"It was like I was awake for the very first time. There was just you. Only you. I know you felt it as well, didn't you? And now you are here with me." Both of his hands were on my face pulling me closer to him. Our lips were so close. "I want to kiss you and I want you to kiss me back. I want to be more than just your friend. Every day. Forever."

I didn't know how to reply. I never do in moments like this.

This is usually where I fall over or burst into hysterical giggles or even just run a mile in under four minutes but I didn't this time. I had felt it too. In that moment all I wanted was his mouth on mine but I still had to give him an answer. I had to tell him — what? "Aydin."

"Sssh, no talking."

Or I could just shut up and let myself go.

Aydin lowered his head and brushed his lips lightly against mine and, where our last infamous kiss in London had been filled with lust and hunger, this one was something else. It was sweet and tender, and it held a promise of something great. A possibility?

He wrapped his arms around my waist and pulled me against him. My breasts smashed against his chest, my hips into his, and he leaned down to kiss me once more. Any doubts disappeared. I opened my mouth to urge him inside. Our tongues tangled together and I wrapped my arms around his neck, lacing my fingers through his curls at the base.

"Aydin." I made a weak attempt to pull away. "Your family could see us."

"I don't care."

"Okay." Who was I to argue?

Our kiss quickly deepened and he pulled away from me. I almost groaned in protest, but then his lips were against my ear. He tugged on it gently. His heavy breathing sent shockwave after shockwave straight to my lady bits. I was definitely in trouble.

"Am I still an asshole?"

Salep and Ginger

I moaned softly in reply and pulled his mouth back down onto mine. He turned and pushed me back against the tree and cupped both my breasts, his thumbs grazing over my frozen (literally) nipples.

"Beautiful," he murmured, as he leaned down and gently bit my right nipple through my dress. I nearly lost it. His hand crept lower, brushing lightly over my stomach and the hem of my dress.

"*Baba?*"

Aydin broke away and looked back towards the house.

"*Baba? Neredesin?*"

He called out to her across the courtyard. "*Geliyorum, tatlım.*" He looked at me and adjusted his cock, which bulged in his jeans. "My daughter is wondering where I am. We should go back in."

"Of course." I straightened the bottom of my dress before walking back toward the door. I looked over my shoulder and winked at him. "Oh and Aydin? I think you might always be an asshole."

He wiggled his eyebrows in reply. "And a Creeper."

I burst out laughing. "Don't you worry, I haven't forgotten your Creeper status."

I slipped through the door, shaking the snow off my head, then sat in a chair just inside the threshold and brushed the snow from my boots as best I could. After my tantrum a few minutes earlier I didn't want to call even more attention to myself by tracking snow all over the room.

Jane Gundogan

Aydin followed me in and immediately checked on his daughter. So, he was an attentive father. My ovaries did a little flip inside my uterus.

Down girls! My clock hadn't begun to tick yet. Or maybe it had. I had to wonder if I was ovary-acting. Ha! I cracked a smile and rolled my eyes at myself, but I couldn't stop the warm feeling in the pit of my stomach as I watched Aydin speak softly to his little girl.

When Emine was settled with some pencils and a colouring book, Aydin took my hand. "Come with me to the kitchen."

"Not a good idea. I've been known to burn water."

"I'll keep you far away from the stove, I promise." Aydin chuckled and ushered me towards the double doors. "I just want to show you where all the magic happens."

The kitchen was large, and indeed it needed to be to accommodate Refika and the three other women who were all chopping, kneading and stirring, oblivious to our sudden appearance in the doorway. Pots bubbled and steamed on a large stove sending fragrant wisps into the air. Beside the stove was a large open grill where metal skewers, filled with meat, sizzled loudly. Every inch of counter space was filled with platters and dishes ready to be delivered to the waiting masses.

My stomach growled angrily at the aroma and I tried to sooth it with a rub.

Aydin threw his head back and laughed. "Your stomach is very demanding."

I shrugged. "It makes most of my big life choices."

"I'd better be quick then." Aydin introduced me to his cousin

Melek, who stood beside Refika at the grill. I watched as they both grabbed the metal skewers filled with meat and replaced them with skewers stacked with tiny, red chillis. Aydin grabbed a chilli and popped it in his mouth. "Cooking is my passion. I love being in the kitchen. I love the preparation, building up the flavours until its perfect. The sound of the cooking meat, the smell of the fragrant spices, and the colours and feeling of the fruits and vegetables. It makes me hungry. It makes me happy. Look at this *köfte*. It is perfect. I promise you there is nothing better than meat cooked over coals."

Melek handed me a *köfte* on a fork to taste. The meat melted in my mouth. "Amazing." I took another bite. So tender. So much flavour. "How do you get it so juicy?"

"It is our family secret." She nudged me lightly. "You marry my cousin, Ginger, and perhaps then I can tell you."

"I'm seriously tempted Melek, especially if I get fed such delicious food every day."

Aydin blushed red, and Melek and I both giggled at his reaction until he scowled at us. "You are ganging up on me?"

"Girls gotta stick together and all." I winked at him and his blush deepened. It was adorable.

Aydin grabbed my hand again and pulled me out the kitchen door.

"Aydin, you're such a baby!" Melek called out, as we disappeared through the door. "He's always hated being teased, even when he was a little boy."

I looked up at him and gave him my most sultry look. "Just so you know, I would never tease you."

The words weren't even entirely out of my mouth when the door to the main house opened and a ridiculously good looking couple appeared. "You called. We came," the young man announced dramatically. "Is it too late to eat?"

"*Oh, ha!*" Aydin grumbled, mostly to himself.

The couple paused in the doorway waiting for all eyes to fall on them. The woman looked familiar. Very familiar. Of course, I had seen her somewhere before. On Aydin's phone.

Shit. It was the ex-wife!

Not only was it the ex-wife, but it was the ex-wife wearing my AllSaints dress, AND it looked so much better on her!

This was seriously going to be the worst dinner party ever!

CHAPTER 11

It's All Fun And Games ... Until Someone Loses Their Heart

Around us the room erupted in rapturous joy. Dinner, the Texans, and I were temporarily forgotten as the family celebrated the new arrivals with a frenzy of cheek kissing, hugs, cheering and even a high pitched wavering sound that Refika made with her mouth, "AYAYAYAYAYA". I half expected Xena Warrior Princess to swing down from the rafters.

Once the frenzied excitement wore off and a semblence of calm returned to the family the ex-wife fixed her gaze on Aydin from across the room. While his face had creased up as though he was in physical pain, hers gave away nothing. It was as smooth as ice and probably just as cold. She crossed the room and slipped one arm around his waist, attaching herself to him in a proprietary manner as they spoke in Turkish. Her blue eyes then fell on me standing beside Aydin. She blinked once, twice, as she scrutinized me with a tight smile. She then laughed as though Aydin had just told her the funniest joke in the world and sashayed away, swinging her considerable assets.

If the floor had opened up right there and then I would have happily crawled in, rather than spend another second in that room. I had even lost my appetite (I know that seems impossible to believe but I really had) and after looking at how the ex-wife filled out my AllSaints dress I really could stand to skip a meal or three.

The Texans were loving every moment of the drama. Cel leaned close to Jack so she could whisper in his ear, but her whisper wasn't quite soft enough not to travel to me. "I'm thinking that the Australian is the girlfriend and the other one is the wife."

"The attractive woman with the long-haired man?"

"Yes. The ones that just arrived."

"And they're brothers?"

Wait! What?

"Honestly Jack, you don't listen to anything do you? The long-haired one is Refika's son, the gorgeous one is her nephew, and the woman who *was* married to the nephew is *now* with the son!" She caught me watching her and blushed. "It's rude to gossip. I apologise."

"Gossip? What gossip?" I grinned and slid down the abandoned bench until I was seated right beside her. "It sounds like you know a hell of a lot more about what's going on than I do — so feel free to spill the tea."

While Cel filled me in with all she knew about the new arrivals we watched the family dynamics from the safety of the bench. Once greeted the older men ignored the couple entirely and returned to the doorway to puff away on their cigarettes. The women, however, were all very excited and chatted loudly as Simge moved around the room greeting everyone. Aydin had retreated to the bar and poured himself a drink. He took a generous gulp from the glass as he watched his ex-wife closely. The muscles on his jaw was tense, his mouth pulled into a hard line. Did he still harbour feelings for her? Was that why he returned to Istanbul ("some decisions must be made")? Was she one of those decisions? And how would I factor into all of this?

On the other side of the room, Refika was just so happy to have her son there that she looked ready to burst. She couldn't leave him alone as she tidied his hair and dusted non-existent fluff off his shoulder. He laughed as she fussed over him. He turned and wrapped his mother in a bear hug. He kissed her on both cheeks over and over then put her down and crossed the room. He slid his arm around the ex-wife's waist.

Cel was right, the ex-wife and the cousin were together.

Holy shit!

What type of woman must she be to run off with her husband's cousin? And while I'm pointing fingers at people, what type of person must his cousin be?

The cousin did seem genuinely entranced with Simge and rightly so, for she was truly spectacular. In fact, she had the whole room mesmerised as she swanned around with her perfectly proportioned breasts and fantastic gams in *my* bloody dress. Even Cel and Jack gawked at her as she sashayed across the room, her face animated as she spoke to people, her perfectly contoured makeup applied to enhance her blue eyes and full, pouty lips. This was a woman that certainly knew how to work with the assets God gave her.

"She's stunning." I murmured to Cel as I watched Aydin's ex-wife chat with Melek, who seemed ready to bust a gut in her excitement.

"Sure she is." Cel agreed. "But then, so are you. In fact, I think that dress suits you mighty fine as well."

Women's intuition can be so spot on sometimes because Cel sensed I was in desperate need of a little boost, as I self-consciously pulled at the sides of my too-short dress. I hated Leyla right then for convincing me to buy it. I also hated my Sicilian grandmother for her height (I stopped growing at five foot five) and the pizza shop on the corner of my street (for the extra junk in my trunk). My boobs, however, were still impressive, in fact I even caught the cousin appraise me from head to toe in a way that made me blush slightly.

Simge turned her attention back to Aydin and waved him over. I was more than a little disappointed to see him rush back to her side. She had some kind of magnetic effect on everyone here. Except for me. I wanted to see her squished under a snow plow or frozen at the bottom of the river — either would work for me.

I watched them closely as they talked in low voices to each other. Every few moments he would turn to check on Emine or me before returning to their whispered conversation. The cousin joined them but it was clear he was intruding and finally excused himself. He went to the bar and poured a drink.

"Anyone like one?" He held up the glass in his hand. His eyes roamed the room until they landed on mine.

I was game. Anything to take my mind off of what was going on across the room. "What is it?" I straddled the bench as best I could in my too-short mini-dress and swung my leg over before joining him at the bar. I examined the smoky, white drink that he was now sipping.

"A Turkish staple, well in our household anyway. It's called *rakı*."

He handed me his glass and I took a sip. "Ugh!" I made a face that was most certainly hideous and my eyes began to water as though I'd just been doused with mace. "Oh my... cough cough... God! Did I... cough... just drink licorice?" I managed to splutter between gagging.

The cousin watched me with mirth as I reached for a napkin and started to scrub my tongue in the desperate effort to remove what was, in my opinion, most likely poison, from my tastebuds. "What are you doing?"

"Dying. Need... water."

He looked around for some water but finding none passed me a glass of wine instead. I gulped at the wine (a very nice Merlot) and swished it around my mouth as though it was mouthwash before swallowing it. "Thanks... I'm okay... cough... better now".

"You're going to live?"

I made a very dramatic sigh and grinned at him. "It was a close call but I think I'll make it."

He chuckled and held out his hand and I shook it with gusto. "I am Deniz. Refika is my mother."

Now you've probably already realised that I can make a tit of myself in any situation and that's just what I proceeded to do. Foot in mouth and all that. "And you're dating the ex-wife?"

I clapped my hands over my mouth as soon as I'd said it. Can we just blame the *rakı*?

For a moment Deniz looked decidedly shook but he recovered nicely and grinned. "Sorry, who are you again?"

"I'm Ginger, but my friends call me Ginny."

"Ginger? You're not *the* Ginger from London, are you?" Deniz's eyes grew wide and it was his turn to choke on his drink.

"I guess." Had Aydin had already mentioned me to his cousin?

"And you're here visiting Aydin?"

I paused for a moment as I considered my reply. I mean if I was *the* Ginger from London and if Aydin had already told Deniz about me then I guess I could stake a claim on him officially — even if I wasn't entirely sure exactly what I getting myself into.

"I'm on my way to Australia for Christmas but thought I'd stop in and visit Aydin on the way."

Deniz's mouth dropped open. "I had no idea."

I threw my arms in the air and sung out, "Surprise!"

Both Aydin and Simge turned as the sounds of my whoop and Deniz's laughter rang out across the room. Aydin eyebrow lifted in a what-are-you-up-to-now look but his ex-wife scowled, both hands firmly on her hips and coldness in her eyes. I don't know if she was annoyed that I was talking to Deniz or whether she also knew I was *the* Ginger from London but from the look on her face it was clear that she did not like what she saw one little bit.

The smile dropped from Deniz's face almost immediately as he caught his girlfriend's reaction. "Oh, this is going to be very bad."

"How, exactly?"

"Please excuse me. I must return to my fiancé."

Fiancé? And the hits just keep on coming!

He left me standing alone and crossed back to his girlfriend, sorry fiancé, who had her finger poked into Aydin's chest, now. Their body language was so tense that it made me tense just watching them. Did I really want to deal with this sort of drama in order to be with Aydin? I didn't know. I wasn't going to be stuck to be in the middle of some crazy love triangle, but actually this was way worse. This was a love square.

I gulped down the rest of my wine, poured myself another glass, and re-joined Jack and Cel on the bench. "Did you know that the ex-wife and Deniz are engaged?"

"Really? You know my mama would say that that man was all hat and no cattle!"

I giggled at Cel's turn of phrase. "Well I don't know about that but Deniz is definitely an attractive man."

"Sure 'nuff but he doesn't really come close to your guy, does he?"

He may not be quite as gorgeous as Aydin but Deniz was no slouch in the looks department either. He was a little taller than his cousin and although you could tell he worked out he was more wiry than muscular. Maybe he was a runner. He had taken off his jacket to reveal a white t-shirt. I could see the top of an elaborate tattoo under his tee. I'd never been a big fan of tattoos but that hint of colour was nothing if not sexy. His hair was a mass of thick, glorious curls and with his prominent nose and dark skin I can say without any hesitation that

Deniz definitely had oodles of 'cattle'!

Aydin and the ex-wife's voices raised up across the room and I leaned over to Cel and muttered, "Apparently, this is going to be bad."

"Oh that's not true, hon. I think this is going to be sensational!" Cel winked at me. "It all depends on how y'all look at it. Just enjoy the show."

The three of us sat back and waited for what was no doubt going to be a great hullabaloo. I sipped my wine and tried in vain to interpret what was going on, when Emine sat down beside me and grasped my free hand tightly. "My mother and father are fighting."

"Are they?" I glanced back over at her parents before bending down to her. "I think they're just talking."

"No." For a five year old she was surprisingly switched on to her parents behaviour. "They are angry. It happens a lot."

"Does it?"

She shrugged and peered up at my hair. "I like your crown. You look like a princess."

"Thank you." I smiled at her. "I like your hair. We're both curly-tops, did you know?"

Her eyes widened. "Are you really?"

"Would you like to see?" She nodded shyly, so I unravelled my bun and shook lose my curls so they fell down my back. Emine squealed with joy and reached up to twirl her chubby fingers through them.

"We *are* the same."

"Would you like to try on my crown?"

I slipped Leyla's diamante rosette headband onto Emine's head and she scooted off the bench and ran to a mirror before squealing in delight. "Oh, so pretty!"

"Now you're a princess. Would you like to keep it?"

"Can I?" Another squeal. "Thank you."

I laughed at her enthusiasm as she raced across the room to show her parents.

"*Anne. Baba. Bak!*" Simge, aka Aydin's ex-wife, aka Deniz's fiancé, aka Emine's *Anne or* mother (that woman has way too many titles), bent down to examine the sparkly headband in her daughter's hair. Emine pointed me out to her mother who stared at me with an intensity that was unsettling. I gave her a little wave, then drained the rest of my wine in one gulp. Again. Liquid courage and all that. I was sure I'd need it before the night was over.

Simge removed the headband from Emine's hair and crossed the room to me. I set my empty glass down and tried not to fidget as she scrutinised me. "*Merhaba.*"

"Hello."

"You are English?"

I stood up and smiled my brightest smile at her. "Australian."

"I am Simge Kaya." She announced herself in a captivatingly husky voice. The tight smile on her face contradicted her friendly-ish tone.

"It's nice to meet you Simge. I'm Ginger and this—" I indicated to the Texans beside me. "— is Jack and Cel."

"Cecelia." Cel put her hand out with a smile. "It's lovely to meet you."

Simge rudely ignored Cel's offered hand and instead pointed at my dress. "Oh look, we are wearing the same dress. How awkward."

"Yeah." I giggled nervously. So far everything about this evening had been awkward.

She handed me the hairband. "Thank you for your, er, gift, but my daughter cannot accept anything from the guests."

"Oh, but she ain't no guest," Cel piped up, a sneaky glint in her eyes. "Are you, honey?"

"I... don't think..."

Mayday! Mayday!

"Now's not the time..."

Abandon ship!

"The thing is... Aydin... and I..."

I was about to crash and burn!

"Aydin?" Simge repeated, and momentarily lost her innate calm as she side-eyed me.

T...IM...B.EERRRR!

Efendim?" Aydin appeared from nowhere, took one look at the developing situation and ushered his ex-wife to the otherside of the room. And by the sounds of it Miss Muck didn't like that one little bit, in fact it sounded like she was ripping him a new one, loud enough to be heard over the buzz of the room. Deniz rushed over and put his arm around his fiancé in an attempt to calm her, but she shook him off and continued to argue with Aydin. Finally, Refika stepped in. "*Yeter!*"

Immediately, the three fell silent and turned to Refika with guilty faces. She marched over and spoke to them so quietly that I had to strain to hear anything at all, which was pointless anyway because of course, they were being lectured in Turkish. This whole situation stunk like a dead skunk, and I sank back down onto the bench, happy to not be included in Refika's lecture. Her wrath seemed mighty, indeed!

Eventually Refika stormed off to the kitchen while Aydin and Deniz joined the men across the room. Simge sashayed across to the bar and poured two glasses of red. She returned to my side and handed me one. That was my third, no, fourth, glass of wine. I'd be ugly drunk if I drank anymore, but I accepted the offered glass regardless. "I do apologise." She raised her chin and flipped her hair behind her shoulder. The move was meant to be disguised as casual, but I could tell she wanted me to know she was superior. "I did not realise that you were already such an important part of *our* family."

Determined not to show any weakness, I plastered a glittering smile on my face. "Of course."

"Perhaps we can get together while you are here in Istanbul so we can get to know each other a little better?" Her smile did not reach her blue eyes, which seemed to burn pure hate but she disguised it well for the sake of everyone around us.

"That would be lovely."

I would rather eat the wine glass.

Satisfied with her perfunctory apology, she turned, whipping her sleek, blonde locks in my face and joined Aydin and her fiancé across the room. She wrapped her arms around them both as she looked back at me with a raised eyebrow and a curl to the corner of her mouth. "Oh darling, I had forgotten how handsome you are."

Aydin seemed totally embarrassed by her and mumbled his reply. "Thank you."

She sighed, her lips twisting into a pout. "How do I look?"

Deniz leaned in and kissed Simge on the cheek. "You look beautiful, *canım*."

Simge dismissed Deniz immediately. "I did not ask you, Deniz."

Her behaviour was nothing short of a declaration of war.

"She's a greedy one, ain't she?" whispered Jack. "With her hands on both of them."

"I wouldn't mind being the meat in that particular sandwich myself." Cel wiggled her eyebrows at her husband.

"Even though that's a very —," I cleared my throat, trying not to laugh as Cel practically drooled, "— vivid image, I'm just going to say it, none of this is okay."

"I know! I'm having the best time." Cel leaned towards me and whispered excitedly. "But I think you've got yourself one hell of a problem here."

"So it would seem."

"You know she's famous here in Turkey."

"Really?"

"You didn't know, sugar? She and your boyfriend are both famous."

"Noooo. You must be mistaken."

"I'm sure I'm not. She was on a television show here, I'm not sure of the name." She turned to her husband. "Do you remember the name?" Jack shook his head. "It's a popular show, and she met your boyfriend while they both worked on it. Now she stars in movies."

"Are you sure?"

She nodded and leaned into me and whispered, "He gave it all up. Walked away from the whole enchilada."

Married? Divorced? A child? And now he's famous? What else is he hiding? How am I supposed to trust someone who has lied straight to my face over and over again?

"I guess that explains all the Facebook followers. How do you know?"

"Refika told me all about who was coming tonight. She is very proud of her son who had captured the heart of 'the most beautiful woman in Turkey'."

"Damn it!"

"Sure, that's one way to say it. You're smack in the middle of a right pickle."

As I watched the theatrics I bloody wished I'd snuck off for a kebab, or maybe stayed hidden in my room. Hell, I rather have stayed at the fecking airport. All preferable options. Aydin was again in deep conversation with his cousin while Simge stood close by them, beaming. It seemed we had a pot-stirrer amongst us. She looked very happy with the chaos that she caused Aydin. And me.

Refika came in from the kitchen followed by Melek, both overloaded with platters of food. "*Hadı, otur. Akşam yemeği hazır.*" She then turned to me and the Americans. "Dinner is served."

CHAPTER 12

It's Called Eating Your Feelings

The table groaned under the weight of so many different dishes, there was hardly room for the utensils. I sat down beside Cel and internally squealed as I salivated over the sight of all the different plates of food laid out before me, but I couldn't forget that Aydin had lied to me, again, and that took the shine of what looked like would be an amazing meal.

Aydin sat at my other side and pushed his leg against mine. I glared at him. "Quit it."

He bent close to me and whispered in her ear. "What's wrong?"

"You lied to me."

He looked confused.

"You were an actor?"

"I did not lie to you, Green Eyes."

"An omission is still a lie."

"How do you tell someone that you were, at one time, a

model?" Aydin reached out and caressed my chin as he took my hand. "It does not come up easily in conversation."

"A model? I thought you were on television."

Note to self: Google Aydin Kaya.

"I did some modelling when I was younger, to earn money so I could go to culinary school. Then the television show came along. But that is my past. I am much better at being a chef."

"Well, it makes sense that you were a model. You're much too handsome for your own good." He crossed his eyes, pursed his lips and struck a ridiculous pose. "Okay, okay, Zoolander. But seriously, how were you ever on television? You blush constantly."

His eyes locked onto mine and he replied, his seductive, husky tone dripping with promise. "Only you make me blush."

I grinned and even Simge's tinkling laughter at the other end of the table could not diminish the sudden surge of happiness that surrounded me.

"So you forgive me?"

"Hmm..."

"If it will help you make up your mind, you could take my plate of food and dump it all over me."

"Tempting, but no." Yes, yes I know I channelled Julia Roberts / Anna Scott right at that moment, but it totally worked. "How about you tell me about the food instead."

"My favourite subject."

I looked at him with wide-eyed innocence. "Really? I had no

idea."

"Nice distraction by the way." He tipped an imaginary hat at me, and I grinned and tipped an imaginary hat back at him. "Alright, well, where do I even begin? Turkey is home to many cultures. We are the bridge between Europe and Asia. We are both the east and the west." He placed his hand on my back and rubbed gently. His palm was warm, even through my woollen dress. I looked up into his chocolate eyes and tried not to giggle like a school girl in front of Simge, because, of course, she would have a field day with that. No, I had to stay cool, calm and collected, even though this simple touch sent tingles to my lady bits and quickened my pulse.

"This is what makes Turkish cuisine unique, exotic and I think we can all agree delicious."

"The food looks excellent, Aydin. Is this what you serve at the restaurant?"

"Yes. It is a typical Ottoman Turkish cuisine. We make everything you see here, as well as kebab, chicken, and seafood."

"So, when you were in London, what did you do?"

"Apparently, he was doing you." Simge murmured from the other end of the table, but it was definitely loud enough to be heard by all.

Heads turned and all eyes were on me. Even though I was horrified, I couldn't let her win. I was mid-chew, so I licked hummus off my lips suggestively and looked Simge straight in the eye. "Lucky me."

Simge's eyes narrowed, then they flashed with fury at me. "*Orospu!*"

I had no clue what she had said but Aydin's reaction was immediate and it was fierce. He was out of his seat and charged around the table to confront his ex-wife. Simge didn't seem too concerned as he rounded the corner towards her, in fact the half smile on her full lips made me think she was rather enjoying the chaos that she had caused.

Deniz slid off the bench and grabbed Aydin forcefully by the arm. "Mind yourself, cousin!"

Aydin ripped his arm out of Deniz's grasp and bent down until he was eye to eye with Simge. His voice shook, anger lacing through each word. "Ginger is here as my guest and I will not allow you speak about her like that!"

Simge's smile slipped slightly and she distanced herself minutely from Aydin. I doubted that anyone had ever spoken to her that way before but as much as I appreciated Aydin being my hero I didn't really need anyone, him included, to stand up for me. This was one Aussie chick who could take care of herself!

I took a deep breath, gathered my courage and stood up. "Actually Aydin, would you mind if I said something?"

It was as though they were watching the final at Wimbledon and the entire table turned their heads in unison towards me. It was time for me to channel my inner Serena Williams and serve up the match point. I forced myself to smile sweetly at Simge, although it was probably more of a demented grin. "Now I don't know what you just called me but I'd wager it wasn't too nice."

Simge's smile was still fixed firmly in place but she lifted her wine glass and her eyebrow as an acknowledgement.

"Let me just tell you a little something about me, Simge. I don't like confrontation. I really don't. (I'd rather have a UTI). It's just how I'm wired but do you want to know something I dislike even more? Rudeness, and I think you've been incredibly rude, both to me and to my friends, but what's even more appalling is that you've been incredibly disrespectful to Refika and Melek who have worked so hard to prepare this beautiful meal. Now you might be Turkey's answer to Kate Winslet or whatever but that doesn't mean you're all that and it also doesn't mean you can speak to people any way you like. Frankly I think you're behaving like a total bitch!"

Game, set and match to Ginger Knox!

Everyone held their collective breaths as they waited for Simge's reaction. Aydin, however, looked like he was trying very hard not to laugh.

"This kitty has claws, Aydin. You had better treat her well!" Simge laughed lightly as she glossed over my insult. I had to applaud her performance. She really was a great actress. She would go far in Hollywood.

Not an apology but how many fake apologies could one person give in a night. I smiled tightly and sat back down. No need to embarrass myself any further.

I really was Ginger The Brave or maybe I was Ginger Out Of My Freaking Mind!

There was awkward silence for the beat of three and then the entire table started talking at once. Potential disaster had been momentarily diverted to everyone's relief.

Aydin slid back down beside me and kissed my cheek. "And here I was thinking I could be your hero."

"I just get really cranky when I'm hungry." I shrugged and leaned into him. "And right now I'm starving."

"We had better feed you then." Aydin started spooning food onto my plate and chuckled. "Or you might turn on me!"

Platters were emptied and more platters appeared on the table. Aydin made suggestions of which dish to match with which *meze* or salad and he was right on all counts. The food was delicious but all I could think of was my performance in front of Aydin and his family.

Couldn't I have thought of a more appropriate word than bitch in that moment? Scrag? That might have worked. Shrew? Seemed rather Shakespearean. Termagant? Would've probably required an explanation. Nope, I totally stand by what I said. Simge Kaya was a bitch! But I also knew that Simge Kaya was now an enemy.

She would definitely make me pay for humiliating her, but, thanks to the three (or was it four) glasses of wine, plus all that adrenalin coursing through my veins, I didn't really give a hoot at that moment.

Bring it on!

Eventually the last platter was emptied and the table was cleared, but before I could catch my breath (or discreetly burp), Refika and Melek returned with dessert.

"Ooooh," I groaned. "I don't think I can eat another thing."

"Didn't you once say to me that you were hungry all the time?"

I nudged him and giggled. "I think you might actually have achieved the unachievable. I'm finally full."

"I don't believe that!" Aydin passed me a plate filled with the sweet dessert, and I admit I hoovered it down pretty quickly despite being so full.

"I guess you liked it, then?"

"I loved it. All of it." I lifted my glass of wine and called down to Refika. "Thank you for such a delicious meal Refika, and thank you for inviting me tonight."

Refika blew me a kiss. "*Afiyet olsun.*"

Deniz lifted his glass of rakı. "*Şerefe.*"

The Turkish men at the other end of the table lifted their glasses in reply. "*Şerefe.*"

Aydin clinked his glass against mine. "Cheers!"

I leaned forward and whispered in his ear. "Panties."

He choked on his drink. I patted him gently on the back as his face turned red and smiled innocently at the rest of the table. "Looks like someone's eye's are bigger than their stomach."

With dinner over I had hoped I could make a stealthy escape, but I quickly realised that the night wasn't over just yet.

The table was cleared away, and Aydin and Deniz pushed it against the wall opening up space in the centre of the room. Refika's husband pulled out a guitar while his friends magically supplied a drum and a little oboe.

With a cheer, Refika threw a small white handkerchief in the air which was picked up by Deniz who began to dance from side to side, shaking his shoulders to the rhythm of the drum. Soon everyone was dancing: Refika and her sisters almost immediately, followed by Simge, Emine and Melek. Jack pulled Cel up and they stepped into the circle and started following the steps. Left, right, left, skip, dip, left, right. Now I understood Aydin's dancing style back in London. It's definitely part of the Turkish way to get funky. Aydin joined the dance between Emine and Simge. My stomach lurched. I couldn't help it, but a wave of ugly jealousy washed over me. I didn't want it to be obvious that I was watching them but my eyes were glued as they danced past. Simge knew it too. She leaned towards him to whisper something in his ear. He smiled. She twisted and turned, slightly out of beat, and her boobs grazed his chest. Totally on purpose!

Deniz whooped at me as he went past and dropped the hankerchief in my lap. I wrinkled my nose at him. "Noooo."

He nodded, "*Evet!*" and shook his shoulders at me. I laugh-snorted and shook my shoulders back at him. He grinned (mostly because my boobs would have shimmied like a stripper) and pulled me up to dance. He hooked my finger to his and I spun the handkerchief around in the air as we lead the line around the room. Left, right, left, skip, dip, left, right.

I didn't know how long we danced for, the music never missed a beat, but eventually Deniz pulled himself away and I gratefully followed him. We sat back down on my bench.

"So how long will you be here for, Ginger?"

"Just a few days I think."

He nodded. "I want to apologise for Simge. This is not an excuse, but she has been in a bad mood all night."

I snorted — again. "It's no big deal."

"Yes, it is. Please let me explain." His English was nowhere near as good as Aydin's and his forehead wrinkled as he tried to find his words. "Simge is very, er, protective of Aydin. I am too. We do not want him to be hurt."

They should have thought of that before they started boinking each other.

"Aydin and I have been best friends since we were babies. But of course we had to be, we are family. And then Aydin met Simge and, well, perhaps we are not best friends anymore, but we will always be family."

"Right. And now it is you and Simge?"

"Yes." He smiled at me sheepishly. "As it should have been."

I searched my brain for something appropriate to say. "So, when's the big day?"

"It will be on Saturday."

"This coming Saturday? In two days Saturday?"

"Yes. And you should please come. You are very welcome to join us."

"I don't think I will be here then, but thank you." I knew full well that I would be about as welcome as a venereal disease.

"No, you must attend. You can come with Aydin. It is important for all of us. You are family now too, eh?"

I wondered if Deniz's invitation was more about his guilt, rather than for either Aydin or Simge's benefit. Or perhaps it was to prove to Simge that Aydin had moved on with his romantic life because it was bloody obvious that she still harboured some pretty intense emotions for him. I watched Aydin and Simge dancing with the rest of the group and wondered whether Aydin even knew how he felt about his ex-wife.

"Seriously, thanks, but finger's crossed I will be on my way to Sydney by then."

"That is a shame. But you are here now, and it is obvious to me that Aydin cares for you very much."

I grinned at his comment but didn't trust myself to say anything out loud.

"You know you are the first girl that he has brought home since —"

"Since the divorce?"

"Yes."

"Well, I've been told I'm quite a catch."

"And funny. My cousin likes that, you know." Deniz glanced over at his fiancé before his eyes held mine. "It is good that you are here. Aydin was upset that he had to leave London. He wanted to see you again, but now he must stay here in Turkey until we come back from America."

"You're going to America?"

"Yes. We leave after the wedding."

"For your honeymoon?"

"Yes, but also Simge has a part in a movie that is filming there. We all hope that this will be the start of many good things for her in America!"

"Los Angeles?"

"Chicago."

"Windy."

"I'll pack a jacket." Deniz laughed loudly. Simge caught my eye and immediately left the dancing line to join us. She took Deniz's drink out of his hand and took a sip, then fixed her ice cold, blue eyes on me. "Are you going home for Christmas?"

I wanted to smack that fake smile off her smug face, but instead I threw my hair over my shoulder and raised a brow. Two could play this game. "As soon as I can get into the air." I put my own rather mediocre acting skills to good use and sighed longingly as I gazed off into the distance. "Christmas in Australia is amazing. No snow, no rain, just oodles of sunshine, fabulous parties and wonderful friends. I am sorry to miss your wedding though, it's on Saturday, isn't it?"

"Oh?" She was definitely surprised that I knew about her upcoming nuptials.

"Deniz just invited me. He's just too sweet." I patted his arm. "You had better treat him well."

I was sure Simge saw through my theatrics especially as I used her own words against her, but it was her squinted eyes and pursed lips that made me grin. I had gotten under her skin. Good! She deserved a taste of her own medicine. The subtle art of manipulation could ruffle anyone's feathers. I may not have been a movie star, but I was Ginger Valentina Knox, dammit, and I rocked this dress just as good as her, curves and all!

He patted her hand. "Of course I did, *aşkım*. Ginger is almost part of our family."

I batted my eyelashes at her innocently in an attempt to piss her off. "To think, one day we might be like sisters."

She leaned towards me and looked at me hard in the eyes. "I am sure some people might find your sassy attitude appealing but I can promise you that I am not one of them."

"I'm absolutely crushed."

This time it was I who sashayed across the room. Aydin was sitting beside the fireplace with Emine and I sat down beside them. Emine climbed onto my lap and started to twirl my hair in her little fingers. "Ginger?"

"Yes, sweetie?"

"When do you go away?"

"In a day or so."

Emine started bouncing up and down on my knee and clapped her hands. "Maybe you and me and *Baba* could go and visit the palace?"

My eyes opened wide in surprise. "There's a palace?"

She nodded her head so vigorously that Leyla's headband (which must have been returned to her by her mother) slid precariously to the side. I set it back into position and kissed her on her soft, cheek. She smelt like baby powder and sugar snaps. My ovaries started doing push-ups as my heart skipped a beat.

Check yourself Ginger before you wreck yourself! Children were not on my agenda anytime soon, but then again Aydin wasn't on my agenda either and now? Ugh!

"It's not really a palace like in Cinderella, but it is still very pretty. It is behind the wall." She pointed to the tall wall in the courtyard.

I raised my eyebrows at Aydin for his input. "You know Emine, I wondered what was behind that wall. I would be honoured if you could show me."

He addressed his daughter, but smiled to me. "Of course, *aşkım*. We shall go in the morning before it gets too crowded."

"Maybe we could have some *salep* as well, *Baba*?"

"*Salep*? You mentioned that to me in London. It's a drink, isn't it?"

"It's my favourite." Emine smacked her lips loudly. "I like it with, er, um, *Baba*?"

"Cinnamon."

"Yes, but *Baba* has it with —"

Aydin answered his daughter in a husky voice that was directed at me. "Ginger. I really like ginger… on my *salep*."

Heat flushed my face and it wasn't from the fire. His double entendre was altogether sinful.

Emine squealed and pointed at me. "That's your name!"

I giggled and ran the back of my fingers down her soft cheek. "It is."

"In Turkish it is *zencefil*."

"So I hear. I think I will have to try some *salep* with *zencefil* as well then, because it's my namesake."

"If you behave yourself Emine, then we might have some *salep* as a special treat."

Satisfied with tomorrow's plan Emine skipped off, leaving us alone. Aydin looked at me with a twinkle in his eye. "Did you enjoy yourself this evening, Ginger?"

"Definitely eye-opening, that's for sure."

"Is that a yes?"

"Hmmm, where do I even begin?" I tapped my finger against my chin as I mock contemplated the evening's events. "Let's see, you *were* married. You're *now* divorced. You *are* a father. Your ex-wife *is* a bitch. You *were* an actor slash model but you're *now* a chef. There was *wonderful* food however, some *crazy* dancing... and a *lot* of drama. It really was quite a show."

"It was a bit of a disaster, and I know I screwed up at least once."

"Only once?"

"Maybe twice."

"I did have a good time though."

"I'm glad." He wrapped his arm around me and I leaned into him. The night was slowing. I desperately needed some sleep. I covered my mouth as I yawned. "Tired?"

"It's definitely been a long day."

"Let me walk you back to your room then."

Trying to leave was almost impossible what with having to say goodbye to each and every family member followed by another round of hugs, kisses, *"iyi akşamlar"*, *"güle, güle"* and promises to visit them before I left Istanbul.

I winked at Simge as Aydin and I walked toward the door together. "Time to call it a night. I'm incredibly jet-lagged, but thank you sister, for such a memorable evening."

Simge glared at me. If looks could kill, I would be dead where I stood, but I was pretty sure I had won this round!

Aydin opened the door for us and I smiled up at him as we shuffled through the snow to my room. We stood at my door in awkward silence, neither of us really sure what to say.

Too much had happened in the last few hours — to be honest, I wasn't quite sure what to make of it all. Too much to process. Too much confliction and doubt.

This morning I was on my way to Sydney for Christmas, then my fortune changed and I found myself stranded in Istanbul with the man who just might be the love of my life. Along with his ex-wife. And his daughter.

My head pounded, although I wasn't sure if it was from all the drama or whether I was quite probably still suffering from the hangover kicked off by Hugh Grant's antics the night before. The only thing I knew with any certainty, was that every cell in my body was desperate to be in his arms again.

As if on cue, Aydin wrapped one strong arm around my waist and pulled me to him. "I don't want tonight to end just yet."

My vision blurred and my heart began a frenzied beat in my chest. Aydin wanted me to invite him inside, I could tell. If truth be told, I wanted to do just that as well. I had never wanted a man so much before. But I knew we shouldn't, and certainly not with his ex-wife and daughter practically next door.

Jane Gundogan

I grinned up at him. "I just don't get it. You're so nice, and she's so —"

"So Simge?"

"Did you just use her name as an adjective?"

He chuckled. "She is jealous."

"Of me?" I laughed. "Why?"

"Because she can see that I have real feelings for you."

"Oh? Does she realise that she's getting married in two days and that means that she waives any proprietary rights to her ex-husband, however cute he might be?"

Shut up, Ginger!

"Why thank you, Green Eyes." Aydin kissed the top of my head and widened his grin. "I don't want to talk about her. I want to talk about you and me and that incredibly large bed that is behind this door."

I shook my head and opened my door to put as much distance between us as I could stand. "Sorry. Not going to happen. I'll see you tomorrow."

He sighed and raked his fingers through his hair, a ridiculously endearing habit that made it increasingly difficult for me to say no to him. "Yes, of course. But before you go, there's something I need to do first."

"What's that?"

He stepped closer, closing the gap between us, then reached up and held my face in his hands. He licked his lips and brushed them lightly on mine, then, oh then, he pulled me close so that the heat of our bodies sizzled against each other. He opened his mouth and his tongue sought out mine. He moaned and pressed his erection into my hip.

How did he get hard so fast?

Aydin broke the kiss and our hot, mingled breath steamed out into the frigid night air. "I should go." His voice was gravelly and he cleared his throat, almost whimpering as I pulled away. "Emine and I will see you in the morning."

I nodded. "Goodnight." I slipped inside, closing the door behind me. Leaning against the door, I closed my eyes. A one-night stand with Aydin Kaya was the last thing that I needed.

Oh no, no, no, Ginger! A one-night stand with Aydin Kaya was EXACTLY the thing I needed!

CHAPTER 13

But I Don't Wanna Be A Princess

I woke slowly and stretched my limbs and marvelled at just how comfortable I was. I also marvelled at the fact that I didn't have a hangover. I wasn't sure if it was thanks to the enormous, cosy bed that I had slept in or maybe it was those decadent sheets, but someone really should notify the Vatican because if that wasn't some kind of miracle, then I don't know what was. I pulled the fluffy duvet back over my head, not quite ready to start the day, when the silence was broken by what could only be described as melodic chanting. It seemed to be coming from all around me. It was eerily beautiful, like a lullaby, and my eyes grew heavy again, soothed by the sound, and I had to pinch my arm to fight the temptation to fall back asleep.

What was I doing lying around in bed?

I was in Istanbul!

And I was going to a palace with Aydin — and his daughter!

Yikes!

Aydin had a daughter! He was a package deal. Aydin and Emine.

Ugh, and his ex-wife, the bloody movie star!

A pro's and con's list began to form in my mind.

Pro: Aydin was quite possible the most perfect man on the planet.

Pro: I was pretty sure that Aydin liked me.

Pro: I was pretty sure that I liked Aydin.

Pro: Emine was a cutie-patootie *and* I think she liked me.

Con: I just used the words 'cutie' and 'patootie' together! *insert eye roll here*

Con: Aydin lived in Istanbul and I lived in London... or Sydney.

Con: His ex-wife was a total bitch.

Bonus Pro: But she *was* leaving.

Conundrum!

With Simge out of the picture, maybe I could stay in Istanbul a little longer. And would Aydin want me to stay in Istanbul with him? Or was I just a holiday fling? What about Emine? Speaking of Emine, did I want to potentially be a step-mother and all that goes along with that particular moniker? And what if we had our own child — or children? Did I want children (my ovaries shouted a very resonant "yes" to that hypothetical)? Did he even want any more children? How would this even work? But all my jumbled thoughts meant nothing. The real question was whether I was genuinely ready for this relationship or any relationship for that matter?

The term "being at a crossroads in life" had never been more true than for me at that moment.

I pushed aside all my internal angst and grabbed my phone to check my emails and messages. I wasn't at all disappointed to find out that there was nothing from the airline, but there was way too many from both my bratty friends back in London and several from my stressed out sister back in Sydney.

I quickly wrote to Sadie that I was alive and well and I had a roof over my head. I didn't update her on Aydin though. I really didn't need that kind of negativity.

There was also a message, no, wait, there were messages — plural — from Henry. Fecking Henry!

I opened the first message. Why? I don't know. Curiosity? Maybe. Morbid stupidity? More likely but it really does lead me to wonder what would make a normally intelligent woman ignore that feeling of dread that you get the pit of your stomach and open a message that she knew full well was going to be painful.

> **Henry:** I miss you. I'm sorry.

And then this happened:

> **Henry:** So I guess yr not going to speak to me.
>
> **Henry:** I said I'm sorry.
>
> **Henry:** I just want to fix this.

And then things started to go downhill:

> **Henry:** Who do you think you are?
>
> **Henry:** You think you can do better than me?
>
> **Henry:** Fine. I give up. I don't care anymore.

Until finally:

Henry: Delete my number.

I laughed out loud at his last message — and did exactly as instructed. Delete contact? YES!

Look at me being all emotionally mature and shit!

Time was getting away from me so I examined my clothes and, satisfied that my new Mavi jeans and black turtleneck, along with my gorgeous, red jacket, would be the most sensible attire for playing tourist, I showered, then opened my phone again to quickly update everyone back in London:

Ginger: You guys dropped me into the middle of a right mess! I should be very angry with you—

I stopped for a moment, to consider what I wanted to write. Aydin was a model, a television star, married (and divorced) from a right royal bitch, and had a daughter. But most importantly I liked him. A lot. More than a lot.

I started typing again, but there was just too much to say. It would've probably taken me all morning to write what had happened since the moment we met at the airport. Instead, I wrote: —

— but I can't because I'm happy. Incredibly happy. I wish that I'd met Aydin earlier. Who knows what will happen, but right now I'll be in Istanbul for at least another day or so – I may as well enjoy it.

Ginger: So rather than curse each of you, I will wish you a Merry Christmas and will see you on the flip side!!!

Meg: OMG I knew it! I knew Aydin was the one.

Courtney: Do you guys know what time it is?

Nate: How was he in the sack?

Ginger: Get your mind out of the gutter Nate!

Nate: That means she did it.

Ginger: That means shut up!

Meg: I'm doing a happy dance for you right now FYI.

Courtney: Am I the only one trying to sleep?

Nina: Make wise choices xo

Nate: Does anyone else think Meg might be drunk?

Ginger: Does anyone else think I should un-friend Nate?

Meg: Me.

Courtney: Definitely me and now I'm going back to sleep. Boink away Ginny.

Nate: Come on guys.

Nate: Guys???

My stomach growled, which surprised me considering the amount of food I had woofed down the night before, so I made my way over to the main house for breakfast. Cel and Jack were already sitting at the large table.

I sat down and was awed by the sheer volume of dishes filled with food being placed before us. "This is breakfast?" I whispered to Cel. "It's like she's trying to outdo dinner last night."

"Yes, it's huge, isn't it? A Turkish breakfast or kah-vahl-tuh," she said, in her unique twang, "is always out of this world. Fill up on it. I promise it'll keep you going through to dinner, although I'm still full from last night, to be honest."

"I thought I was as well, but my growling stomach told me otherwise. It was delicious though."

"So was the dinner show."

"Yeah that was a little wild, wasn't it?"

"I think you handled yourself very well. I don't know if I could have kept my temper with that woman."

"It was difficult, I promise you."

'Kah-vahl-tuh' was an extravaganza of bite-sized Turkish delicacies in tiny dishes. There were different varieties of cheeses, olives, tomatoes, cucumbers, freshly baked bread, multiple types of condiments and a delicious fried cheese pastry all served with a freshly brewed glass of *çay*. As soon as one plate emptied, Refika appeared with another. "I'm going to be huge by the time I leave here."

"Nonsense, Ginger." Refika reached down and grabbed a handful of my muffin top thanks to my incredibly tight jeans. "You could stand to put on some weight. You are too skinny."

"Oh no, I don't think so." I smiled at her as politely as I could, while I grimaced underneath. "I think rather the opposite is true."

Cel agreed with a nod. "She said the same to me."

"Ladies should be, how do I say, *balık etli*. It means fish fleshed."

"And that's supposed to be a compliment?"

Refika looked horrified that she might have unintentionally upset me. "I did not mean to offend you, Miss Ginger. It is very much a compliment."

Jack put down his newspaper and stared at both of us before gesturing in a rather crude manner. "It means ladies need more cushion for the pushin' and all that."

Cel squealed and slapped his hand away. "Oh my Gawd, Jack!"

I had to stifle a pang of envy as I caught the long look Cel exchanged with her husband. They were mad for each other and they showed their happiness with every smile or look that passed between them. I wanted to experience that kind of love. With Aydin? Maybe. But also, maybe not.

The reception door opened and Cel nudged me out of my thoughts. "Prince Charming has arrived."

I looked up and smiled at the sight of Aydin and his daughter standing in the doorway, rugged up for the cold weather. Just seeing him again made my heart skip a beat. It was a crime just how handsome that man was. Only he could make a pair of jeans and a winter jacket look sexy.

Emine rushed over to hug me. "*Günaydin*, Ginger!"

"And good morning to you, Emine. What a lovely way to start my day."

"Are you excited to go to the palace?"

"I am. I've never been to a palace before."

Emine stared at me for a moment and then her smile fell slightly. "You're hair is pretty today."

"Thank you."

"*Baba* did mine."

It was evident that Aydin had attempted to style her jet black curls into what I could only presume was a bun but had bombed out bigtime at that particular fatherly task. It looked more like an Amy Winehouse failed beehive. What was he thinking?

I knew only full well how a disastrous hairstyle could ruin the day of even the happiest of five-year-olds. My mind flashed back to my fifth birthday party when my sister had fashioned my hair into what we thought was a very fetching pompadour. It drooped almost immediately and I ended up looking like someone had thrown a bowl of spaghetti over my head. Sarah McGowen had taunted me for the whole afternoon calling me 'Noodle Knox'. That charming moniker stayed with me throughout my entire school life. I still plotted Sarah McGowen's demise.

I had braided my own hair into a fishtail that morning, mostly to keep it under control, but also the probability of contracting pneumonia was very real so I hadn't washed it. I smiled sympathetically at Aydin's daughter. "Would you like me to braid your hair? Like mine?"

Emine's gloomy face vanished immediately and she beamed at me. It made my heart pitter a little and patter a lot! I really wanted Aydin's daughter to like me. "*Evet.* Yes, yes please."

Aydin moaned as I released her hair from his failed beehive. "I'm not even going to tell you how long that took."

Emine looked up at me very seriously. "It took forever, Ginger."

I chuckled as I got to work. "Well I'll have it fixed in a jiffy."

Aydin watched the two of us with interest before he reached over and popped an olive in his mouth. "My aunt is going all out with *kahvaltı* by the looks of things."

I snorted as I started to pull Emine's hair into sections. "She told me I need to put on some weight."

"Wouldn't hurt you."

"Seriously? I'd be huge."

He shrugged his shoulders, dismissing my self-diss. "You'd still look beautiful to me." He dropped a kiss on my head and disappeared into the kitchen.

Cel nudged me in my squishy bits. "He's a keeper, Ginger."

"I don't know about that. Besides, I hardly know him."

"Doesn't matter. You two belong together. I'm a little psychic, you know."

Jack spoke up from behind his newspaper. "She is."

"I am."

"I've literally only known him for three days, including today, and we spent the first two days arguing with each other!"

"Oh, Ginger!" Emine squealed as she wiggled in her chair making it more than a little difficult to put the final touches to her hair. "You should marry *Baba* and live with us!"

Jack coughed from behind his newspaper while Cel laughed heartily.

"Er…"

Aydin chose that moment to come back into the room. I knew my face burned beet-red. "*Hadi*."

"Ginger, *Baba* is ready to go. Are you finished yet?"

To cover up my embarrassment of having nearly been caught discussing our potential nuptials I nodded mutely and began to fuss with my breakfast plate while Emine jumped up and ran to look at herself in the mirror. She turned back to the table a struck a pose. Both Cel and I oohed and aahed our approval as Emine modelled her new hairstyle before she ran to her father who helped her into her pink jacket.

I grabbed my own jacket, wrapped my scarf around my neck and slipped on my gloves. I was ready for today's adventure.

Aydin opened up the door for me, waving his hand with a flourish. "After you, my lady."

"You're really trying to be my knight in shining armour, aren't you?"

"Better than being your Creeper."

"I'm beginning to like my Creeper." I murmured and glanced over my shoulder to see Cel make kissy-face as she waved goodbye.

"I hope you don't mind walking."

"Not at all. Is it very far?"

Aydin shook his head. "Topkapı Palace is, as Emine said last night, right behind my aunt's pansion. This wall —", he gestured to the immense stone wall that continued all the way along the street, "— surrounds the palace grounds. We enter just around the corner at Gülhane Park and then it's just five minutes up the hill."

Emine skipped ahead of us but every couple of metres she turned and motioned for us to keep up with her. "Too slow. Come on, come on."

Aydin smiled as he watched his daughter bounding ahead. "She is very excited. She really likes you."

"I really like her. She's very sweet."

"I think so." He leaned his head towards me. "I know there were apologies made last night but I wanted to also apologise for Simge's behaviour."

"You don't have anything to apologise for but I've gotta say she really didn't take to me, did she?"

"I know I said that she was feeling a little jealous, but I admit that she has never had *that* reaction before."

"To any of your other girlfriends?"

"Are you my girlfriend now?"

I'll be whatever you want me to be.

"No!" My cheeks heated at my dirty thoughts. "I meant, any other female acquaintances that you may have had in the past."

"You're babbling."

"I know."

"And you're blushing."

"Stop it!" I ran ahead to walk with Emine. As we turned the corner, a tram rushed past us, and I grabbed Emine's hand and pulled her back from the curb. "Woah!"

Aydin caught up and bent down to speak to his daughter. He didn't shout, but instead he spoke quietly to her in Turkish. He stood back up and looked over at me. There was relief written all over his face. He mouthed, "Thank you."

I nodded slightly and mouthed back, "No problem."

Emine looked suitably chastised as Aydin took her hand. Rather than make a big deal out of it, I stepped in alongside Emine and said, "What's your favourite part of the palace, Emine?"

By the time we had reached the large opened gate that lead to Gülhane Park I had learned that Emine loved the gardens (but mostly in spring when there were loads of colourful flowers) and the jewellery on display. She also loved the stories that the guides told and the bright colours of the rooms.

I gave myself a mental high-five. I was totally acing this stepmother gig!

Now safely in the park, Emine ran ahead while Aydin and I took our time walking up the hill. I slipped on some ice at one point and grabbed onto him, almost taking us both down in the process.

"You are seriously clumsy. I am surprised you haven't broken your head."

"Maybe I have."

He pulled his gloves off and threaded his fingers into my hair, massaging my scalp as he examined my skull. "No, your head seems perfect to me."

"You're trying your hardest, aren't you?"

His eyes were heavy as he gazed into mine. "Ginger, I only have a little time with you, then you will leave me. I am not going to let you go without a fight."

"Aydin—"

"You are very important, both to Emine and to me."

It was probably the nicest thing anybody had ever said to me before. "How can you possibly know that? We've only spent a total of about twenty-four hours together."

"I already told you I knew as soon as I met you that you were important to me." He caught me off guard and kissed my lips. "You need to understand this, Ginger."

I looked into his eyes. What I saw there both frightened and excited me. Was I supposed to embrace this, or run away? I shivered; my body reacted to his presence, or to my dilemma, I didn't know. But what I did know was that my punani was hot and raring to go and would be prepared to jump on board with whatever I ultimately decided to do.

Aydin pulled his hands out of my hair and rubbed them up and down my arms. "Cold?"

I didn't have to tell him that my body was involuntarily reacting to his hotness, did I? I just smiled. That should do it. A non-answer.

He wrapped his arm around me and we continued up the hill. "Better?"

I smiled wider, my cheeks blushing ferociously.

Ahead, Emine was patting a small, ginger cat that was sitting on a park bench. "Someone's found a friend."

"Oh, Emine." He muttered in Turkish before he let out a long sigh. "There are cats everywhere in Istanbul. This is not surprising to me. Emine has tried to sneak more than one cat into the house before."

I went over to pat the little cat. "She's cold, Aydin."

"And hungry, Baba."

"And not coming with us." Aydin admonished both of us and walked ahead.

I grinned at Emine. "Maybe we can come back and check on her later."

Emine nodded enthusiastically at my plan.

We entered Topkapı Palace through a small gate. I took Emine's hand and was happy to concentrate on the museum and palace grounds rather than think about how I wanted to screw Aydin stupid. Emine was excited to show me around and pointed out her favourite pieces in the museum as we made our way through each room.

"You are right Emine." She pulled me from room to room. "It's not really a palace like Cinderella, but it is lovely."

"I wish I was princess here."

I had to suppress a grin as we had just entered the Harem. I can't imagine that the women that lived behind the walls of the harem loved every moment living there, although if Aydin were the Sultan, then I would be perfectly happy to be his beck and call girl. Over and over and over again.

Aydin bent down and whispered in my ear. "Did you know at one time, the Sultan had over three hundred concubines living here? He was a lucky man."

I snorted in reply. "Wow, that sounds… dreadful. I mean, does anyone really need that many concubines?"

He grinned dangerously at me. "I would only need one concubine and I would spend my life making sure that she was satisfied in every way."

Oh. My. God.

"Well, if you ever become the Sultan, let me know and I might just apply for the job."

He was quiet for a moment before moving closer to me. "I think you would be the perfect candidate for the position, any position you like."

Ho-ly shit!

After I scraped myself off the floor, I took a few deep breaths. This man, this ridiculously attractive, sexy, funny man, was flirting so hard, and with me! And he was doing a damn good job at it, I might add.

I had to remind myself we were in public and that jumping his bones there and then in the Harem would probably be frowned upon. Well that, and the fact that his daughter was only a few display cases ahead of us. I threw him my 'come hither' eyes and laughed at him. "Creeper!"

He looked suitably hurt. "Again with the Creeper! I'm starting to wonder if you like me at all Ginger."

I began to giggle uncontrollably as I watched his face scrunch up in mock sadness. "Don't worry, Creeper, I like you just fine."

I grabbed his hand and squeezed. Yep I like him just fine.

"*Affederseniz.*" A soft, female voice echoed from behind us. I turned my head, grateful for the interruption. Whatever took me away from examining my feelings that were swirling around in my head, pushing my heart to beat faster, my face flush and my lady bits to tingle. Yes, I was grateful for the interruption.

A young woman popped out from between two mannequins dressed in golden armour. She smiled at Aydin and they chatted for a few minutes before he put his arm around her as her friend took photographs on her phone. Other than a curious look by the friend, I was thankfully ignored throughout most of the encounter. A few moments later, she waved goodbye and moved into the next room. She had barely gone ten seconds before we heard squealing.

I grinned at his bright, red face. "Hey, Mr. Movie Star Man!"

"Quit it."

"You really *are* famous, aren't you?"

"Not at all!"

"Bollocks." I waved him off. "Let me ask you this then. Does the paparazzi follow you around as you do your grocery shopping?"

"It happened once."

"Have you ever received a love letter from a secret admirer?"

"No, but I once received over three thousand tweets from a woman who confessed her love to me. I had to disable my account."

"Bloody hell!"

He wiggled his eyebrows at me. "Sometimes they can be a little, er, suggestive with their plans for me and my body."

They all wanted to climb on his penis as well!

"I bet they are. Alright, one final question. Have you or have you not ever had a strange woman appear on your doorstep, or even between two mannequin soldiers, to squeal at you?"

He laughed. "Surprisingly, that one happens quite a lot!"

"Yep, well I hate to be the one to tell you this, but you are kinda famous."

Aydin chuckled and held his hands up in surrender. "Okay, okay. I'm famous and women all over Turkey love me."

I nudged him hard in the ribs which only made him laugh harder. "Jeez a little full of yourself, aren't you?"

He grabbed me around my waist and pulled me in tight. His eyes blazing, he bent his head to mine. "Tease."

His lips touched mine lightly and then with a passion that wasn't quite appropriate for a public place. When we parted, his hot breath swept over my face. "I told you that I would never tease you."

It was becoming increasingly difficult to pay attention to my surroundings with Aydin beside me so it was almost a relief when Emine begged her father to stop for *salep* as we passed a tiny cafe in the outer garden.

Happy for any distraction from my Aydin fantasies, I chose a table at the rear of the cafe which gave an unobstructed view across the Bosphorus to Asia while Emine immediately ordered for the three of us along with some *peyniri tost*. By the time the *salep* arrived Emine and I had given up trying to count the number of boats on the water (as well as the number of minarets on the land) and I turned my attention instead to the teacup that had been placed before me. In it was a milky froth, similar to a latte, with shavings of ginger on top. I sniffed the air. There was the sweet scent of cinnamon along with something else, something I couldn't quite place.

"Before I drink this, can you remind me what's in it? I mean, I drank some *rakı* last night, and it was awful."

"You have no idea what you are missing." I had scrunched up my face at the memory of last night's *rakı* and Aydin chuckled. "*Salep* is made from the root of an orchid. That gives it its unique perfume. There is also a little mastic in it, orange blossom, and, of course, cinnamon, or pistachio, or your namesake, sprinkled on top."

"Strange."

"Be adventurous, Ginger. I promise you will love it."

I blew on the steam rising from my mug before took a tentative sip. I let it sit in my mouth for a moment before swallowing. "It's very sweet... and a little grainy. Thick but... oh! It's delicious."

"Phew! I'm relieved. I wouldn't know what to do if you hated both *rakı* AND *salep*." Aydin leaned over and gave me a quick kiss. "Next time I might get you to try some *boza*."

"Bozo? Like the clown?"

"No, *Boza* with an 'A'. It is a fermented drink."

"So, it's beer?"

"You are so Australian."

We fell into a comfortable silence as we sipped our *salep*, both of us lost in our own thoughts. Well, I was lost in my thoughts; Aydin was busy keeping a watchful eye on his boisterous daughter who was busy exploring the palace walls with a little blonde girl that she had friended.

I could hear Emine explaining in English why she was going to marry a prince and live in the palace when she grew up. "You know Emine's language skills are very advanced."

"We have always spoken to her in English. With her mother wanting to work in America and Europe it was important that we all had, that we have, good English."

"So, what will happen with Emine when Simge leaves?" I couldn't separate the feelings I had for Aydin when it came to Emine and Simge. I wanted this man right now, that much I knew, but with all that came with him, it left me confused.

"Emine will stay with me. Simge will be busy working and Deniz is not quite as good an uncle as he could be. Plus, she has school."

I pondered over this. Aydin had to stay in Turkey with Emine and I needed to return to London or maybe I'd move back to Australia. Either way any chance of a real relationship seemed almost impossible.

"Ginger." He reached for my hand, brought it up to his mouth and kissed my fingertips. "Is there any hope that you will stay a few more days here with us?"

I let out the tiniest of sighs as his lips pressed against my skin and shook my head. "I think there will be a flight tomorrow or maybe the day after."

"The thing is —" He stared past Emine down to the Bosphorus in the distance, "—the thing is, I've not felt this way about someone in a very long time."

"Since Simge?"

"No not even Simge. I did not have this overwhelming feeling of happiness with her. With Simge it was exciting. She was taking over Turkey. She was very famous. And so was I, because of her." He shrugged. "I got caught up in the fame."

I nodded, encouraging him to go on. "My first crush was on a girl named Filiz. I was fourteen. Every time I saw her, I swooned."

"You swooned. Really?" I giggled at the old-fashioned term.

"I did," he replied indignantly. "I am proud of my feelings. They were real, and I loved her very much."

"And what happened to Filiz?"

"Let's just say that she didn't feel the same way about me."

"Ah, unrequited love. It's a bitch."

Boy, she must be sorry now!

"But now I have this feeling again."

"I make you swoon?"

"You do. And I want you to stay a few more days so I can swoon and you can catch me."

"I might just let you fall."

"You would let me fall? After all the times I have picked you up?" He poked me. "Next time I will leave you right where you land."

I laughed loudly, and Emine waved goodbye to the little blonde girl and came back to the table before climbing onto Aydin's lap. "*Baba*, can we go now?"

He pointed at her sandwich. "You haven't eaten your toast, Emine."

She slipped the wrapped cheese toast into her pocket. "Oh, that's not for me. That's for the cat in the garden."

I clapped at Emine's ingenuity. "Your daughter is quite a genius."

"Or an evil mastermind."

With one final look at the impressive view of the Bosphorus and Golden Horn Emine and I went off in search of the little cat in the park. Aydin trailed behind. After following kitty's little pawprints in the now slushy footpath, we finally found it sheltered under a wooden bench. Emine opened up her toasted sandwich and pulled small pieces off for the cat who sniffed at Emine's hand nervously before grabbing what was offered.

When the sandwich was gone, Emine looked up at me with fear in her eyes. "Do you think she will be okay here by herself?"

"I'm sure she has some friends close by, but perhaps you can come back another time and check on her?"

Emine was disappointed. I was pretty sure she wanted me to hide the kitten in my coat pocket but took my profferred hand anyway, and we walked back to Aydin who had waited for us at the gate. He took Emine's other hand and we retraced our steps back down the hill, the near-perfect family. All that was missing was a little boy with dark curls and green eyes.

My ovaries gave me a nudge. Baby. Baby. Baby!

"Emine is staying at her mother's tonight." Aydin snapped me out of my internal drama and shot me his lopsided grin. "Would you like to have dinner with me?"

"You mean, like, on a date?"

"Yes, I think its time we go on a date, don't you?"

"Are you going to make me swoon?"

He chuckled and leaned over Emine in to whisper in my ear. "I'm hoping to do more than that."

I scoffed in mock outrage but nodded enthusiastically. I didn't know how much more time I would have here in Istanbul, but I (and my horny bits) knew that I wanted to spend whatever time I had left with him. "Yes, please."

"Eight o'clock?"

I nodded as I bent down to Emine. "Thank you for a wonderful morning. I had a great time."

I wiggled my nose at her and Emine giggled. "Me too." She wrapped her arms around my neck tightly. "*Baba,* can we keep her?"

My heart contracted and I looked up at Aydin for help, but he had turned his head away. "Aw, sweetie. You already have my heart."

I tried to untangle her fingers from around my neck but she wasn't having it. "No, I want to keep all of you."

Aydin bent down and dragged Emine off me. "Come now, *aşkım.* Let Ginger go. She is very busy this afternoon."

There was a lump in my throat and I didn't trust my words so I just nodded and waved.

As Aydin took his daughter's hand, he winked at me. "And try to stay out of trouble, will you?"

I produced a weak smile for Emine's benefit. "I can't promise anything."

As I watched them walk away Emine turned and waved one final time. My heart was torn as I wondered when, or if, I would ever see her again. I turned towards Leyla's shop, after all, I had promised to update her on dinner; but most of all, right then I desperately needed a friend.

CHAPTER 14

Introducing ... The New Ginger

"*Merhaba!*" I popped my head through the shop door and surprised Leyla. "I said I would come back, and here I am!"

"Ginger! Hello to you, too!" Leyla hugged me tightly before kissing me on each cheek. "How did it go last night? I bet you knocked them all dead!"

"Not quite."

"Did you tell the donkey that you were not falling for his charms?"

"I'll tell you the whole story, but first let me ask you something. Have you ever heard of Simge Kaya?"

"The actress?"

I nodded.

"Of course. She is very famous."

"What's her story?"

Leyla passed me a magazine with a photograph of Simge on the cover. I flipped through the pages until I spotted Simge's smug face staring back at me.

"She was on 'One Life' here in Turkey, but she was recently offered a starring role in a real Hollywood movie! I think it might be James Bond… or maybe Mission Impossible. Something with that famous actor, you know the one."

"Is that right?" I put the magazine down. "Is she married?"

"She was married, but that was years ago. She is getting married again, though."

"What was the story with the ex? Do you know anything about him?"

"Aydin Kaya? They were very much in love. But then she left him for another man. Oh!" Leyla's eyes widened with realisation. "Aydin. Aydin? Your Aydin?"

I couldn't help but grin. The look on Leyla's face was priceless. "Well not my Aydin. Just Aydin."

"*Aman Tanrım*! Oh my God! You and Aydin Kaya? This is incredible."

"I'm as astounded as you are."

"Oh, Ginger! I said he was a donkey!" Leyla moaned before she stood up and stomped out the storage room muttering to herself the whole time. "Aydin Kaya! A donkey! Aydin Kaya is no donkey."

I took a seat on the sofa and opened the magazine to the story on Simge. I studied the photographs of this beautiful woman that Aydin was at one time in love with and compared myself to her. Talk about feeling like the consolation prize. There was no way I could compete with the likes of Simge Kaya. The main photograph was of her dressed in a gold, strapless gown at a movie premiere. She looked beautiful, laughing and posing with other beautiful people. There was also a photograph of her and Deniz on a yacht drinking champagne as well an older one of her with Aydin on their wedding day. The story was written in both Turkish and English (lucky me) and was all about her upcoming nuptials. There was also an in-depth analysis as to whether her ex-husband would try to stop the wedding. As sources exclusively revealed, Aydin was still very much in love with the goddess that is Simge Kaya!

I continued to flip through the magazine until a photo of Aydin caught my eye. He was dressed in a formal suit and looked ridiculously gorgeous. I surreptitiously ripped the page out and slipped it into my handbag, just for proof mind you, and not at all because I'm a crazed fan.

Leyla reappeared, with *çay* and biscuits. "Sugar?"

"One, thanks." I re-examined the photograph of Simge and Aydin. "Simge is very beautiful."

"As are you."

"Thank you, but I am sure not in the same league as Simge."

"Only confidence makes Simge Kaya more beautiful than you or me. She thinks she is beautiful and so she is beautiful."

"She was wearing the same dress as me last night."

Leyla looked as mortified as I had felt. "Oh, Ginger!"

"I know." A groan escaped my lips, and with my small glass of tea in hand, I proceeded to relive the whole evening for Leyla who squealed intermittently and oohed and aahed every so often.

By the time I finished, Leyla looked wiped out. "What a story."

"I'm calling the whole evening a complete disaster!"

"So Simge Kaya is a bitch? I guess that makes sense." She stared off into the distance, then refocused and grabbed my arm. "Marry Aydin Kaya and stay here forever. Just imagine, I could be best friends with Aydin Kaya's wife, and you could wear all my designs when you went out. I would become famous as well!"

I swatted her hand away. "Don't be daft!"

"And tonight you are having dinner with Aydin Kaya?" Leyla had a dreamy look in her eyes. "So what are you going to wear?"

"Probably these." I indicated the jeans I was wearing.

Leyla looked more horrified at my fashion choice then when I said Simge was wearing the same dress.

I grimaced. My credit card was about to take another battering. "Alright, what would you suggest then?"

Within moments Leyla handed me the softest pair of leather pants and a black cashmere sweater with a peek-a-boo cut out at the neckline that exposed just a hint of breast.

"These just came in this morning. You will look amazing without looking like you are trying. You need to look fabulous for Mr. Aydin Kaya."

"Just Aydin."

"Yes, yes just Aydin." She sighed dreamily before re-focusing. "Plus, I think it will snow tonight, so you need to dress for the weather."

"Not again!" I groaned. "I'll never be able to get out of here at this rate."

"Is that such a bad thing?" Leyla seemed amused by the fact that I wanted to leave Istanbul and the hot-as-hell-super-amazing-ridiculously-stupendous, Aydin Kaya.

"Of course not. I guess I need to accept that my trip back home isn't going to happen."

"I'm sorry."

"Me too. I've got a suitcase full of clothes I haven't had a chance to wear."

"Yes, but look how well it has worked for my bank balance!"

"Not so much for mine." I grumbled under my breath before disappearing into the change rooms.

The thought of tugging and fighting with leather pants wasn't what I had planned for my visit to Leyla's, but as I slipped one leg and then the other into the scrumptious leather, I knew I had found my outfit for tonight. I stepped out to find Leyla holding a pair of gorgeous diamante hoop earrings. I wiggled my finger at her, but she shook her head. "Don't worry, Audrey Hepburn. It is costume jewellery." They totally completed the outfit.

I took one final look around her shop. There was still one thing missing. "Leyla?"

"Yes, *canım*?"

Jane Gundogan

"Do you stock underwear?"

"You don't have enough?"

I grinned sheepishly. "I didn't bring the right, er, kind."

She lifted her eyebrows at me and grinned. "Why yes, I do. In fact, you are here at a great time as we just got in our new year stock. They are still in the box. Come and see if you like something."

I went out to the back room with her and she opened a large box on the floor. Bras. Camis. Teddies. Bikinis. G-strings. Even garters and girdles. A lot of lace, very sexy and it was all in shades of red. I don't know why I had thought Turkish underwear would be PG-13, but Leyla's box of goodies was rated R for raunchy!

"I wasn't expecting such a variety."

"It is a tradition in Turkey to wear red on New Years for good luck."

I picked out a few items. No more daggy, cotton panties for me, thank you very much!

"Now, what will we do with your hair?"

"I was going to leave it in the braid I think, otherwise it will be a whole thing to wash and dry and style." I flicked my fishtail back over my shoulder. "It's just too hard without my conditioner and dryer."

"Not true. Come with me." Leyla deadbolted the store's front door, took me out the back and up a rickety staircase next door. She opened a small, blue door. A hair salon. Here?

Leyla called out as we entered and a young woman appeared from a back room. She openly scrutinized me before having a lengthy conversation with Leyla. Satisfied with themselves, they waved me to the chair by the shower hose.

Now, this would be the point in any great rom-com where the obligatory movie makeover montage would take place. It would be a fun-filled five minutes all to the beat of a boppy, empowering song sung by Taylor Swift or Cindi Lauper. Leyla and I would dance wildly while I was transformed from a nerdy book girl to a hot babe. Sadly, that did not happen, despite the Turkish pop music being piped through the room, and instead I closed my eyes and prayed that Leyla's friend could perform a miracle on my frizz and tame the mane.

"Leyla?" I whispered nervously. "I don't want to come out a blonde or anything."

"Relax Ginger. Serap will merely release the beauty that you already have."

"If so say so."

After being poked, proded, massaged, plucked and blow dried, I was finally allowed to look at myself in the mirror. "Okay... just... wow!"

"You look amazing Ginger!"

"*Cok güzel*. Very beautiful."

I stared at the beautiful woman in the mirror, aka me, and saw someone I had never met before. Staring back at me was a beautiful stranger. The woman's hair was reset into large curls that fell halfway down her back. Her eyebrows were arched slightly higher and her hazel — no, Aydin was right, they were green — eyes were smoky and made up with kohl and oodles of mascara. This woman's skin was somehow glowing, and her lips were red and sensual. Yes, this woman was beautiful and confident. Maybe I really did have my very own rom-com makeover.

Leyla decided to walk with me back to the pansion and we linked arms as we shuffled our way along the footpath. I want to say she walked back to the hotel to spend time with me, but who was I kidding? Of course she wanted to meet the fabulous, the magnificent, the sexy as hell, Aydin Kaya!

We went straight to the main house where we were greeted by Jack and Cel who, along with Refika, had already planted themselves in front of the fireplace with a glass of wine. Jack whistled when he saw me. "You are looking fine."

Refika scrutinized me closely before nodding her approval. "My nephew is a fortunate man, and you are a fortunate woman too. Yes?"

Leyla and I both giggled in agreement.

Refika left the room for a moment before returning with another bottle of wine (for us), a two-tier teapot filled with *çay* (for her) and *pasta* (for everyone).

"Pasta? Like spaghetti? I don't think I should eat anything. I'm supposed to be going out to dinner."

Refika grabbed my cheeks and squeezed them fondly. "Such a silly girl. No *aşkım*. Cake. There is always time for cake."

I nodded, confused, but more than a little relieved to see that the cake wasn't made from spaghetti. Instead, it was a sweet, syrup-soaked semolina cake. I leaned over and whispered to Leyla. "I'm going to be huge by the time I leave Istanbul."

She looked me up and down matter of factly. "You are a little skinny."

"What is it with everyone here telling me I'm skinny? Back in Australia, I would be considered plus size."

She looked at my elevated eyebrows and laughed. "I believe men much prefer women a little larger. My father says it means they are good breeders."

I coughed, choking on my wine. "Leyla!"

"Don't be shocked. Everyone is looking for someone to procreate with. It is how the world turns. Believe me, I know. I have been looking for years."

"Let me just get through tonight. I'll worry about procreating another time."

She squealed, barely containing her excitement. "With Aydin Kaya!"

I blew out hard, puffing out my perfectly-blushed cheeks. "You're completely out of control!"

Actually, it was I who was a little out of control as I mulled over the very real possibility that Aydin and I might actually see each other in our birthday suits before the night was through. Don't get me wrong, I was all for a little shtupping, or maybe even a lot of shtupping, but there was a lot of pressure riding on that shtupping and, in the end, it was all that I, and my depressed vagina, could think about.

I had gulped down my first glass of wine, which hadn't helped to alleviate my fears at all, and was well onto my second by the time my date arrived.

Aydin's appearance was preceded with a cold blast of air from the open door and an excited squeak from Leyla. When I looked up, he was leaning against the frame watching me with that gorgeous lopsided grin of his. He removed his jacket which he folded over his arm and strode across the room like he was strutting down a catwalk for Armani. In his black sweater and matching beanie, he really did look like a model, the scruff on his chin adding to his naturally fabulous good looks, but that beanie really had to go so his curls could fly free. I lost myself for a moment as I imagined Aydin naked. Sexy naked. A gasp unwittingly escaped my throat. He raised his eyebrows with a knowing grin. I swear that man could read my mind!

It took only three strides for him to reach my side. He pulled me out of my chair and wrapped his strong arms around my waist. He leaned forward to brush his lips across my mouth. For a moment I forgot that we had a very attentive audience and as tiny sparks rippled across my skin. My nipples tightened as his tongue slipped between my lips and entwined with mine as his grip on me tightened.

I don't know how long we kissed for, it could have been for only a moment, or it could have been for an eternity, but when common sense finally returned and he released me from his embrace, I stood breathing heavily, trying to remind my brain that I was in a public place. Ripping off Aydin's clothes to ravish him might not be the most sensible thing to do at that moment.

"Good evening." The hunger in his eyes was unmistakable as they roamed down my body and back up. "You look beautiful."

"So do you." I desperately wanted to touch his hip, his strong arms, his hard ass. I kept my hands to myself. Stupid audience.

"Ahem." Jack coughed into his wine glass while Cel and Leyla gaped at us with their mouths open wide.

Aydin was sheepish as he finally acknowledged our audience. "My apologies." His voice was deep and scruffy, and I wondered if anyone else heard the longing in it that I did. "I forgot myself for a moment."

He turned to his Aunt and kissed her hand before lifting it to his forehead.

"What is he doing?"

Leyla replied. "*Sevgi, saygı, sadakat.* It means love, respect, loyalty. It's traditionally how the we give respect to our elders."

"That's a lovely sentiment, isn't it?"

Before Leyla could say anything else Aydin turned his dark, sexy as hell, gaze on her. I held my breath in anticipation of Leyla's reaction to meeting the great Aydin Kaya! The shock on her face hadn't faded in the slightest as he approached her, in fact she looked like she was about to faint. Oh yes, this was going to be great!

He bent down, extended a hand, and grinned wickedly at her. "You must be the one and only Leyla."

This was the first time I had seen Leyla not wholly in control of herself. "Merhaba... hello... hi."

To me Aydin is just a chef, and perhaps the love of my life, but to Leyla, and to most of the women in Turkey, he was more famous than Brad Pitt. She attempted to stand, but the three glasses of wine coupled with her meeting the stupendous Aydin Kaya caused her to trip over her own feet and land on her bum in front of him. I watched as Aydin's face changed from embarrassment to confusion before it finally settled on barely contained laughter. "Why do people always end up on the floor around me?"

I had to give props to Leyla because she rallied quickly. By the time she was back on her feet she had already batted her eyelashes at him. "Sorry. I am not usually this clumsy."

He took all her fan-girling in good graces though and laughed it off, even when she started taking selfies of the two of them. It was definitely time for me to save his hot ass before she started to grope him.

"Right." I grabbed my jacket and scarf. "Time for us to go, I think."

I hugged a still-dazed Leyla goodbye who whispered in my ear. "Go get him, girlfriend!"

Aydin clasped my hand and pulled me to the door. "It was good to meet you, Leyla."

"Yes. Yes. You too, Aydin Kaya!"

I glanced back at Leyla, already on her phone no doubt telling anyone that would listen that she was just in the company of the famous Aydin Kaya!

CHAPTER 15

Philophobia: The fear of falling in love

A ydin's small white car was parked at the gate. With his free hand, he opened the passenger door and I slid inside. "Thank you, kind sir."

He winked at me. "I know how to treat a lady right."

"Oh, yeah?"

Getting into the driver's seat, he started the engine, revved it a few times and grinned at me. "Ready?"

For a moment I was lost as the image of Daniel Cleaver revving the engine of a red sports car flooded my mind. I shook my perfectly coiffed curls and forced myself back to reality. That seemed like more of a Bridget Jones moment that a Ginger Knox one. No need for the fantasy. I had the reality of a gorgeous man sitting opposite me, despite the fact my reality drove like a nine-year-old behind the wheel of a bumper car. I thanked God for the invention of seatbelts as we bumped over the cobblestones and screeched out onto the main road. "So, where are we going anyway?"

"It's a bit of a surprise."

"I love surprises. Keeps life exciting." I shifted in my seat and caught him sneaking a glance at my boobs in my cashmere peek-a-boo sweater, which was totally the reaction I wanted. The twins still had it but coupled with my hot new candy apple red bra, they were just the right amount of plump and perky — and definitely nowhere near my knees which was a huge bonus. "Will Bozo the Clown be there?"

Aydin chuckled and reached for my hand, entwining his fingers in mine. "It's *boza* and no, there will not, but there will be a very nice glass of red waiting for you."

"You sure know the way to a girl's heart, well, my heart anyway."

He lifted my hand to his mouth and gently kissed it while keeping his other hand firmly on the steering wheel and his eyes on the road. I caught my breath as tiny sparks ignited across my skin. It might have been cold outside, but it was heating up nicely in the car. "You will not be disappointed, Ginger."

"I can't imagine myself ever being disappointed with you, Aydin."

"If you keep talking like that we will never make it to the restaurant."

It was game time and I was flirting hard. I pushed a curl behind my ear and fluttered my eyelashes at him. "Is that a promise?"

Aydin dropped my hand and gripped the steering wheel like it was his job. We whizzed past the park that we had visited that morning and continued up to the crest of the hill before turning off the main road. He slowed the car down to a crawl as we drove down another cobblestoned alley, finally coming to a stop behind an rather old, four storey building. Hmmm.

Emboldened, my flirting went up a couple of notches. "Another alleyway, Aydin? What *do* you intend on doing with me here?"

"Ginger." His voice was low, a warning, but his gravelly tone only made me want him more.

I gazed at him innocently and smoothed out my sweater. "Yes, Aydin?"

He looked around the small carpark. All empty. All dark. He reached over and dragged me across to his seat, turning me in his arms so that I straddled him. I wiggled in his lap, rubbing myself against what was no doubt a very hot rocket in his pants. I wondered how much more he would stand for before he screwed me right then and there. "Give me your lips."

Yes, sir.

Bossy Aydin was hot as hell!

My mouth opened and he kissed me hard. He was in total control. I moaned as my tongue met his. There was nothing better than kissing this man. His lips on mine became my whole world, and I wanted this kiss to go on forever. I ripped his beanie off freeing those luscious locks of his and immediately wrapped my fingers in them, twisting and twirling his curls. He held my face in his hands and pulled my lips off of his, then turned his attention to my neck, biting me softly which sent shockwaves straight to my lady bits, already primed for a big night. I arched as his hands slipped under my sweater when, without warning, my back nudged the car horn. "HOO-NNNKKK!"

We both jumped at the sound of the horn and pulled away from each other.

"Shit!"

A light came on behind me. We were the perpetual deer in headlights. Thank God the windows had fogged up giving us just a little privacy. I wasn't sure if we could be arrested for getting hot and heavy in a car in Turkey, but I certainly didn't want to find out. Flashes of Midnight Express ran through my mind. I pulled down my sweater and threw myself over to the passenger seat.

A voice called out from the open doorway. *"Kim o?"*

We both sat as still as statues as we waited for the door to close. I held my breath, confident that my breathing was so loud that the person in the doorway would know that we were only a pair of jeans and leather pants away from fornicating in his carpark. Aydin hissed and whispered under his breath. *"Git ya!"*

Finally, the light turned off and the door closed. I giggled with relief. "Now what?"

He took a deep breath as his eyes roamed over me. "You are driving me crazy, Green Eyes."

"Right back at you, Creeper." I leaned forward and kissed his cheek while slipping my hand into his lap to brush the rocket in his pants.

He leaned his head back against the headrest, closed his eyes and blew out hard. "I think that's enough excitement... for now."

I squirmed in my seat. "For now."

"Right. We had better get a move on. Just give me a moment."

I waited for him to get himself under control. "Just so you know, we're skipping dessert."

"Absolutely."

Aydin opened his door and came around to open mine. He took my hand and led me over to the small, metal door. "Stay calm. Okay?"

Wait! What?

He opened the door and we walked into a large, commercial kitchen. I was a little shocked and very, very confused.

Finally, someone spotted us in the doorway. "Aydin!" then the rest of the staff yelled their hellos to him as well.

They all laughed and smiled, hugging each other and slapping each other's backs while they subtly, and some not so subtly, gave me the once over. The door of a walk-in refrigerator opened and an attractive, older man appeared carrying a platter of meat. I immediately knew that this was Aydin's father. He was tall and slim like Aydin and he had the same chiselled cheekbones and delicious jawline. This man could have been the George Clooney of Turkey, if there was such a thing, with his silver-fox hair and dark skin, but he had something that even George didn't. A fabulously thick and perfectly maintained moustache.

Aydin's father placed the platter down on a bench and openly scrutinized me before he offered me his hand. "*Hoşgeldiniz!*"

"Hello." I shook his hand formally.

"*Baba*, this is Ginger. Ginger, this is my father Mehmet and this

—" he gestured to the kitchen around us, "—is our restaurant."

"Oh, wow!" The wave of terror that washed over me when I realised I was meeting his entire family at that moment threatened to wipe me out, but I took a deep breath and plastered a bright smile on my face.

Once I had been thoroughly eyeballed, everyone returned to their stations. I took the opportunity to look around the large kitchen. The industrial-sized oven was over-crowded with bubbling pots and simmering skillets beside a massive open grill filled with meats and vegetables on sewers being watched over by two very harried staff members. In the corner, an older man held an enormous pizza peel and I watched him pull large, puffy bread out of a stone oven. Beside him, another man was chopping a mountain of vegetables. It was totally chaotic, but from my many hours of masturbatory love with Gordon Ramsay, I knew that everything would come together when it was time to plate the dish.

Yep, I knew the terminology, baby!

Aydin pointed out two of the young men by the stove and grill. "These are my brothers Engin and Hasan, but they are a little busy right now burning someone's dinner."

He yelled at his brothers in Turkish and pointed to the grill. They turned their attention back to their task just in time to save some delicious looking pieces of meat from becoming charred. Aydin laced my fingers with his and pulled me along behind him as he walked over to the grill. With his free hand, he picked up a pair of tongs, flipped the meat over and gave his approval. One of his brothers plated it up while I watched.

At that moment my stomach growled. Loudly. I was mortified.

Aydin chuckled and rubbed my belly. "I guess you're hungry?"

"Who wouldn't be when being in the presence of all this delicious-smelling food?" Good recovery, Ginger.

"We better get you fed then."

He led me through a set of double-swinging doors and we stepped out into the dining room. I looked around in fascination. It was all very typically Turkish. Hundreds of colourful Turkish lamps hung from the ceiling casting a rainbow of light over the happy patrons. The dark, red walls were filled with pieces of art depicting Turkish scenery — markets, mosques, and bridges — but my eyes were drawn to another painting, this one was a portrait of a woman, with familiar dark eyes staring back at me. It had to have been painted here, in this very room, as the ceiling had the same hanging lamps and the walls the same dark red. Her face was familiar, and yet I knew I had never met her. I stopped for a moment to examine it carefully.

"This is lovely." I pointed the painting out to Aydin.

"That is my mother. It was painted a very long time ago by a famous Turkish painter."

"She's stunning."

"Yes, she was." Aydin gazed at the painting with a tinge of sadness. "She passed away a few years ago now. Car accident."

Damn it!

"I'm sorry."

He shrugged. "Of course."

He took my hand and we climbed two flights of stairs. Each level was filled with happy patrons, no doubt enjoying their delicious meals. When we finally arrived at an enclosed, glass rooftop, I was surprised. It appeared to be little more than a storage room with a single table set for two. The only illumination from dozens of candles set around the room that gave the place a very romantic glow, although it was the view out the window that was truly stunning.

The whole of Istanbul was on display before us, a flickering sea of fairy lights. Absolutely magical. The Bosphorus Strait and Asia was to our right, while behind us was the was the jaw-dropping magnificence of two extraordinary structures, an enormous, domed mosque bathed in light and the other building that, I think, might have been a church or maybe it was another palace, but regardless, the rivalry between the two buildings was difficult to ignore. They were both overwhelming with their massive proportions, but amazingly they co-existed side by side.

"What do you think?"

"I think its beautiful."

"I think you're beautiful."

This kind of compliment would have normally embarrassed me, but right now, here opposite Aydin, I accepted it with grace. "Thank you."

"Wine?"

"Do you really need to ask?"

He laughed and poured a glass for both of us. "We only use this level in summer, but I thought you would enjoy the view from here."

"I do. It's breathtaking."

He raised his glass and threw me a sexy grin. "Panties."

I made a face at him. "Is 'panties' our thing now?"

"If you've made 'Creeper' a thing I think I can make 'panties' one as well."

"Alright then, Creeper." I tapped my glass against his and repeated the word. "Panties."

Our eyes locked and we both smiled. I cleared my throat. "So, how long has your family had this place?"

"Just like my Aunt's *pansion*, this restaurant has been in our family for many generations."

"And you work with your father and your two brothers?"

"Yes, but also my sister's husband works here, and their two boys."

I took a few steps closer to the glass dome, swirled the wine in my glass and took a sip. "Tell me about the place you want to open."

"I have land just outside of Bodrum."

"Which is where?"

"On the Aegean coast."

"Nice."

"It's stunning." Aydin came up behind me, put his arm around my waist and splayed his hand out before us as we gazed at the city below. "Picture this... a restaurant right on the water. You can hear the waves lapping gently and gulls calling above. Several verandas and terraces, climbing vines of colour with jasmine and grapes with thousands of twinkle lights and a canopy of bougainvillea overhead. It will be *the* place to visit when you holiday in Bodrum."

"It will also have fabulous cuisine, cooked by master chef, Aydin Kaya."

"Indeed." He grinned at me as a waiter delivered our first course. "Come. Let's eat while it's hot."

Aydin pulled out the chair for me then caressed my shoulders as he got me settled. "Having spent time in London and seeing how the restaurants there operate, I know I can incorporate some of their ideas into what I want my restaurant to be, to make it a more hands-on experience."

"How so?"

Aydin sat at the table, his eyes sparkling in the candlelight as he spoke of his dream. "What do you know about gastro-tourism?"

I shook my head. "Nothing."

He unwrapped a linen napkin, ripped off a piece of puffy, hot pita and slid it across fresh hummus. "Open."

I opened my mouth and he placed the bite inside. This was my chance. I wanted to taste more than his tongue, so I closed my lips around his finger and sucked off the hummus. His eyes grew wide.

"Ahem, er, gastro-tourism provides visitors with unique experiences that highlight kitchen culture. Visitors will come to not only experience some great food but also learn how to prepare it themselves, which will include visiting village markets, local farms and dairies to purchase ingredients."

"That sounds amazing."

"I hope to move down there before the summer to start work. Now that Simge is leaving, I must also find somewhere for Emine and I to live until the restaurant is ready."

"You're going to live at the restaurant?"

"Yes, I will build my home above the restaurant. I hope you will visit me there. Would you?"

"Oh, well, maybe." I stuffed another piece of bread into my mouth negating any further reply. Could I live there with you? My cheeks grew warm. If only Aydin knew that had just popped into my head. Oh, Ginny, what are you thinking?

"Yes, I think you will." He poured another glass of wine before turning his attention to the two buildings out the window. "Shall I play tour guide again?"

"Please. I promise I won't fall asleep this time."

"When did you fall asleep?"

"In the car."

"Right. I didn't mind that. You were snoring softly. It was adorable."

Don't blush, don't blush, don't blush!

"You must already know that Istanbul has at one time been the home of the Ottoman, the Byzantine, and the Roman Empires." His assumption that I knew anything about Turkish history made my face redden even further. I nodded and tried to keep up as he talked about the imposing red building lit up to my left. "That is the *Hagia Sophia*. It was built over 1,500 years ago and it was at one time a church. Then it was a mosque, but now it is a museum. Perhaps you will have time to visit it while you are here?"

I nodded as I continued to graze on the various meze that kept appearing at our table. "Maybe."

"And this —" He pointed at the mosque opposite, "— is *Sultan Ahmet Camii* better known to tourists around the world as the Blue Mosque."

"Oh right. I've heard of it, but it's not blue."

He grinned. "Correct. It got its name from the *Inzit* tiles of blue ceramic that adorn its inner walls."

"Could I go inside?"

He nodded.

"Even though I'm not Muslim?"

"Of course. Just as I visited Westminster Abbey in London, mosques are open to everybody regardless of religion." He grinned again, his lopsided smile that I had become a little obsessed with. "Now onto more important issues. Have you been able to arrange your flight yet?"

"I've still not heard back from the airline, so it looks like you'll be stuck with me a little while longer."

He reached for my hand and kissed it. "That makes me very happy, Ginger. The happiest I've been in a long time."

As we sipped on our wine I found myself telling Aydin things that I had never dreamed of telling anyone. I spoke about my parents divorce, about how ugly it was and how I hadn't been in contact with my mother for years. I gave him the low down on my first kiss, the first time I got drunk and even my first hickey. I talked about Sydney and how much I missed living by the water — and all that glorious sunshine. Full disclosure, I even admitted to my unhealthy addiction to romantic comedies and Hugh Grant. And nothing I said put him off, not even a little bit.

Aydin then spent an extraordinary amount of time trying to convince me to stay with him in Istanbul which made me spend an extraordinary amount of time trying to think of a reason why I shouldn't, in fact, stay in Istanbul. I mean, except for my life back in London. Or Sydney. But Aydin, oh yes, it wouldn't be too hard for me to be tempted to stay right here forever.

Before I had the chance to get lost in the fantasy, Aydin's father appeared at the top of the stairs curiously carrying a clay pot in one hand and a curved sword in the other. He theatrically placed the pot on our table and then proceeded to swing his sword in circular motions. He spun around before flipping the sword into the air and catching it with ease. I held my breath as Mehmet swung it one final time, breaking the clay pot open with a flourish to reveal a delicious-looking lamb casserole which he plated up with grilled vegetables and couscous. "This looks delicious, Mehmet."

He slapped his hand against his chest and spoke slowly as he endeavoured to find the right words. "Please, you must call me *Baba*."

My face burned bright as I repeated myself, "This looks delicious... *Baba*."

"Okay, okay, eat, eat. *Alfiyet olsun!*"

He waved goodbye and disappeared back down the stairs leaving us to our meal.

We ate slowly, laughing, sharing stores and savouring every delicious bite. My gaze kept returning to his face as I ate. His hair was mussed up, thanks to my fingers, but somehow that muss only made him look even more beautiful. I bit my lip as my hazel eyes — no Ginger, when you're with Aydin your eyes are always green — met his melted chocolate ones before they travelled lower still to his soft lips, hidden amongst the scruff on his chin. His mouth continued to form more words, and I tried to concentrate on those words, I really did, but his tongue kept making an appearance ever so often which made it impossible to think of anything else.

Football ... something... Tarkan... someone... lips... mouth... TONGUE!

My heart thundered so fast I thought I might have had a panic attack. I looked around for an open window. Or maybe a door. I desperately needed air! I fanned myself with my napkin.

"Hey!" Aydin stopped talking and reached across the table for my hand. "Are you okay?"

I nodded, unable to speak.

"Tell me what you are thinking."

"Nothing."

"I don't think that's true. I wonder if perhaps you are starting to like it here. I am thinking that you won't want to leave. Maybe you might prefer to stay with me?"

Don't let yourself get carried away, Ginger!

"Why do you keep saying that?" My words might have come out a little more forcibly than I had intended. "This is nice Aydin, but this isn't real life. How could it possibly be?"

"It could be if you wanted it to be."

"Someone has got to maintain some common sense here because there is only one outcome."

"And that is?"

"The very real likelihood that somewhere down the track we are both going to cause each other a lot of pain."

"You are wrong." His jaw tensed and he pulled his hand from my grasp. "Would you like to know what I think?"

I raised my eyebrows but didn't reply.

"I think you fall in love with the most unexpected people at the most unexpected times. And I fell in love with you. In London. The first time I saw you."

Keep it together, Ginger.

"Not possible."

"What I feel for you is so deep it overwhelms me, Ginger. And I believe you feel the same way about me. You just may not know it yet... or you do know it, but you are too scared to admit it."

I gave him an indignant huff. "You don't know what you're talking about."

Fact: he knew *exactly* what he was talking about.

I had a choice to make. Either be drawn into this whole crazy romance, or tell him to chill the hell out and make a run for it. My brain wasn't going to be much help and, lets be honest, my heart has never been known for its stellar decision making skills, so that left my vagina in complete control of all my decisions. Of course my vagina was yelling its approval of all things Aydin. Yes, yes, YES!

Aydin rose from his chair and held out his hand. "Now, if you still want to skip dessert maybe we could go for a walk before I take you back to my Aunt's."

"Yes, yes, YES!"

Stupid, not-so-depressed vagina!

We stopped by the kitchen to thank his family for dinner. *Baba* wiggled his resplendent moustache at me. "If I were thirty years younger, Miss Ginger, I would steal you from my boy."

"*Baba*, If you were thirty years younger, I think I would let you."

He laughed and hugged me tightly. "You come back and visit me, yes?"

"I hope so."

Just like last night it took an extraordinary amount of time to say our goodbyes to not just his family but also customers in the restaurant but finally we made our escape and crossed over the street to the park.

Despite the light snow and the late hour, there was a surprising number of people out and about. Tourists walked by taking photographs, lovers embraced tightly in an attempt to stay warm, and families enjoyed the winter atmosphere while they sipped on *salep* or nibbled on roasted chestnuts that were being sold by vendors scattered around the square. Aydin wrapped his arm around me pulling me into his chest. "What are you doing tomorrow?"

"It's Christmas Day."

"Not here."

"Oh? Okay, well I might come back here and have a look around."

"And tomorrow night?"

"What do you have in mind?"

"Will you join me at Deniz and Simge's wedding?"

I stepped out of his embrace and looked at him like he had just grown another head. "Oh, hell no!"

"Ginger, please? I would like you to come as my guest. You will be very welcome."

I paced back and forth, mumbling under my breath as I weighed up my options. Simge definitely wouldn't want me there, that's for sure and Deniz only wanted me to come out of a sense of guilt. But if I did go I would get to spend another night with this beautiful man standing before me, hot lopsided grin and all. Who was I kidding? The only one that mattered was Aydin. He would protect me if anything went awry.

He grabbed my hand and pulled me in close. "Ginger, I'm not asking you for a kidney. It's a wedding. It will be fun, I promise."

I took a deep breath, holding it for what seemed like forever until I blew it out so hard I felt faint. "Alright, but I bet Simge will be livid."

"You are my family now."

"Not *really*."

"You will be. In time."

Holy hotness. My heart raced in my chest. Marriage? I wasn't even his girlfriend yet. Surely, the panic showed on my face.

Aydin chuckled as he bent down to kiss the top of my head. "What *am* I going to do with you?"

"Dunno."

As I looked up at him, I wanted him to kiss me so badly, my lips tingled for his touch. He wrapped his arms tightly around my waist.

"*Aman Allahım sen çok güzelsin.* You are so beautiful my darling. My Ginger."

His lips grazed mine; light and soft at first, but it quickly turned into something deep and lustful. His hands were in my hair as he kissed my neck, my earlobe, my cheek, while my hands roamed freely under his sweater, hidden from view by his thick jacket. He didn't even flinch when I ran my cold hands across his chest before I slipped to his abs. As my fingers skimmed the top of his pants he moaned into my mouth. "I think it's time to go."

"Agreed."

As Aydin pulled me along toward the car, I looked back at the view behind me, wanting to remember this moment. It really was a picture postcard with the snow gently falling and the Blue Mosque behind us and I couldn't help myself. I grabbed my phone and took a selfie of Aydin and me before posting it on my Instagram. I even tagged Aydin for good measure.

I wanted to give them something to talk about. Whoever "they" were.

CHAPTER 16

Sex is Fun. Love is Funner.

We both knew that entire night had just been foreplay to what was to come next. Aydin really slammed the pedal to the metal as he raced us back towards the pansion. In those few minutes, there was a lot of nervous humming (on his part), breathless giggles (on my part) and furtive glances (by both of us).

He pulled the car to a stop and let it idle. I was nervous and I rummaged through my handbag looking for the key. That gave me a precious few seconds to calm my completely frazzled nerves. Purse? Passport? Lipgloss? Magazine article? Shit! Couldn't let him see that. He'd think I was some kind of crazy stalker. I stuffed that down the bottom of my handbag and continued to rummage around until — yes! I dangled the key in Aydin's face.

Our eyes locked, but no words were exchanged. Who was going to do it? Who was going to make the first move?

You, Ginger!

Do it! Do it! DO. IT. GINGER!

"Shut up!"

Shit!

"Sorry?"

"Talking to myself." To cover up my embarrassment, I leaned over to Aydin and kissed him lightly.

"You are too crazy, Green Eyes," he whispered against my mouth before his lips crashed against mine again. It was intensely hot — sexy hot — and, as his tongue slipped past my lips, my brain, my heart and my out of control vagina had all taken up the mantra. "Do it! Do it! DO. IT. GINGER!"

I reluctantly pulled myself away, and raised my eyebrow mischievously. "Are we planning on staying out here all night or do you think we should go to my room?"

I jumped out of the car and tapped my foot on the wet sidewalk, looking at an imaginary watch. I didn't have to wait long, because Aydin was out in an instant, slammed the car door and immediately disappeared from sight. "Oof!"

"Aydin?"

A moan came from the cobblestones. I carefully walked around the car to find him on his hands and knees. He stood up warily and wiped himself off. "Stupid ice."

I laughed and gazed at him with wide-eyed innocence. "Why do you men always end up on the ground around me?"

Aydin swatted me on my bum and chuckled. "Because you are so beautiful."

We both walked tentatively across the icy courtyard to my

room, neither of us wanting to break any bones before all the hot, sexy, sex. I handed him the key. He clicked the lock over, pushed the door open and stepped back to allow me to enter the room first. I gasped. On every surface were candles, their soft, flickering glow making the place look like an enchanted fairyland.

I threw my arms around his neck. "How did you do this?"

He shot me his super sexy, lopsided grin. "I have many secrets."

The fireplace was lit and a bottle of wine waited beside the bed along with two glasses. I also noticed a small, leather bag beside the bathroom door. Aydin was well prepared, and only a little presumptuous, but I was totally onboard with it.

I needed to pee, which I knew from my nearly thirty years on earth was a sure sign of nerves, so I excused myself to the bathroom.

I closed the door softly behind me and turned on the faucet to run. I freshened up my downtown and gave the toilet a solid flush. At that moment I was grateful that I had my summer toiletry bag sitting on the counter. There was just enough scented lotion left, and I rubbed my body all over. Ginger was going to smell like a tropical island tonight. I hoped Aydin liked coconut. I looked in the mirror and gave myself a little pep talk. "This is it, Ginny. This man loves you. Get over yourself and let him. At least for tonight."

When I came out of the bathroom, Aydin was standing by the fireplace. He had opened the bottle of wine and poured us each a glass. I pulse sped up as he gazed at me, his eyes bright in the flickering candlelight.

We both began to talk at once.

"Thank you for taking me to your restau—"

"I hope you enjoyed—"

We both started laughing, which broke the tension a little. Aydin stepped toward me and opened his arms. I immediately fell into his embrace. His fingers caressed the skin between my sweater and leather pants. "Ginger?"

"Yes?"

"I want you more than I have ever wanted anyone in my life. You are my past, my present, my future, my everything, and I will vow to spend my life making you smile every day."

My heart exploded with... something. Was it love? Dunno. It might have been acid reflux. I opened my mouth to reply, but he put a finger on my lips. "I know this is hard for you. You don't have to say anything, just let me love you. I want to love you."

Our hands were everywhere at once. The wine forgotten, Aydin tugged my sweater over my head as I shook off my boots. He pulled down the zipper of my leather pants and began to peel them off of me, which proved more difficult than I had expected. I giggled and he chuckled as he pulled and tugged, then he lifted me onto my enormous bed and lay me down. It seemed as though the lotion had created a sort of suction and the pants clung to my skin. He tugged at the pants from the bottom. We laughed at the ridiculousness of it all, but Aydin didn't stop until I was released from my leather restraint. I reached forward and dragged his sweater and t-shirt over his head and dropped it to the ground. His jeans were next and I unbuckled them and pushed them down over his firm ass. They fell to his feet leaving nothing between us but my spanking new and incredibly sexy, candy apple red bra and panties, and his rather pristine, (who does his laundry?) white boxers.

"Oh man." He fingered the red lace.

"What?"

He sighed dramatically. "If you must know, I was really looking forward to seeing you in your nice, safe, cotton… panties."

He grinned at me wickedly as he traced the hem of the lace on my breast.

"I'm happy to go and change, but someone's going to need to help me take these off first."

"I always wanted to be a boy scout." He wiggled his eyebrows and gave me a salute. "Ready to be of service."

I laughed at his comment and settled myself back onto the pillows. Aydin leaned down and pressed a wet kiss to the inside of my thigh. His warm lips against my cool skin were like bursts of fire as he kissed his way up my inner thigh. His hot breath now hovered over my drenched lace panties.

He lifted himself up and crawled up my body until we were eye to eye. His cinnamon chocolate eyes were now dark with desire. "Do you want me?"

"Yes." Even though I wanted to shout it from the mountaintop, it came out as a soft whisper.

"Ginger?"

I cleared my throat. "Yes."

"Aşkım?"

I wanted him so badly right now that I yelled it this time. "Yes! I want you, Aydin. Right! Now!"

The laugh that came from his throat was a sound of pure joy. He kissed me with that passion that was uniquely Aydin, filled with so much love and emotion it brimmed over and spilled out everywhere. With him, I was safe, adored, loved. This man was in love with me. I still couldn't believe it, but it showed in how he touched me. He moved his hands down my body, his warm palm sliding against my cool skin. He trailed his lips down from my mouth toward my neck, stopping to nibble on my ear and I moaned as his tongue slipped in. I ran my fingers up and down his back, his muscles tensing as my hands moved lower, my fingers feathering across his stomach. He was hovering above me, his body taunt, his muscles bulging as he held himself up.

"Do you know what you are doing to me?"

"I hope it's the same thing you're doing to me."

"Damn right it is!"

He lowered himself to me just enough to run his tongue down my neck and over my collarbone, then he laid beside me. His fingers traced the top of the lace on my bra over my breast, before he slipped down a strap. He kissed my shoulder, then slipped down the other strap. I lifted my back as he unclasped the bra, releasing my girls. He moaned at the sight of them.

"Ginger, you are truly a beautiful goddess." He bent down and left a trail of wet kisses across my breasts, grazing his tongue across one nipple before taking it into his mouth. He sucked at it gently then nipped it, pulling his head away to watch in awe as my nipple hardened at his touch. He turned his attention to my other breast and treated it with the same love.

"*Meleğim.*" He breathed again. "My angel."

After paying homage to my breasts he moved lower, kissing my stomach and the insides of my thighs, until finally, I felt his hot breath again against my panties. The sensation was too much. I was ready to explode before he'd even had any face time with my girly parts that were desperate to meet his acquaintance. He pulled gently at the red lace, sliding it slowly down and dropped my panties on the ground. One bonus of thinking I'd be spending my Christmas holiday in a bikini was that I was smooth and waxed and perfectly manicured, so when Aydin spread my legs apart and whispered "amazing," I knew that my very excited foo-foo was at its absolute finest, and ready for an introduction.

With Aydin gazing down at my most precious flower, that lopsided grin pulled his lips up to one side. At that moment I was indeed in heaven.

"Close your eyes, *aşkım*. I want you to only feel my love on your body."

I wanted to watch his beauty adore me, but I let my eyes flutter close at his request. And I was so glad that I did. I was already slick and hot and so ready for his hands as they rubbed and teased but when he put his mouth on me, I just couldn't wait any longer. I spread my legs wide as he finally slipped a finger and then another inside me while he continued to suck and lick and tongue me. I writhed under him, my fingers tight in his curls, holding him as his teeth grazed my nub, sending sparks of electricity through my whole body.

I arched my back as his fingers plunged in and out, gentle at first before the momentum built, over and over, probing, pushing, searching for that elusive spot until finally... oh, yes. His fingers were so long and strong and hit that perfect spot causing me to gasp, sparks of colour exploding behind my closed eyelids. Oh, God. Oh, God. Oh, God!

I let out a lustful moan as I gyrated against his face, each stroke of his fingers pushing me further, his lips and his tongue sucking and licking and biting the centre of my world, demanding my body to pulse until I gasped for air.

And there it was. The Big O. Orgasm. O God. O My. Olly Olly Oxenfreeeee!! O! O! OOOOOOO!

There was nothing in the world but Aydin and I... and his tongue... and his fingers... and his lips. And it was amazing.

Out of breath, I opened my eyes just as Aydin kicked his boxers across the room. Wait! Let me rephrase that, 'Naked Aydin' kicked his boxers across the room.

I admired my view of Naked Aydin as he climbed up my body. Naked Aydin was everything I had fantasized about and more. He was a goddamn piece of artwork. His skin was glistening with sweat and his muscles rippled with every move he made. I ran my hand through the smattering of dark hair on his chest and chiselled abs, before my gaze was drawn downward to his neat bush of pubic hair, and rock hard cock. I gasped at its size. It was definitely larger in girth and length than I had remembered from our previous meeting but I was definitely up for the challenge.

I pulled myself up on my knees and kissed him deeply. Our tongues met and tangled together as we let our passion build. Aydin moaned, and I manoeuvred him backwards onto the bed. I straddled him, pressing my folds on his shaft until I was open and grinding my slick juices on him. He bucked, and a low growl rumbled in his throat as he tried to push himself inside me. I dragged my hips reluctantly away and felt his cock buck furiously against my leg. "Not yet, babe."

Like the cat that had caught the canary Aydin grinned that sexy grin of his up at me. He settled himself on the pillows, his arms thrown casually behind his head. "Oh, boy!"

I slowly slid my whole body along his, sweaty skin against sweaty skin. I was so ready to sink myself down onto his already bucking shaft but instead I turned my attention to his neck which I nibbled, his collarbone which I licked and his nipples which I sucked until they puckered. "Do you like that?"

Aydin moaned in reply. Moving instinctively, I ran my fingers over his abs and kissed at the soft hairs that trailed from his belly down to my ultimate prize. I caught his eye and licked my lips suggestively. He moaned loudly in anticipation. "Please, Ginger."

"Not so fast." He jerked beneath me as I moved even lower down his body. I kissed his hips and his inner thigh before raining tiny kisses on his tight balls, inhaling his musky scent as I did. He was already so hard that as I grasped the base and slowly traced a pulsing vein up a bead of pre-come had welled on the head. His cock was begging to be licked and there was nothing more on this earth that I wanted to do at that moment. His breath drew in with a hiss as I took him in my mouth. Salty. Delicious.

"Oohhh, Green Eyes." He reached for my head and started to rock his hips as he pushed himself in deeper, feeling him hit the back of my throat. I licked and sucked him, alternating my speed with each pass. I pulled away and watched him buck, his cock desperate to return to heat of my mouth. He cried out so I took him again, but this time let him set the pace. In and out, in and out. My tongue teased him as he withdrew and sucked deeply as he thrust back in. He was close. I closed my eyes and sucked harder, swirling my tongue on his head, the desire to taste him overpowering me.

"Ahh... mmm... oh...*evet*... Ginger... that feels too... you need to... wait... aarrghhh!"

He managed to pull himself away and gently lay me onto the bed. The crackle and rip of a condom packet broke through the haze of my arousal and I watched in awe as he rolled a condom down his thick length.

His eyes met mine and I nodded giving him the permission that he wanted. He leaned over me, positioned his hips between my spread legs and slowly pushed into me. I moaned as he entered. His girth stretched me slowly until I was filled with him. We became one.

I moved my hips faster and faster, driving him deeper into me. He shuddered as our rhythm increased. I arched my back, my breasts pushing into his chest and he repositioned himself so he could press his lips to them. "So beautiful."

I wrapped my legs around him, my ankles hooked behind his thighs, which allowed me to take him even deeper, massaging my secret spot with each thrust. I was already lost, moaning Aydin's name over and over as he pumped into me but the pure joy of the moment was more than my bruised heart could handle. This wasn't sex, this was making love. The sheer power of that emotion completely overwhelmed me. This was something I had never experienced before. We moved as one as tears fell from my eyes. Tears of absolute joy, of happiness, and of finally experiencing the love that Aydin wanted to give me. He leaned down and kissed my tears.

Aydin's body stiffened, his eyes squeezed shut, his brow furrowed and his jaw clenched as he repositioned himself to increase the pressure, creating a different sensation for both of us. He was close. I tightened my thigh muscles, taking him as deeply as I could, giving all of myself to him.

"*Seni seviyorum*. I love you," he whispered over and over until I felt his orgasm erupt within me. He kept thrusting through his orgasm, keeping time with me until that warm tingly feeling began to build within my body. I couldn't hold back and within moments the tingling was replaced by tiny sparks of lights that swirled and spun around me. I closed my eyes as the sparks became more vivid but even with my eyes shut tight I watched as the sparks became bolts of lightning shooting through me until I reached my inevitable conclusion. "Aydin, oh, Aydin! Don't stop... don't... stop! Oh-O-O!"

O-O-O-orgasm, or more precisely — encore-gasm. Soar-gasm. Hit-me-in-my-core-gasm. Give-me-more-gasm. Je-adore-gasm. I could keep going but, well, you get the drift.

I held onto Aydin as I rode the storm-gasm (last one, I swear). I could feel every inch of his cock, every thrust as he stroked me, every surge of pleasure that felt like no other I had experienced before. He brought his mouth down onto mine and, as I tongues met, I moaned into his mouth, both of us panting, while our orgasm slowly ebbed.

Good God damn!

"*Aşkım*." Aydin rolled onto his side and lightly kissed my neck as his hand absently caressed my breast. I snuggled into him and closed my eyes as he sighed into my ear. "I could just lie here with you like this forever."

I knew I should have been lost in the after-glow of amazing sex but my eyes sprang back open at 'forever'.

Forever is a long time. A very long time.

Henry and I were going to be forever.

I scowled at myself as my bliss evaporated which allowed my rational brain, my bruised heart and euphoric lady bits mull over the evening's events.

Brain was, as always very level-headed but Heart feared the emotions that Aydin had stirred in me. These were feelings that I had sworn to protect so I would never be hurt again. And there were other feelings as well, stronger feelings that had sparked a new kind awareness. Was it love? Maybe. I was definitely feeling things that went beyond anything that I had felt for Henry. But could I even be trusted to understand my emotions when I had been so utterly wrong last time? Worse still, what if it was love and Aydin broke my heart? I didn't think I could survive it, especially if he were the one to do it. My Euphoric Lady-Bits just finished my thoughts with what seemed like her new mantra, "But the sex? Good God damn, the sex was mind-blowing!"

He watched me with great fascination as my three conflicting body parts fought over 'forever'. "What are you thinking about?"

"You've got to stop asking me that."

He boosted himself up against the headboard and made himself comfortable with another pillow behind his neck. I gazed, mouth agape, as the sheet dropped down to his hips and revealed his total ab perfection. "So tell me."

My brain threw in the towel, and my heart was also about to lose its battle. My euphoric lady bits was the clear winner of this round. Damn Aydin and his hotness!

"Okay." I was overcome by a sudden burst of shyness as he scrutinized me, completely naked. "Aydin…"

"Ginger…"

Warmth crept up my neck, and I felt my cheeks redden. "I have a confession to make. Wait, no, it's not a confession, it's a statement." Taking a deep breath, I summoned all my courage and blurted it out. "I think I have feelings for you."

He smiled his sexy, lopsided grin at me. "Great, I think."

"I'm not sure what feelings they are, exactly, and I don't know if I can trust these feelings really because it could be all just an overreaction to the mind-blowing sex but… ." I was tongue-tied, "…this… I… sheesh… I dunno… this all seems to be moving a little too fast for me, and honestly, I don't know what to make of it all."

He ran the back of his finger down my cheek. "Relax, Ginger. I will wait until forever for you because I love you." I must have looked aghast, or perhaps terrified beyond all reason because he chuckled softly. "And that's not such a bad thing, you know."

"Please don't say 'forever'."

"Why not? I mean forever. I will want you forever. I will love you forever."

I took a deep breath and let it out slowly. "I've been told forever before."

"I'm not him."

"I know, I know." I took a deep breath and let it out slowly. "It's just, my judgment wasn't so good the last time I gave my heart to someone. He utterly humiliated me. Looking back, he even used me. I have to admit I'm very hesitant to open up. I don't want anything like that to happen again."

Aydin he kissed me on top of my head. "Ginger, you're going to be okay. I will take care of you. I will protect you. I will love you. Forever."

"I'm just…"

He brushed my tangled curls back from my face and kissed my forehead. "Scared. Yes. I know. And I already know you love me as well. I've never doubted it for one minute, even if you don't recognise it yet. I see it every time you smile at me, or when I look into your beautiful, green eyes. I see it when you are with Emine, the way you treated her when we were together. But if you must know, I knew you loved me when you were throwing dagger eyes across the room at Simge. At that moment, I knew you were mine."

I groaned in embarrassment. "I admit I might have been a little jealous."

"A little?" He wiggled down under the duvet and pulled me against his chest. "You looked like you wanted to throttle her."

"No jury would've convicted me if I did."

"Crazy girl." He chuckled sleepily. It wasn't long before his breathing slowed and he drifted away, snoring gently. Cocooned in my Aydin burrito, I closed my eyes and willed myself to sleep. The sooner I fell asleep, the sooner it would be morning — and I was hopeful that the morning would start with a bang (double entendre fully intended).

CHAPTER 17

A Bitch Will Always Be A Bitch

Bang. Bang. Bang.

A sharp knock on the door woke me. It was either too bloody early or too bloody late as the room was pitch black. I absently reached for my mobile to check the time. Ugh, too early. A shiver ran down my spine. It was also too bloody cold. There was nothing but smouldering ashes in the fireplace, and the room was distinctly cooler than it had been when we had been in the throes of passion.

Aydin didn't stir so I wrapped myself in a crumpled sheet, shuffled across the floor and peeked out the window. It was Simge. Decked out in a black jacket, skin-tight pants, and ankle-breaking high-heeled boots, her hair perfect and her face entirely made up, she looked like she was on her way to a photo shoot. Not bad for two in the morning! Meanwhile, I was butt naked (apart from the sheet), remnants of Serap's makeup smeared across my face, a nasty-looking beard rash and had the aftermath of excellent sex hair. Basically, I looked like I'd just been royally fucked, which I had — a lot.

I opened the door a crack.

"What do you want?"

"I need to talk to my husband." She glanced at my sheet. "Privately."

Of course she knew that Aydin was in my bed. How could she not? "He's asleep."

"Then I will speak to you."

"Give me a minute." I shut the door in her perfectly made up face.

I scooped up my jeans and Aydin's sweater from last night and pulled them on as quickly and as quietly as I could. Although I didn't feel the need to imitate Simge with a full face of make up I attempted to make myself look halfway presentable. I pinned my curls into a bun before washing away the remnants of Serap's makeup. There wasn't much I could do about my beard rash. I shrugged at myself in the mirror. "You'll do."

I slipped out of the room and crossed to the main house where I found Simge beside the fireplace, smoking a cigarette. I sat down opposite her and waited. For a while she said nothing, she just continued to puff away. Finally she looked me straight in the eyes. "I think you are enjoying yourself with my husband."

What was it with these people referring to their "ex's" as though they were still married? "Don't you mean your ex-husband?"

"Yes, but he still loves me, and I know this. You may share his bed tonight, but you will never have his heart."

"If you say so." I refused to let myself get dragged into an argument with this shrew. "What do you want, Simge, because I don't think you really want to know about my sex life."

"Yes, you are right." She flicked cigarette ash into the fireplace. "It is straightforward. I need you to leave my family alone. Go back to London or Australia or somewhere else and don't come back here again!"

My heart lurched into my mouth. "Excuse me?"

"Leave Aydin alone. Leave my daughter alone. You will do me this favour."

All I could do was laugh at her audacity. "I don't owe you anything Simge, and I certainly won't be doing you any favours. You have been unforgivably rude to me from the moment we met. Give me one good reason why I shouldn't march back to my room, wake Aydin and tell him what you just proposed."

"Because you care for him." She curled her pouty lips into a saccharine smile, smarmy and unaffected by the tone of my voice. "And because I could make life very difficult for him."

There was nothing she could say that would make me leave Aydin. The feelings I had for him were real and damn it, I would fight this bitch to the death if I had to. It looked like my brain just made the decision that my heart was too scared to make alone. I loved him. I loved Aydin.

"I am sure that you know I have been offered a role in a movie. In America. Deniz and I will be leaving in a few days."

"You mean after your wedding?" I reminded her sarcastically. "Which is tomorrow isn't it? Or is it today?"

Simge stood up and fixed her icy gaze down at me. I had to crane my neck to look up at her. She really was freakishly tall in those heels. "I have been wrestling with the decision that I had already made regarding my daughter."

"Oh?"

"I was going to leave Emine here with her father but, perhaps it would be better to take her with me. I don't really want her being a witness to any unsavoury behaviour."

"But you already agreed to leave her with Aydin."

"Did I?" She shrugged. "Minds can easily be changed. Now I think my decision will be based solely on whether or not you disappear from their lives."

"So let me get this straight, if I leave, you will leave Emine with Aydin. Is that right?"

"Yes."

"But if I stay here you will take her away from him."

The smirk on her face made me see red. She was a succubus, feeding off the drama that she had caused. "Aydin's happiness is entirely up to you."

"Why do you care?" I jumped off the seat so we were face to face. Well, more like face to top of my head but you know what I mean. I lifted my chin to glare up at her. "You don't want him. You are marrying his cousin for God's sake!"

"Perhaps, but you are not going to have him either."

Checkmate to this bitch!

The corner of her mouth curled up in a wicked smile. "So? What will you do?"

Something snapped inside me and I knew exactly what to do.

I raised my hand and slapped Simge hard across her cheek. There was a moment of regret as as she teetered on her five-inch heels but that moment was nothing compared to the dread I felt when the door opened behind me.

"Ginger? Are you alri—?" Aydin's concerned question died on his lips. His eyes darted between Simge and me and my very red handprint that had been freshly imprinted on Simge's cheek. "What's going on here?"

Busted!

"Your girlfriend just assaulted me, that's what's going on." Simge dramatically shrieked and covered her face. "If my career is ruined because of her—"

Aydin looked at me and I shrugged in reply before he turned back to Simge. They began to argue in Turkish, both of them yelling and gesticulating wildly before she turned back to me and shrieked. "I think I should report this to the police."

"Shut up, Simge." Aydin sighed the sigh of a man who had seen these theatrics many times before. "Ginger why don't you go back to the room. I will follow you in a moment."

"I don't—"

"Please, you will do this for me?"

"Fine." I blinked away the tears that threatened to spill over and walked out, slamming the door behind me.

The next twenty-five minutes were spent pacing the room as I waited for Aydin to return. My mind invented countless reasons for his prolonged absence, none of them great, so by the time the door finally opened I was nearly sick with worry. I wrapped my arms around him, sighing in relief as I breathed in his scent. "Oh, Aydin." I murmured against his lips. "I'm so sorry."

He sat down on the bed and leaned against the headboard. "What am I supposed to do?"

"Can I just say something?"

"Of course."

"Do you want to be with Simge?"

He looked into my eyes. "No."

"Because she's still in love with you, you know that, right?" He shrugged in reply. "And if you do still love her then I'll leave and the three of you can be a family again."

"I am not in love with her. Do you think that I am?"

"Honestly, I don't know what to think. All I know for sure is that it shouldn't be this hard."

"I do not love her, I can promise you that." He shook his head. "Sometimes I want to hate her, but I can't. She's Emine's mother."

"I understand."

He sighed, and put his head in his hands. "She's threatening to take Emine with her."

"She told me." I climbed onto the bed beside him and wrapped my arms around him pulling him to my chest. "She also told me that she would leave Emine here if I left Istanbul."

Aydin squeezed me tighter. "I don't know what to say."

"I do."

He looked up at me with desperation in his eyes. We both knew what had to be said, but I also knew that he would never be the one to suggest it. "Please don't say it, Green Eyes."

"I'm going back to London."

I was the heroine in my own movie, prepared to sacrifice my own happiness with a selfless act, although I really didn't want to be the better person at that moment.

And I guess not every rom-com had a happily ever after, did it? I mean, look at Roman Holiday. Audrey Hepburn definitely didn't stay in Italy with the hotness of Gregory Peck, did she? Nope. She moved the hell on with her life knowing that she was as rich as fuck and would probably marry some equally attractive prince from a neighbouring country. And damn it, I was Audrey Hepburn! Wasn't I?

I waited for Aydin to beg me to stay, to tell me that he would fight his ex-wife rather than have me leave, but he didn't, so I guess that established that I had made the right decision for everyone.

I stroked his hair like you would stroke a child and whispered over and over. "It's okay. You're okay. I'm fine."

Eventually, he pulled back to look at me. His eyes were red and he wiped the remainder of a tear away. "I just can't lose my daughter."

"Of course you can't."

We lay together, wrapped in each other's arms until Aydin dozed off. I slipped out of his embrace and tip-toed to the chair. Silent sobs shook my body as I sat huddled in the cozy chair beside the smouldering fireplace. I had finally found my leading man, and he was fucking amazing. Totally gorgeous, funnier than he knew, the best damn kisser, one hell of a great lay AND for some crazy reason he really loved me. Damn it. And despite my reservations, I loved him as well, but rightfully, he loved his daughter more, which just made him even more magnificent in my eyes (and in my ovaries). If only this could last forever.

But it couldn't.

What type of woman would agree to walk away from all that?

A stupid git that goes by the name of Ginger Knox, that's who!

I climbed back into bed and wiped away my remaining tears. There was no more time to waste on tears. If I were going to go, I would go out with a bang.

And with a bang in mind, I slipped my hand under the covers, trailed my fingers across his chest and abdomen to his boxers, and to my very much desired destination, which I happily found it was already granite hard. Aydin opened one eye.

"Good morning."

Aydin groaned, his voice thick with sleep. "I don't think it's morning."

He propped himself up on his elbows as I dragged his boxers down over his hips and legs. I threw them across the room before pulling his t-shirt over his head. I ran my fingers through his wiry bush before my hand came to rest wrapped around his cock.

"We should probably talk."

I wasn't going to change my mind. "No need."

"Green Eyes... please." The tone of his voice was a warning, but the look in his eyes was something else.

I rolled on top of him and straddled his waist. "So talk already."

"I don't think I can concentrate with you sitting on me."

"Your loss, buddy." I braced my knees on either side of his hips, lifted myself up and lowered myself, inch by magnificent inch, down onto him.

I rode him slowly, arching my back. He sat up and kissed me, our tongues tangled as we explored every crevice of each other's mouths. I could feel the urgency and desperation in Aydin's kiss as he made love to my mouth. Did we have the same thoughts? Did we both wonder if this would be the last time that we kissed each other? The last time we would make love?

It was raw with passion. I could never have imagined such an erotic kiss, a kiss that not only gave but took. It was a kiss that made me so wet, so tight, that as I rode him, my body spasmed in readiness for what was to come. Aydin moved his lips to my breasts, raining kisses over them before he closed his mouth around my nipple and tugged. I gasped and he reached up and pinched my other nipple. Damn it, I nearly exploded then and there.

He moaned and tried to thrust harder, but I wouldn't allow it. I tightened my grip on his cock with my muscles and mentally thanked Cosmopolitan for reminding me to do my daily kegels. His eyes burned into me as I controlled his movements. He fell back onto the bed, entirely under my spell while I rode him.

I bit my lip and moved my hand to my wetness. Around and around I slowly rubbed myself in time with the movement of my hips. Pure ecstasy washed over Aydin's face as he watched me pleasure myself. I had to remind myself that I wanted this to go slowly, to savour the little time that we had left together but between his cock and my fingers I knew I wouldn't last long.

His hips thrust up to meet mine, his cock filling me deeper and deeper. One. Two. Three. And I came all around him. Lost in the kaleidoscope of rapturous orgasms, my fingers and his cock working in unison to send me twisting and tumbling in a heady swirl of nirvana, ecstasy and lust.

Aydin took advantage of the moment and flipped me over. He plunged straight into me from behind, and I gasped as the waves of pleasure continued to wash over me, my muscles tightening around him like a vice. With a final guttural groan Aydin slammed home hard, his orgasm erupting, spurting his seed into me. It was exquisite and I mashed my face into the pillow so my screams were muffled as the waves slowly subsided.

Aydin collapsed onto my back, his exhausted cock still cocooned in my overjoyed muff. He pushed my damp curls aside and kissed the back of my neck. "Good talk."

I nodded into the pillow. "Very productive."

Nothing else was said. Within minutes Aydin rolled away and was snoring softly. I lay beside him, wide awake and wondered how I had gotten myself into such a mess. I wanted Aydin, forever. Yes, you heard me. I said FOREVER. My yin was very much meant to be with his yang. I was meant to be his.

But I had to leave him behind.

Jane Gundogan

And that really sucked.

CHAPTER 18

A Piece of My Heart

I woke to the now-familiar sound of the *muezzin* from a nearby mosque, as the faithful were called to prayer. Despite my late-night visit from Simge, followed by some incredible pre-dawn sex, it still felt early. I dozed off again, cocooned in Aydin's arms, but was abruptly woken by the sound of my mobile chirping loudly.

I wanted to stay there, happily cocooned in my Aydin burrito, but I rolled over, grabbed my phone and checked my messages.

The airline had finally gotten back to me. It seemed I could either fly back to London tomorrow, or I could catch a flight to Dubai on Tuesday, arriving in Sydney on Wednesday. There was really no point in flying to Sydney when I had to be back at work next week. So, London it was.

I tiptoed across the room with my iPad and slipped into the bathroom. Sitting on the toilet, I followed the airline's instructions to book my return flight to London for tomorrow morning.

That was that then. I was going back to London. Without Aydin.

Jane Gundogan

Despite the heaviness that had settled in my chest, I slid back into bed and watched him sleep. I wasn't surprised to see that he was still lost in his dreams. That right there was a man that had definitely earned a lie-in.

My mind wandered back to our mind-blowing love making last night and again this morning. I couldn't even begin to compare it to anything else. Nearly three years of sex with Henry was alright, and sometimes even great, but with Aydin, it awoke something in me. And as he snored surprisingly loudly, I longed for his eyes to open so we could do it again. And again.

A psychologist might have surmised that I was self-sabotaging with the allure of the now-forbidden fruit making it all the tastier, but I didn't care. My last day with Aydin was not going to be a pity-party for one. I was going to make the most of it, and that included getting out and exploring more of Istanbul.

I threw back the covers and nudged Aydin with my toe. "Merry Christmas!"

He rubbed his sleepy eyes and yawned. "It's still early."

"I don't care. Get out of bed so we can go and be all Christmassy. I saw a man selling roasted chestnuts near the mosque, so that's our first stop today!"

"Today?" He looked confused. "Today is Deniz and Simge's wedding."

"Surely you're not still going?"

"I must. Deniz is my cousin."

For a moment, I couldn't draw a breath. I was something beyond furious. Here I was sacrificing our love for him and his daughter, and all I asked for was one final day. I shook my head. "I don't understand you at all. From the beginning, you've made it clear you wanted to be with me. You said that you loved me. I bloody well have to wonder if you know what love actually is, and yes, maybe I'm not all that clear on what love is myself, but one thing I can bloody well tell you, is that if you love someone, you want to spend every moment with that person and not with your bitch of an ex-wife, especially when that person is going to leave soon!"

I climbed out of bed, went to the bathroom and, to really get my point across, slammed the door as hard as I could.

I turned the shower on and let the water beat down on me. I wanted to cry but crying wouldn't change anything. Aydin was an adult. He could make his own decision just as I had made my decision to leave. I just couldn't fathom why he would want to spend what little time we had left with his ex-wife rather than with me.

So I took my time. I shampooed and conditioned my hair and even tidied up my eyebrows to delay re-opening the bathroom door. I didn't want to go back into the bedroom and argue with Aydin, but after I had brushed and flossed my teeth, there really wasn't a lot else for me to do. I wrapped myself in the fluffy bathrobe supplied by the pansion, then made a turban out of a towel to dry off my hair. I took a deep breath and opened the door.

Aydin was dressed. Which made me even angrier.

"Going already?" I glowered at him. "You're really are a love 'em and leave 'em kind of guy, aren't you?"

"Ginger, you are being unreasonable."

He took a step towards me and caressed my cheek with the

back of his hand. My anger thawed ever so slightly as the sparks of electricity filtered from his hand to my face. Damn him!

"Unreasonable?" I laughed derisively. "Simge even said this was how it would be."

"Sımge doesn't know what she is talking about." Sadness laced his voice. "I must go to the wedding. I am their witness."

"It's your ex-wife's wedding, Aydin. You're a smart guy. I shouldn't have to explain this to you."

He smiled at me as his eyes roamed over my body wrapped up in the plush bathrobe courtesy of the *pansion*. "You look very nice."

"Don't try to change the subject!" He made an attempt to grab me, but I dodged out of his way.

He took another step forward and smirked. Ugh! My heart nearly melted there and then. "Stand still!" He caught me in his arms and slid the bathrobe off my shoulders. It dropped to the floor and I stood in front of him glaring — and naked. He reached up and unwound the turban from atop my head, releasing my curls. They cascaded down my back and over my breasts. His eyes were nearly black, and his voice husky. "Now you look even better."

Any residual anger dissolved as he clamped his mouth down on mine, kissing me with a passion that left nothing unsaid. Lust swirled around us, pulling us toward the bed. It was clear he wanted me again, and I would give myself to him. Every time. I had no self-control anymore where Aydin was concerned. "Don't think I'm going to forget that I'm mad at you."

"You are mad at me?" He chuckled. "I didn't realise."

I moaned gently as he kissed my neck. "Shut up."

I couldn't get enough of him as he kissed my cheek and my ear. His lips and tongue felt like an electric force on my skin. He lifted his face back to me. For a moment, indecision flashed across his face. He sighed, and tiny frown lines appeared on his forehead. "You deserve better than me."

I scoffed at his suggestion. "You don't even realise how much you have already given me."

His hands ran down my body, grazing my mound before they came around to rest on my ass. He squeezed it gently. "I have caused you nothing but pain."

"A little, maybe, but you've also made me a better person. You've taught me how to feel… to… to love… again, and for that, I will always be eternally grateful." My arms tightened around him. "And any pain that I may suffer will not be caused by you. You, Aydin, are an amazing man, despite your bloody awful taste in women."

"Present company excluded."

"Naturally."

He sighed. "I have to go."

"Well, if you have to go." I slid my hand down his jeans, his erection plain to see as it strained to escape. I bit my lip and fell to my knees. I unzipped his jeans and slid them down to his ankles. Aydin was rocking it commando style. I approved wholeheartedly.

I immediately took him into my mouth and to the back of my throat. I held it there for a few seconds until Aydin groaned and then I released him from my mouth and looked up at him with a sly smile. "But do you really have to go right now?"

"I can't… I have to… oh Ginger."

He fell back onto the bed and I returned my attention to his cock, clamping my lips back over the head. Without removing my mouth from his member, I twisted around until I was straddling his face. He pulled me down onto him and flicked his hot tongue up and down my slit, lapping my juices like a cat. I nearly shattered as he sucked on my labia and pulled my lips into his mouth. I licked and sucked his cock, matching my movements to Aydin's tongue. He bucked and I tasted his pre-come. He was close. I continued to ride his tongue, writhing on his mouth. I wanted to come on his face, for him to lick me clean. I groaned against his cock. "I'm going to come again."

"Yes, Ginger. Come all over me, love."

I undulated myself against his face, rubbing against his rough growth on his chin as his long tongue continued to love me. He thrust his hips up one final time, and exploded in my mouth. I continued to keep pace with him as my own orgasm rocked through my body. I was soaring to the stars once more. I pulled myself off his cock and screamed. "Yes! Yes! Yes!" My orgasm kept crashing over me, wave after wave, as Aydin licked and sucked me until I was finally spent.

I rolled over and collapsed on the bed. He scooched around and grabbed a pillow, slipping it under my head. We kissed as he lay down beside me. "I'm really going to be late."

I chuckled. "Yeah, you are."

We lay there and exchanged tender kisses, him playing with my hair while I circled his nipple with my finger. Then he sat up and looked into my eyes and his face arched into worry. "I want to do this with you for the rest of our lives."

I sighed and shook my head. "Please stop, Aydin."

"Wait! Let me explain. What I mean is that, if you want to leave, I won't stop you, but I don't want you to leave because of Simge."

That was definitely my opening to tell him I had my return flight booked, but as I watched him beside me, I just couldn't bring myself to do it. I sighed. "It's way too complicated. I would never jeopardise your relationship with your daughter."

"I can get a lawyer."

"You'd have more success if you got a hitman." I just couldn't think about it anymore. I closed my eyes and grew sleepy in my post-coital haze.

When I opened my eyes again Aydin was freshly showered and standing next to the bed. "I'm really leaving now."

I kicked the covers away and wrapped my bare legs around him. "Stay."

"I know what you're trying to do."

"What?" I gazed up at him innocently.

"Make me miss the wedding completely. I need to go. Deniz is waiting to pick up our suits." He kissed the top of my head. "And you shouldn't waste another minute lying in bed."

I groaned and reluctantly let him go. "Fine. Get out of here then, before I might be inclined to have my way with you again."

"Will I see you later?"

Aydin looked at me with hope in his eyes. Will he? I honestly didn't know. He was the one that was about to walk out the door to go to his ex-wife's wedding. "I hope so."

"You sure you won't come to the wedding?"

"Probably not a great idea to have me in the same room as your ex-wife right now."

He opened the door before looking back at me, laughing and grinning from ear to ear. "I can't believe you slapped Simge. I know people that would have paid money to have witnessed that."

"Think of it as my wedding present to you."

He shut the door behind him. I could hear his laughter as he crossed the courtyard.

CHAPTER 19

Medusa's Gaze Won't Get Me Stoned

As much as I would have preferred to stay buried under the avalanche of decadent sheets and delicious duvets in my enormous bed and be the star of my very own pity-party, Aydin was right, I had to get my ass out of bed and get moving. So much to do. My first stop was to Leyla's shop to tell her I was leaving. I then had to somehow condense the additional twenty kilos of clothing I had purchased (alright perhaps not quite that much) and squeeze them into one teeny-tiny suitcase before I went out to explore. To top it all off it was Christmas Day and I wanted to enjoy it!

Dressing quickly, I had to apply quite a bit of concealer to cover the dark circles under my eyes before I made my way over to the main house. Jack and Cel were already at the table tucking into their *kahvaltı*.

"Merry Christmas," I called out as I walked into the room.

"Merry Christmas to you too, darlin'." I slid onto the bench next to Cel who eyed me closely. "You okay, sweetheart?"

What a loaded question that was.

"I'm fine. Just a little tired."

"Busy night?" Jack joked from behind his newspaper.

"Shut up, Jack." Cel admonished, before she turned back to me. "Glad we got to see you this morning. We'll be leaving this afternoon."

"Oh no!" I was genuinely upset about the loss of my two new friends.

"And now we won't find out how the story ends."

"What story?"

"Why yours and Aydin's, of course! This has been like the cherry on top of a big slice of Istanbul pie. It's been a fabulous drama."

"Honestly, I don't really need all this drama in my life."

"Well, I think you handled yourself really well at dinner the other night. If it were me, I would have given that girl a right smackdown."

I leaned into Cel and Jack. "If you must know, I got the opportunity to do just that last night."

"Did it feel fabulous? I bet it felt fabulous."

I grinned. "I've got to admit, it felt pretty damn good."

Jack popped his head out from behind his newspaper. "And you made it into the paper as well."

"What?"

Cel and I both jumped up and tried to grab the newspaper from

Jack, but he wasn't having any of it. "My newspaper, ladies! Back off!"

We both sat down on either side of him while he flattened the paper on the table.

There I was in black and white (and colour). And not just one or two photos, there were five of them including my Instagram post!

I scrutinized the photos. I don't know why famous people are always banging on about the paparazzi because these photos were actually pretty good. If I ignored the fact that they had totally breached our privacy and instead focused on the images themselves, then I had nothing to complain about. There we were, a couple in love, strolling past the fountain and wrapped in each other's arms. My Instagram photo that I uploaded told another story, however. In that image my lips were puffy and kiss-swollen. Hello! I could even see my hard nipples through my sweater while Aydin looked at me like he would devour me whole. That was a photo of a couple that was gagging for each other — and it showed.

"Holy shit!" I hid my face in my hands. "I'm so embarrassed."

"I wonder what it says?"

Behind us, the front door flung open and Leyla rushed in, weighed down with an armful of newspapers. "*Aman Tanrım!* You are famous! Did you know you are famous?"

"We know."

"I never should've put up that stupid photo."

Leyla handed newspapers to Cel and I and thew herself down beside me. "Ginger, don't be silly. Aydin is just so popular. He is followed by the paparazzi constantly. Always. Who he dates, what he does. It's news!"

Cel nods knowingly. "Like Kimmy and Kayne!"

"Jesus, what a comparison!" I frowned at her.

"And you looked so hot!"

We all leaned down to re-examine the photos. "You think so?"

Jack nodded. "Hell, yeah, you do!"

Cel and I both swatted him with our newspapers. "So what does it say?"

Leyla translated the story:

> On the eve of Simge Kaya's wedding to fiancé Deniz Yılmaz, her ex-husband, Aydin Kaya, 35, was spotted with a mystery woman in Istanbul last night. The actor was seen grinning ear-to-ear as he was photographed with the much, much, larger than life woman, who took time out from their romantic interlude to snap a rather smug photo of the couple, which she uploaded to her public profile.
>
> With Simge's wedding due to take place today we have to wonder whether Aydin Kaya has actually moved on or whether this bizarre coupling is a last desperate play to win his ex-wife's affections. This reporter is guessing that the latter is true because the star could have his pick of any woman in Turkey. Why else would he be seen with someone so completely unsuitable?
>
> Stay tuned.

I swallowed the lump in my throat. "Scathing."

"Don't pay any attention, Ginger. You look amazing in those photos." Cel screwed up her newspaper and tossed it to one side. "And we all know the truth so it doesn't matter what's written about you anyway."

Jacked nodded in agreement. "Fake news!"

"I still can't believe I met Aydin Kaya last night." Leyla sighed and stabbed at an olive with her fork dramatically. "And I made such a fool of myself. I always thought I would be very sophisticated if I met someone famous, but I failed completely, didn't I?"

Both Cel and I chuckled at Leyla. "Totally."

"He is just so beautiful."

I agreed with her sentiment wholeheartedly and sighed. "Yes, he is."

"You are so lucky."

"Not as lucky as you might think."

"What?" Leyla dropped her fork in shock. "What do you mean?"

"The airline contacted me. The airport was re-opened last night and there's a flight out tomorrow morning."

"You can't leave now! Everything is happening now."

"I can, and I am, okay?"

"Oh, darlin'! Why didn't you tell me?" Cel looked at me with concern. "Was it the smackdown?"

Leyla looked from Cel to me. Breakfast was forgotten as she realised that she was missing a massive piece of the puzzle. "What's going on?"

"Nothing. I just had a tiff with Simge last night."

"A tiff?"

"She socked her."

"Tiff? Socked? I can never understand what you *yabancılar* are talking about!"

"Alright, I'll tell you everything but promise me you will stay calm."

"I can't make that promise."

Leyla had already proven to be an excellent listener to my personal drama, so I took a deep breath and blurted out the whole sorry debacle (staying well within the boundaries of PG-13) to both her and Cel. Even Jack put down his paper and sat, his mouth agape, as I updated them on the past few hours.

"And you agreed to leave?"

"No, I offered to leave."

"And he's letting you go?"

"Well, he doesn't actually know I've got a flight yet."

All three of them shouted at me at once.

"What?"

"What's the matter with you?"

"You have to tell him."

"It's better this way. I go and he can move on *with* his daughter."

Cel and Jack glanced at each other but said nothing while Leyla launched herself at me, giving me a hug. "Oh, *canım*. I'm so sorry. That Simge Kaya! She is just, the…"

"I really hate to blaspheme but think the word you might be looking for is the Anti-Christ," Cel added helpfully.

I nodded in agreement. "She really is."

"But you are here today? Yes?"

"Yes."

"And you are spending it with Aydin, yes?"

"No, I'm not actually." I snipped. "He's with Deniz preparing for the wedding."

"No!"

"Doesn't matter."

"You're allowed to be mad, you know."

"I'm not mad."

Cel piped in. "I'd be mad."

"Can I be annoyed?"

"I guess."

"Or miffed."

"I'd definitely be a little miffed!"

"I don't know what either of you are talking about, but as your self-appointed new best friend, it is my job to help you forget about Aydin Kaya." Leyla dragged me out of my seat and slipped her arm around my waist. "So today you're going to experience the most famous city in the world — Istanbul."

Despite my reluctance (I was still feeling pretty sorry for myself), my grin matched Leyla's enthusiasm. "Definitely. Let's do this!"

After a sad goodbye to Cel and Jack and a promise to update them on whatever disaster befell me next, I grabbed my jacket and was dragged out the door by a very excited Leyla.

Ten minutes later we were mingling with other tourists waiting to be given entrance into a non-descript building that was little more than a door, not far from Aydin's restaurant.

"Be prepared to be blown away." Leyla smiled widely. "You are going to love this."

I folded my arms belligerently. "You know when people say 'you're going to love this', it's usually a disaster."

"You really have trust issues, don't you?"

I snorted, but followed Leyla anyway down a flight of nondescript stairs before arriving at the top of a stone staircase in a massive underground cavern.

My eyes grew wide and I gasped in amazement at the sight before me. "What on earth is this place?"

"This —" Leyla said, as she took my hand to lead me down the stairs, "is my favourite place in all of Istanbul." She stretched her arms out in front of her. "Welcome to *Yerebatan Sarnıcı*, also known as the Basilica Cistern."

Blown away was an understatement. Before me was a subterranean grotto, held up by hundreds of columns. The whole room seemed to have an ethereal glow with its discrete lighting and hushed tones spoken by the visitors around us. I had never seen anything quite like it and I was besotted.

We walked across platforms above the water as Leyla whispered stories of her visiting the cistern when she was younger. "I first came here with my grandfather when I was five. He told me I had mission of utmost importance. I had to find Medusa's head, and I had to look Medusa right in the eye. If I did not turn to stone, then I would be blessed."

"Well, that wouldn't half terrify a child!"

"My grandfather always told me stories of the *jinn* and ghosts. He knew I was fearless."

"Is that what they call 'crazy' today?"

"The first time I visited, there was no lighting. It was just so black, and it went on forever. My grandfather handed me a little torch and sent me on my way. This is one of my fondest childhood memories, and every time I come here, I remember him and how much I loved him." She misted up for a moment and I gave her hand a squeeze. "Close your eyes, just for a moment."

I closed my eyes and stood silently beside Leyla, hand in hand. "Now listen. Tell me what you hear."

"Nothing."

"Right. You hear nothing." Echoes came from behind us and

Leyla rolled her eyes. "Well, now you hear other tourists but my point is that there is so much life above us and yet here we are hidden from the world. And now I pass on to you the charge, *Bayan* Ginger. Find me Medusa's head, look into her eyes and prove your worth!"

Leyla was trying her hardest to distract me, to focus on something other than Aydin — and it worked well. I giggled at her theatrics, and took my mission very seriously. I left Leyla behind and began searching the rows of columns for Medusa's elusive head. Finally, on a hunch, I crossed to the far corner of the grotto.

There she was!

"Found her! And look –" I turned my head sideways and stared directly into her ancient face. " – I haven't turned to stone!"

Leyla whooped loudly which echoed off the cavernous walls, drawing attention from a group of nearby teenagers. One of the girls pointed at us and whispered to her friends.

"Oops. Sorry Ginger. I think you've been spotted."

She grabbed my arm and led me quickly back down the slippery walkway toward the exit. The girls tried to follow us, but we ran up the stairs and out onto the street as a load of tourists alighted from their bus. We took the opportunity to disappear into the masses.

"That was bizarre."

"Well, you *are* dating Aydin Kaya, one of Turkey's most eligible bachelors."

"For a few more hours at least." I looked down at my phone and sighed. Time was getting away from me. "I should probably get back and pack my bags."

"You know what we could do —" Leyla looked at me with a glint of mischief in her eyes. "— we could go to the wedding."

I wrinkled my nose at her.

"We would sneak in the back if you wanted. No one would know you were there."

"I don't need to sneak in. Deniz invited me and so did Aydin for that matter."

"Then let's go!"

I had to admit I was curious, okay more than a little curious. No doubt Simge would look supermodel gorgeous, but she'd still be the most awful human on earth in my eyes. And Aydin would be in a suit. Fifty shades of hotness!

"Fine. We'll go." I giggled as Leyla jumped up and down in excitement. "But we stay out of sight."

"As long as we get to dress up I don't really care."

"Dress up?"

"To fit in, of course. I mean, you don't want to draw attention to yourself do you?"

We returned to Leyla's shop and she immediately began pulling out ridiculously over-the-top evening gowns for me to peruse. "They all seem a little fancy for me, Leyla."

"Believe me, they're not. Wait until you get there, you will see. You can never be overdressed at a Turkish wedding. Never!"

After trying on a few bling-heavy dresses that really didn't suit me, I settled for an orange satin top that gave a glimpse of my midriff and pink satin and tulle ballerina skirt that came to just above my knee. Perhaps I was not as glamorous as Leyla would have wished, but to me it was perfect. Suddenly, Leyla squealed before she rushed out to the storeroom.

Startled, I yelled after her. "I wish you'd stop doing that, Leyla!"

She re-appeared a moment later holding the most divine pair of red suede ankle boots with cut out details. "Sorry. I got excited."

She handed me the boots, which I slipped on and looked at myself in the full-length mirror. I was a fusion of colour. "Taste the rainbow."

"You look fabulous. But there are rules. These are my Jimmy Choos."

For the love of shoes!

I looked at her, aghast. "I can't wear your Choos!"

Sharing Choos is the sign of the truest of friendships!

She put her hand up to stop me. "Yes you can. I want you to. You will wear these, and you will dance and have a wonderful time. You will be like Cinderella at the ball. Now, for your hair."

Leyla delivered me upstairs to Serap who teased my hair into masses of curls on top of my head and did my makeup in smoky greys and pinks finishing me off with some cherry red lipstick. I had to admit, I looked pretty freaking fantastic!

Leyla appeared a moment later wearing a blue, sequin dress and matching Manolo Blahnik's that put her Choos' to shame. She had pulled her hair into a chignon bun at the nape of her neck and her makeup was totally fierce. Total transformation from funky urban fox to ice cold diva in under fifteen minutes! Now that is a useful skill!

"Wow! You look gorgeous."

"I always have outfits ready for any occasion, and this occasion requires sequins, lots of sequins." Leyla primped in the mirror. "Now *hadi*, I do NOT want to miss a thing!"

CHAPTER 20

Siri? How Can I Get Away With Murder?

After a terrifying drive across the city, our taxi pulled up to a very stylish hotel overlooking the Bosphorus. Leyla was beside herself. "Even though this is a hotel, Çırağan Palace is also *the* place to be married in Istanbul."

I screwed my face into a grimace. What the hell? Every second building in Istanbul seemed to be a damn palace!

Getting in was just ridiculous with paparazzi snapping furiously as we drove by. Once we passed them we had to deal with two separate sets of security and that was even before we got to the entrance of the hotel! But once we'd run the security gauntlet, we were whisked down a lavishly decorated corridor and delivered to a similarly over-the-top ballroom by hotel staff.

Waiters, holding trays with glasses filled with champagne, greeted us at the entrance of the ballroom and I happily accepted a drink, chugged it down and grabbed a second glass, returning my empty to the tray. The only way I was going to survive the evening was drunk!

There were already hundred's of overdressed guests milling around, and Leyla was beside herself with excitement. She pointed out Turkish politicians, film and TV stars as they all arrived to celebrate the coupling of the great Simge Kaya and Deniz Yilmaz. This seemed to be the Turkish equivalent of Harry and Meghan Markle's wedding!

Emine spotted us from the stage and rushed over. "This is SO exciting!"

She threw herself into my arms. "Did you know that this is a palace as well?"

"I did."

Emine shook her curls. "Look, Ginger, we both have had our hair done like a princess. Do you like my tiara?"

"You are the most beautiful princess I've ever seen."

"*Teşsekuler*." Emine lifted her arms, and I bent down to face her. She kissed me on both cheeks. "I'm going now. My mother asked me to find you, and I have."

"She did?"

Oh, crap.

"Uh-huh." She nodded and skipped off down the stairs before running up onto the stage.

"Why do you think Simge wanted to know if I was here," I whispered to Leyla out of the corner of my mouth.

"I can't imagine."

"She's up to something, I'd wager." A moment later Simge's

head appeared in the doorway that Emine had just disappeared behind. She spotted me, grinned wickedly and blew me a kiss.

"That can't be good."

Leyla squeaked. "It's Simge Kaya!"

"Pull yourself together, Leyla." I huffed at her. "And so much for us being covert."

"It's hard to be covert when we are this fabulous."

I scoffed. "You, maybe."

"Is fabulous not the right word? Maybe beautiful?"

I laughed out loud at that and Leyla frowned back at me.

"Let me offer you a little best friend advice, canım. If someone calls you fabulous, you own it. When you are called beautiful, you believe it. You don't need to love yourself, but you should. You are fabulous. Do you think Simge Kaya is beautiful? She is, but it is that confidence that oozes from her that makes her so desirable. You may think you are ordinary but Aydin Kaya, the Aydin Kaya, loves you. YOU! He thinks that you are beautiful, that you are fabulous. But I promise you if you don't have confidence in yourself then everything will go to bok!"

"Bok?"

"Shit!"

I sighed. Leyla was right. Pre-Henry I was all sorts of fabulous. I was a strong, independent, sassy young thang that loved life, but when I opened my bedroom door in Notting Hill (adjacent) that sassy young thang ceased to exist. It was time to take control of my life and become that fabulous woman that Leyla — and Aydin — believed that I was.

"You're starting to sound an awful lot like a fortune cookie."

"I don't know what that is, but *sus*." Leyla turned her attention to the stage and smiled brightly. "They are starting."

An older man in white robes stepped onto the stage and called everyone to attention. Leyla and I slid into some free seats as Deniz and Aydin appeared.

Deniz looked very handsome in his black tuxedo, but he fell way short beside the gloriousness that was beside him. I squirmed in my seat as I ogled my guy. Aydin's hair was tousled in a way that looked like it had been done by a professional but had probably just dried like that naturally while his facial hair coupled with the same black tuxedo as Deniz made him look like a Turkish James Bond.

Damn, he was gorgeous!

The blood rushed to my head, and to my already recovered and ready to party again mu-mu, as I imagined Aydin removing his jacket and bow-tie, and slowly, excruciatingly slowly, undoing the buttons on his shirt. In my mind, I heard Joe Crocker warbling, "You Can Leave Your Hat On" and I started to hum, loud enough that Leyla had to nudge me to pipe down.

Deniz and Aydin turned their attention to the side of the stage to wait for the blushing bitch (sorry I meant bride) to grace us with her presence. Moments later, she appeared and the entire room gasped in unison. I clenched my jaw. She looked gorgeous. Well, duh! She was a vision of vintage Hollywood glamour. A goddess who walked amongst us mere mortals. Her dress, a silver beaded masterpiece, shimmered as she walked toward Deniz. The bodice was fitted to display her fabulous breasts, and when she turned to face her groom, the dress seemed to accentuate her pert bum as well. She sashayed across the stage, stopping momentarily to flash a radiant, if not somewhat nervous, smile at the audience.

Deniz stepped forward to kiss her cheek, but she hesitated as she turned to face him. It was a small gesture, and it only lasted a moment, but I still saw it.

She glanced back to Aydin as Deniz walked her across the stage to sit down, but he was oblivious to the building tension. He smiled happily and took a seat. Deniz sat down beside him, and they nudged each other and grinned like schoolboys. I had to giggle at their antics before I turned my attention back to Simge who chose that moment to catch my eye. She mouthed something at me.

What?

I looked around.

She looked at me again, and this time I understood what she was mouthing, "I win."

I realised at that moment what was about to happen. I grabbed Leyla's arm just as the Imam began to speak. "She's... she's not going to do it."

"What?"

The Imam took the microphone, cleared his throat, and began to speak to Deniz and Simge. He then turned to Deniz and handed him the microphone. Everyone broke into applause when he spoke into it. *"Evet."* Yes.

Now it was Simge's turn. The Imam spoke to her before passing her the microphone. She didn't reply. She looked from

Deniz to Aydin before she dramatically burst into tears.

They say love conquers all, but love had never come up against the hurricane-force that was Simge Kaya on a mission.

Pandemonium broke out as around us, wedding guests wailed and gasped while the photographers almost fell over one another to take photos. Simge Kaya had just ditched Deniz Yilmaz at the ceremony!

Across the room, Refika ran onto the stage and threw herself into Deniz's arms, but he pushed her aside as he began to yell at Simge. It was quite the spectacle, and I had to give credit where credit was due because Simge gave an Oscar-worthy performance as she stood beside Aydin and wept forlornly into her hands.

The paparazzi loved it.

I grabbed Leyla's arm. "What's going on?"

Leyla squirmed with excitement as she translated the yelling on stage. "It seems that Simge will not marry Deniz."

"Clearly."

Leyla covered her mouth and gasped. "She is now saying she still loves Aydin."

I should have seen this coming.

"She says that she wants to try again with him. That she thinks that they should be together, that they should be a family."

Deniz's face turned almost crimson with rage. Aydin stepped between them in an attempt to calm them both down.

My heart was pounding against my rib cage, and I wondered if I might be having a heart attack, which was, I guessed, possible but perhaps not probable. "What does Aydin say?"

"I wish he would speak up," Leyla mumbled and leaned forward to hear better. "He does not want this. They are divorced. He has moved on."

"Now she says that she was wrong and that she still loves him." She turned to me. "She is asking if Aydin still loves her?"

"Does he?" I asked, holding my breath, waiting for his answer.

"Yes!" Leyla shrieked. "He says he will always love her. She is family."

My hands shook as my stomach churned. "I think I might vomit. What about Deniz? What does he say?"

"Deniz is angry. Simge wants Aydin. And now he says that Aydin has encouraged her affection."

"That's not true!"

I thought back to Refika's dinner when Simge spent half the evening flirting with Aydin. Had Aydin encouraged her or was he merely trying to keep the peace?

Deniz yelled at Aydin before he stepped forward and pushed him across the stage. Aydin put his arms out to Deniz in an attempt to calm him down, but without warning, Deniz jammed his fist into Aydin's cheek. Caught off guard, Aydin fell back against the table and knocked it over. Deniz then turned to Simge and lifted his arm as though he was going to slap her, but Aydin jumped between them and punched Deniz square on the nose, knocking him to the ground. Aydin threw his arm around his ex-wife to protect her from both Deniz and the surging crowd, grabbed Emine and disappeared behind the curtain.

I sat there, stunned. "That was unbelievable!"

"It was."

"Are they coming back?"

"I don't know."

"What should we do?"

"I don't know."

A good ten minutes passed, and neither Aydin nor Simge returned. Around us, people had begun to leave, and frankly, we had no reason to be sitting there any longer, so Leyla turned to speak to some of the photographers before slipping back into her seat beside me. "They believe that Simge and Aydin have left already."

He left with her?

"Are you sure?"

"No, but that is what the photographers are saying. Would you like for me to go and have a look for you?"

"Fuck this. Let's go." I stood up and headed toward the exit. "I didn't even want to come to the fucking wedding in the first place!"

The photographers spotted me as we returned to the hotel's reception and started snapping. I was news, the now redundant girlfriend, abandoned by the great Aydin Kaya who had run back into the arms of Turkey's most beautiful actress.

Leyla rushed me outside and hailed a taxi. We jumped in as the photographers mobbed the car.

Leyla gave the driver direction back to the *pansion* before falling back into the seat beside me. "What are you going to do?"

"I can't stay there tonight."

"Do you want to come and stay with me?"

"Thanks, but I'll be fine. My flight is at six tomorrow morning. I can easily spend the night at the airport."

We arrived at the *pansion*. Leyla paid the driver, then followed me to my room. "Where's your bag?"

I pulled it out from the closet.

"That's it?"

I nodded.

Leyla opened it up to find it packed to the brim full of my summer clothes. She mumbled under her breath, and I forced myself to smile at her. "You saying something?"

"I'm just wondering how people survive with only one suitcase." She began to re-organise my bag to squeeze in my new clothes into an already groaning bag. "We're going to need something to hold all this together."

"Like some Spanx?"

She wiggled her finger. "Don't you make fun of Spanx. I haven't been out of them a day since 2010. Now that I think about it, Spanx for luggage is one genius of an idea."

"I want half the profit."

Leyla grinned at me before she returned to the pile of new clothes, shoes and accessories that I had accumulated over the past few days. I shook my head. It would be an impossible task to fit everything in my bag. "Just give me a minute while I change."

"Of course."

In the bathroom, I turned the faucet handle until the water warmed and washed the remnants of Serap's makeup off my face. Makeup free, I looked in the mirror and scrutinised the stranger who stared back at me. "Shit." That woman who had beamed back at me only hours ago was now defeated. Her skin had lost that youthful glow. Her shoulders were hunched over as though the weight of the world were upon them, but it was her eyes that disturbed me the most. The dark circles accentuated her pain. She was a genuinely broken-hearted woman. She had loved and she had well and truly lost. "Who the hell are you?"

Her voice was lifeless, and the woman in the mirror shrugged in reply. She didn't know who she was either.

I came out of the bathroom with a clean face, dressed in my comfy travel clothes and carrying Leyla's Jimmy Choo's. "Thank you for trusting me with your Choo's."

"*Rica ederim.*"

"I felt like a princess wearing them."

"You looked like one as well — but your Prince Charming, he will have a lot to answer for."

I sighed morosely. "I wish I had never come to Istanbul."

Leyla shook her head. "Don't say that, *canım*. We would never have met had you not come to stay. Not knowing you would make me very sad."

"I just can't believe he left with her." I absently folded up my leather pants and handed them to Leyla to squeeze into the suitcase.

"We don't know he did that."

"He said he loved her."

"Yes, but for the sake of his daughter. He also said he had moved on."

"I guess."

"I think you are the one forgetting something, Ginger. It is you that are leaving him. And he doesn't even know that you are leaving!"

"I'm doing that for him." I cried, angry that Leyla did not support my decision. "I didn't do it so Aydin and Simge could get back together."

"I am quite certain that he does not want to get back with Simge. Do you think, even for a moment, that a man like Aydin Kaya would let Simge Kaya be assaulted, even if it was by her fiancé? She may not be his wife anymore, but she is still the mother of his child."

"No."

"And would you have wanted him to allow that to happen?"

"Of course not."

Leyla shook her head and chuckled, then patted the overflowing suitcase. "If you sit on it, I might be able to get it zipped up."

"My Italian backside finally comes in handy. *Grazie, Nonnina.*"

She giggled and smacked me on the bum as I climbed up on top of my suitcase. "Aydin did the right thing, Ginger. You will hate yourself when you realise this."

"I guess now we'll never know, will we?"

Leyla abandoned the zipper and looked at me. "Ginger, I say this to you with all of my heart. You are a fool. You are going to let Aydin go over a guess?"

"I have to."

She shook her head before returning to the zipper. "If you say so."

I left Leyla to struggle with my suitcase and walked over to the main house to drop off my key. Deniz was slumped in a chair, a plastic bag filled with ice against his nose and a glass of golden liquid in his bloodied, raw hand. "Ginger."

"Deniz. Hi." He waved the plastic bag in my direction. "I'm sorry about, well, you know, everything."

He snorted into his glass. "Yes, for you too. It was very entertaining though, very Simge."

He indicated his drink, but I shook my head. "No, thanks. I am just looking for your mother. Is she here?"

"She is, but she has already gone to bed. She says she has been thoroughly embarrassed by my behaviour and will probably never leave the house again."

"Your behaviour?" With raised eyebrows, I smiled at him.

"Isn't she being a little dramatic?"

"She has always had a flair for the dramatic." He laughed harshly before throwing back the rest of his drink. "Can I help you?"

"I was going to drop off my key to her. I am leaving now."

"Oh?"

"Yes. I have a flight home."

"And Aydin?"

I shrugged. "And Simge?"

"*Touché*. It seems that they have each other again."

"Apparently. But you know what? I think we will both be better off without them."

"I need you to know that I did not want to fight Aydin or raise my hand to Simge." I could hear the strain in his voice. "It was a reaction. It was wrong, but I just reacted. Now, I will be seen by the public as a monster, a wife-beater."

"No, you won't! Anyone could see that these were extraordinary circumstances. No one would think any less of you!"

"I hope you are right, but we shall see soon enough." He came over and kissed me gently on both cheeks. "What will you do?"

"I think it's time for a change."

"You will return to London?"

"For now, but there's a big world out there."

"So I hear." He took my key and wrapped his arms around me to squeeze me tight. "Travel safe, Ginger."

"You too, Deniz."

As I crossed the courtyard, a taxi pulled up. Leyla and I both struggled to drag my luggage to the cobblestone street. Deniz rushed to our aid and heaved my overweight suitcase into the car before giving instructions to the driver.

I turned to Leyla and hugged her tightly. "I will miss you most of all."

"Promise me I will see you again."

My eyes filled with tears, and my voice choked with emotion. "I promise."

I knew I would never keep that promise.

I had no intention of ever setting foot in Istanbul again.

CHAPTER 21

The Problem With Forever

The taxi delivered me to departures with plenty of time to spare before my flight. After an early check-in, I made my way to the airport's lounge, where I used precious frequent flyer points to pay for access. I found a cozy corner and ordered a cappuccino before opening my emails. The first one was from Sadie jam-packed with her usual unwarranted advice. I could always rely on Sadie for her opinion on pretty much everything.

There was also another message from Henry. There was nothing he could have to say that would be of interest to me. I opened Instagram instead.

Tagging Aydin in that photo had been a colossal mistake. It had had hundreds of likes and way too many comments. It was a good thing that Google translate wasn't so great at translating Turkish because I suspected most of the comments weren't the most positive.

FUCK!

Social media was no longer my friend and, speaking of friends, I opened my messenger to update my unfriended friends (who

I had never actually unfriended).

>GROUP: Burn in Hell
>
>**Ginger:** I don't hate you anymore.
>
>**Meg:** Yah!
>
>**Nina:** Merry Christmas Ginny.
>
>**Nate:** Ho, ho ho.
>
>**Ginger:** Merry Christmas guys.
>
>**Ginger:** So I don't hate you but I am coming home.
>
>**Meg:** What?
>
>**Courtney:** ???
>
>**Ginger:** But I do really really hate Turkey just so you know.
>
>**Meg:** The whole country?
>
>**Courtney:** Or just the bird?
>
>**Ginger:** I'll explain it when I see you.
>
>**Nate:** Was the Turkish kebab just not up to the job?
>
>**Ginger:** Shut up Nate!
>
>**Courtney:** See this is why I don't date anyone for more than a week. Swipe left. Swipe right. It's all good.
>
>**Meg:** Courtney who are you right now?
>
>**Courtney:** I'm living the dream Meggy.

Jane Gundogan

> **Courtney:** Message me your flight details and I'll meet you.

I hoped Courtney was prepared to deal with a broken Aussie in desperate need of support, love and a butt load of booze.

And even though my life had become a complete shitstorm, I stupidly did the unthinkable and Googled Simge and Aydin Kaya. Slowly, I made my way through the millions of hits about their life. The list was being updated continuously, thanks to the non-wedding, and new images appeared every few minutes. I clicked on a photo of Simge smiling for the camera, only moments before all hell had broken loose. I could see the calculation in her eyes. She knew what was about to happen and she relished in it. Bitch! Then another photo caught my eye.

Me! Here! In the airport lounge!

I looked around and spotted a man opposite me hunched in his chair, phone in hand. When I caught his eye, he looked away.

Prick!

I pushed my chair backward and grabbed my hand luggage. I would not cry and give this bastard another photo to sell. I found the restrooms, locked myself in a stall and let a few frustrated tears escape.

Where was Aydin right now? Was he at home with Emine, or worse, with Emine AND Simge? Had he realised that he did, in fact, love Simge, that he and I was just a terrible mistake?

I carefully wiped my red, puffy eyes and blew my nose. Now what? I checked my mobile for the hundredth time.

No messages. No calls. No explanations.

I finished up in the bathroom, slipped on sunglasses to hide my puffy eyes and made my way from the lounge to passport control, doing my best to calm my emotions and keep my tears safely locked away. Who knew where another bloody photographer might have been lurking. The last thing I wanted was a photo of a teary-eyed Ginger Knox on the cover of a Turkish tabloid with the headline, "Aydin Kaya Broke Chubby Australian Girl's Heart."

"Ginger!"

His voice. I turned. Aydin ran the last few steps to me and bent at the waist with his hands on his knees, panting. Dishevelled, with his bow tie hanging from his collar, the breast pocket of his tuxedo ripped and dangling, and his hair adorably messed up beyond belief, he stood before me.

He grabbed my hands which immediately sent those ridiculous and, under the circumstances, completely inappropriate sparks through my body.

Damn electricity.

I pulled my hands away and stepped around him, only to see Emine's teary eyes looking up at me.

"Ginger! We found you."

Low blow bringing Emine with him!

"Hi, Emine."

She threw herself into my arms. I hugged her tightly. "I did not think I would get to say goodbye."

"I'm so glad that you're here, sweetie."

Aydin stepped in and pointed to a chair. "Emmy, can you please go and sit down so Ginger and I can talk for a moment?"

"*Tamam, Baba.*"

We both waited until Emine had found a seat and sat down. He put his hand under my chin and guided me to face him. "You are leaving me?"

"I was there, Aydin." I glared at him. "I saw what happened."

He shook his head in denial, his eyes boring into mine. "You only saw part of it. I had to get Simge and Emine out of there before things got worse. You have no idea what the paparazzi are like here. They are crazy, so I put them both into a car and asked the driver to take them home. When Emine told me you were there I came back to look for you and but you had already left."

"I waited."

"You were gone."

Suddenly there were flashes. As predicted the paparazzi appeared and began snapping. Aydin Kaya was definitely newsworthy today, and let's be honest with ourselves, most people loved nothing more than to watch a good drama unfold in front of them. I tried to hide my face from the camera and push through the ever-growing crowd of photographers that had quickly become unruly, but there was nowhere for me to go. Aydin pulled me behind him in an attempt to keep me safe, but we were surrounded. He began to yell at the photographers, but his anger only seemed to bolster them on, and they surged even closer. The police arrived to move them off; however, in the end, they decided that it would be more sensible to move us to a more secluded spot. Aydin grabbed Emine, and the police hurried us down a corridor and into a small office.

Emine was whisked away to get a drink with a female officer while Aydin and I were shown into a small room at the end of a hall. Once inside the police officer shut the door and stood guard outside. There was nothing else for me to do but to watch Aydin's face, darkened with tension, waiting for me to argue with him. When I didn't say anything he began to pace and I realised that he was hurting as well.

He looked at me fiercely. "You didn't think to tell me you were leaving?"

"It's for the best."

"The best for who?"

I shrugged. I didn't have the energy to argue with him so I changed the subject. "How did you know I was here?"

"Deniz told me you left and Leyla filled me in on the rest."

Bloody Leyla.

"Listen, today might seem like the end of the world —" I looked into his red-rimmed eyes, "— but I promise that the sadness won't last. Memories fade. Feelings change. The only thing that matters is that you'll have Emine with you. You'll soon forget all about that Aussie chick that was stranded in Istanbul once."

"I don't think so."

"I do. You know, that night we first met back in London, you told me how important your family was, and in the end, Emine — and Simge — well, they are your family and that matters."

"I don't want Simge."

"Whether you want her or not, she will always be in your life."

I could see that Aydin had become frustrated as he tried in vain to make me see things his way. "I am telling you now that I don't want Simge. I don't want her. I only want you."

"But you do want Emine? Yes?" I pulled him in and hugged him one final time. "Simge made it clear that if I stay, she'll take Emine away from you."

"Emine loves you."

Tears welled in my eyes. "I love her too, but Simge hates me. She will make this impossible."

"What if I move back to London?"

I shook my head in protest. "You'll never see your daughter. I couldn't do that to you or to her."

"Then stay here."

"I can't take the chance that you might lose Emine."

"I'll never let that happen."

"Some things are out of your control."

An announcement came over the speakers. Although I tried to focus to understand it, I distinctly heard the word "London." My flight was boarding, and I still had to go through customs.

"I've gotta go."

"I won't let you."

I was so frustrated that I started to yell at him. "CAN'T YOU SEE I'M TRYING TO DO THE RIGHT THING HERE GOD-DAMN-IT? SO SHUT UP AND KISS ME SO I CAN LEAVE!"

Aydin was not happy. He also did not kiss me.

"Do you want to know what your problem is, Ginger?" He asked me through clenched teeth.

"Right now you're my problem!"

"No. Your problem is that you are too scared to love."

"Not true. I love love. But when it all comes down to it … I… I just don't feel the same way about you."

A lie. And I hated myself. I knew I had hurt him, but it had to be done. I needed him to hate me. I looked into his red eyes, sunken and sad. I could see the pain that I had just inflicted.

"What? You don't love me now? IS THAT WHAT YOU'RE SAYING?" His voice rose until he was yelling right back at me.

"That's what I'm saying."

"I know you love me! I can see it, but you are too scared of being hurt, so you run away. When I first saw you, I could already see that you had shut yourself off. Is it easier to have no feelings at all than to actually let yourself love or to be loved?"

"How dare you!"

"Prove to me that I am wrong."

"Fuck you, Aydin."

He pulled me close. "No. Fuck you, Ginger."

I tried to pull away from him, but the more I pulled away, the more he pulled me in. His forehead was creased with worry lines, his eyes red from tears. Still hot though.

Was it wrong that I fixated in that moment on how hot he was when he was sad… or angry… or…?

Not now, Ginger.

There was a knock at the door and I was able to pull away as an officer opened the door. He spoke to Aydin and then indicated that I needed to follow him.

"You need to leave now."

Emine ran through the door and took my hand. "Are you sad to be leaving us, Ginger?" Her small voice wavered as she reached up for a hug.

I bent down to her. "I am very, very sad to be leaving you, Emine." I gave her a hug. "You must look after your father for me. Can you do that?"

"I will."

Emine teared up, so I kissed her cheek and hugged her tightly. "Be a good girl for your *baba*."

I stood back up and gazed at the man that I adored one last time. "I can see that you're hurting. Please know that this is killing me, too. I just can't be here anymore. You can't lose Emine because of me."

Aydin bent down and kissed my neck, my ear, and my cheek as his hands swept across my back and pressed me to his chest. I inhaled in his sweet scent. I needed to imprint that scent on my brain, to hold me over until… forever.

Aydin promised me forever.

Finally, he reached my mouth and there was nothing else but his lips, pressed against mine. We kissed until we were both breathless. It was goodbye for both of us.

"Be happy Aydin. I want that for you and for Emine with all my heart."

He nodded and leaned forward to kiss my forehead. "I love you, Ginger. And I will come for you."

He looked at me expectantly. I closed my eyes, shutting out his gaze. I didn't have it in me to endure the pain of looking at him any longer. "Just forget about me Aydin, for everyone's sake."

"*Seni ne zaman unutacağımı sorma, ne zaman öleceğimi bilmiyorum.*" I don't know what he said, but the tone of his voice told me everything I needed to know. He took Emine by the hand and walked away. Emine turned back to me one more time and gave me a small wave with her free hand.

And this time I really was heartbroken.

CHAPTER 22

One Thing Is For Sure ...
Love Stinks (Yeah, Yeah)

The flight home was just as painful as the flight over, but for vastly different reasons. Instead of a stonking hangover, my smashed-up heart sat heavy in my chest, making it hard to breathe. It hadn't just been broken, it had been ripped from my chest and shredded before being handed back to me in a box, the moment Aydin walked away.

It had taken every ounce of energy to make my way through the airport and onto the plane. I know this might sound a little dramatic, but I must have looked like hell with my red eyes and blotchy skin, because when I was delivered to customs by the police officer, I was immediately pulled aside and thoroughly searched before boarding the plane — twice. Perhaps there was concern that I was a drug trafficker or that I suffered from the plague or something, because even when I finally arrive at my seat, my neighbour had a hurried conversation with a flight attendant before he was moved.

Passport control at Heathrow also had a field day with me. Once I'd made it past the drug-sniffing dogs and I'd regaled the customs officer with the story of my heartbreak, it was decided I wasn't an immediate threat to the United Kingdom. They finally stamped my passport and let me enter the country. I trudged to baggage claim, expecting to find my clothes strewn across carousel six, but by some miracle, my bulging luggage had arrived intact. I wheeled my way through the exit and straight into Courtney's waiting arms in a scene very much reminiscent to the first few minutes of Love, Actually… except I wasn't feeling particularly happy at that moment.

I was exhausted and clung to her. "Thank you."

"*De nada.*" She patted me on the back, then held me at arms' length. "How was your trip?"

I glared at her.

"Really? Your messages made it sound like you were on your way to happily ever after, but I don't need to tell you that you look like hell."

"I don't want to talk about it."

Courtney looked me up and down. "You're not sick, are you?"

"I wish that was my problem."

"Fine, but I want details."

"Later."

Courtney drove me home in silence, and under her watchful eye, I crawled into my bed where I slept for a soul-reviving twenty-four hours.

When I woke, she was sitting on my sofa reading "He's Just Not That Into You." "This is rubbish."

I smiled at her. "I know."

"You feeling any better?"

"A little. What day is it?"

"It's Monday night."

"Woah."

"Yep. You were comatose. I thought you were dead at one point, but then Nina came and checked on you."

"Oh? Her diagnosis?"

"Broken heart."

Could one die from a broken heart?

I opened my mouth to reply, but a sob came out instead. Courtney rushed over and hugged me tightly. "You'll be okay, honey."

"Thanks for being here. I honestly don't know how I would have coped in this shitty little room alone."

"I admit the décor of this place is pretty dreary." Courtney pulled me upright. "Now, go and wash your face while I'll make you a cup of tea. The others will be over soon."

Sipping on my tea, I sat down in my wicker chair next to my wilting ficus tree while Courtney fussed around me. Nate and Nina arrived carrying tequila and a bag of lemons while Meg appeared shortly after with three pizzas and a large tub of chocolate ice cream.

"I hate you, Nate."

His face was creased with concern and he nodded grimly. "I

blame myself for this colossal cock-up."

"I blame you too."

"Do you think we should make Nate jump in the Thames as his punishment?" Nina seemed somewhat excited about the prospect of pushing Nate into the darkness of the Thames river.

I laughed, my voice thick with sadness. "It might just help me feel better, and even better might kill him so — yes! Definitely!"

"Do you want to tell us what happened over there?"

I took a few deep breaths, then filled everyone in on the whole sorry mess; from the moment Aydin found me at the airport, to dinner with his family, the catastrophe with Simge, Emine and the non-wedding, and finally to our goodbye at the airport.

Nina wiped away a small tear that rolled down her cheek. "I'm sorry, but this story is a modern-day Romeo and Juliet. Star-crossed lovers, and all."

"You do know they died, right?"

"Do you love him?"

"Look, I know you're all a fan of Aydin's, and so am I, but it's well documented that long distance relationships just don't work. Everybody knows that. So between the distance and his bloody cow of an ex-wife…" I shrugged. "I just need to learn to live without him I guess."

"He's rung, you know." Meg looked at me and bit her lip.

"A few times." Nate knocked back a shot.

"Not just a few times, Nate." Meg sighed. "Constantly. He's been ringing constantly."

"And bombarding all of us with messages!" Courtney held up her phone.

"I know." I passed my mobile to Meg who also blinked back her tears as she read his messages. "Me too."

Nina squeezed in beside Meg to read his most recent message. "Heartbreaking. 'You have changed my life forever. I cannot even breathe without you beside me.' It's a song."

"We just need Adele to sing it. It'll be an instant hit."

I rolled my eyes at the two of them. "You know, when I was young, I thought falling in love would be easy. But the truth is, finding that forever person isn't easy at all."

"Of course it's not easy! Hell, look at me! I dated way too many Mr. Wrong's before I realised that I preferred Miss Right!"

"Mr. Wrong here." Nate waved his arms in the air. "Courts, I've gotta ask, did I make you gay?"

"Probably."

"And what about me? I haven't had a steady relationship in years. Years!" Meg moaned as she stuffed another piece of pizza in her mouth. "Shit, I'm depressed now."

I blew my nose into a tissue thoughtfully supplied by Nina. "I thought that I was in love with Henry, but I was wrong. It wasn't love. At most it was an infatuation. Now I'm *actually* in love with Aydin, but we can't be together. Clearly, I've no clue what I'm doing and shouldn't be allowed to make these types of decisions by myself."

It was time for Doctor Nina and her one semester of psych to analyse me. "We all understand why you made the decision that you did. You based it on love, so of course you know what love is. I don't think anyone one of us would have handled the situation any differently."

"Well, love stinks."

"But then it doesn't."

"But then it stinks again."

Meg jumped off the sofa and dragged me up out of my chair before she wrapped her arms around me. "Listen to me, Ginny. You've had a lot thrown at you over the past few days but none of it really matters. The ex-wife? She doesn't matter. The gossip? It's all rubbish and it will all fade in time. All that matters is how you feel about Aydin. If you are lucky enough to find love you can't let it go. Hold onto it because if you don't you will regret it every day for the rest of your life."

"I don't regret meeting Aydin and I certainly don't regret loving him. I just regret everything else that came along with it."

We all sat in silence, munching on our pizza, all of us lost in our own thoughts. Finally Nate coughed. "He said if you don't call him back, he is coming here."

"I won't call him back."

"Okay."

"And I won't see him if he comes here."

And as though Aydin had heard me all the way from Istanbul, my mobile sounded. We all stared at the phone as it rang out across the room.

"Answer it."

I shook my head and crossed my arms like the petulant child that I was.

"Answer it, Ginny."

"That's an awful ringtone." Courtney grabbed the phone and tossed it to me. "Just answer it so we don't have to listen to it anymore!"

I looked at the four of them. "Fine. But can you all disappear for a bit? I can't do it with you guys here."

"Right." Nate stood up taking Nina's hand. "We're off to the pub."

After the door shut behind them, I closed my eyes tightly and breathed in deep. "Aydin?"

"Ginger!"

"Hi."

"How are you?"

"I'm fine."

I wasn't fine. I knew I wasn't fine. Aydin knew I wasn't fine, but if I said anything else, I probably would've burst into tears.

"I miss you."

The sadness in his voice stabbed at me and I snot-sobbed in reply.

Way to hold it together Ginger.

"Don't cry, *aşkım*."

"I'm not." I mumbled into the phone. "I caught a cold on the plane."

I heard a bang through the phone and I pictured Aydin slamming his fist on a table — or through a wall. He exhaled heavily. "Will you come back?"

I brushed away my tears and gathered myself before I answered. "I don't think so."

"I want you to know that Simge has apologised for the trouble that she caused us. She asked me to tell you that she wants us both to the happy."

"I won't come back."

There was silence.

"Aydin?"

"You should not have had the right to make this decision for both of us."

"Perhaps but it was the right decision for all of us."

"I will come for you."

"Please don't."

I hung up and ignored the phone when it rang again.

I knew I couldn't dive head first into that black hole of grief again. If I did I would probably never be able to pull myself back out again.

Those first few days back in London weren't great, but thanks to perhaps a few too many bottles of wine and regular visits by Courtney and Meg or Nate and Nina or even Courtney and Nina (who seemed to have forged an unlikely friendship), I knew I was going to get past it. I just needed more time.

And then, on the last morning of the year, an intervention of sorts was carried out. I was pushed down onto my wicker chair where I stared sullenly at my friends while they tried to snap me out of my all-encompassing funk.

With Nina leading the way, they reminded me that I was loved and needed by each and every one of them.

I scowled at them. "I'm not going to top myself off, guys."

"We know that Ginger," Nina replied in her most soothing bedside manner. "We just want you to know that we love you and that we're worried about you."

"What do you want me to say? I'm fine."

Meg pursed her lips. "Well we don't think you are, sweetie."

"How so?"

"You're just not the same Ginny that we all know and love."

"Maybe this IS the real me."

I must have looked like I was about to blow a gasket because Meg put her hands up in mock surrender. "Okay, okay, we'll stop. Just know we are here for you, if you need anything or if you want to talk about it, we're right here."

That's just the thing, I didn't want to talk about it. I was happy to wallow in my misery. "Enough! Can't you all just leave me alone?" A single sob escaped my throat.

"Jesus!" Nate slammed his fist down on my countertop. "You've got to stop feeling sorry for yourself."

"Now Nate, let her be." Nina slipped her arm around me. "So what do you want to do? And is there anything that we can do to help you?"

I wanted to go home, to forget everything that happened. I wanted to turn back time. I wanted to forget the pain and return to where I was truly happy, and that was back in Sydney.

"I think I might go and stay with Sadie. I need my family."

Courtney and Meg both objected. "Nooo!"

"We're your family too!"

"Just for a visit."

Okay, so I wasn't entirely truthful. I knew I was a horrible friend but how could I have told them that I wanted to run home with my tail between my legs?

"I just never got my summer." I grabbed Meg's hand. "But I'll be back. I love you guys."

"We love you too."

"You promise you'll be back?"

"I promise."

"And I'm sorry for getting pissy at you, I just want you to be happy," Nate mumbled apologetically, before he added, "But for what it's worth, I think you would've been happy with Aydin."

"Jesus, Nate!"

"Don't say that!"

"It's okay guys. Nate's right. I think I would've been happy with Aydin. But it's done now. And I'm pretty sure I'll be happy again. Someday. I just need time." I was quiet for a moment, then broke out in a huge, albeit forced, grin. "Now, correct me if I'm wrong but isn't tonight New Year's Eve? I think we could all do with a little pick-me-up, or maybe even a complete blowout. What do you say?"

"Tonight's definitely the night for it."

"I'm thinking a little dinner, some fireworks and a few drinks."

"Epic idea."

"Maybe even more than just a few drinks."

Courtney whooped. "YES! Let's throw on some slutty dresses and really go for it!"

"But in the meantime can you do us all this one favour, Ginger?"

"What's that?"

Nate grinned at me. "Get your ass out of that chair and take a shower. You really stink!"

CHAPTER 23

Tragic Rebound Mission

And that's how I found myself on New Year's Eve, again dressed in my AllSaints dress and spikey boots (as well as my freshly-laundered lacy, apple red underwear) leaning against a bar in Vauxhall while Meg flirted with the young Irish lad beside us. I was already tipsy because it was the worst night of the year (did you know?). I was trying my best, but failing miserably as I faked a smile and nodded at Meg and her potential love interest. It's harder than it looks to recover from your heart being irrevocably smashed to pieces.

I grabbed another Tequila Cruda and threw it back. I intended to get wasted.

Nate and Nina had disappeared into the crowd on the hunt for a table while Courtney was already on the dance floor.

"Ginny, get your fat ass up here," Courtney yelled at me, as Prince blasted from the speakers. "Let's go crazy, girl!"

Getting up on the dance floor was much easier said than done in my undoubtedly-more-than-just-tipsy state, and between my high-heels and the disco lights bouncing balls of bright colour in my eyes, I wondered how long it would be before

I ended up on my ass. Squeezing through gyrating couples on my way toward Courtney, someone grabbed my arm and swept me back off the floor. "Ginger?"

I stopped and closed my eyes for a moment.

Aydin?

I spun around, ready to throw myself into Aydin's arms, only to find myself staring into the blue intensity of Henry Hennessey's eyes. "Ginny? Hey! I thought that was you."

"Fuck off, Henry."

My night had officially just gone from bad to shit. I had to swallow down my vomit reflex at the sight of him.

"I can't believe you're here." He smiled at me and tried to wrap me in a hug. "Long time no talk."

"Let's keep it that way."

I pulled away from him and danced over to Courtney where we got our groove on to the new Drake tune, followed by a little Vogue action. When Madonna's disco beat was replaced by a very smooth Justin Timberlake, an arm wrapped around my waist. "How about a dance?" I knew the tone of Henry's voice instantly. It was his seduction tone. After what he did, was he seriously trying this on me?

I turned my head, startled by Henry's expectation. He must have been able to read the expression on my face because he stepped back. "Please?"

Courtney had bailed on our girls twosome and was now dancing with a beautiful blond.

I did want to keep dancing, so I swallowed down the bile that rose in my throat and turned to face the man that I despised. "Fine."

The music seemed to slow and I lost my footing on the slick tiles. Henry pulled me into him. "Ginger, how drunk are you?"

"Very drunk, Henry."

"Thought so."

"So tell me, how's your secretary? Is she here?"

"She quit."

"Aww, Did you need a spoonful of sugar to make that medicine go down?" I threw my head back in laughter. "I'm so sorry. I mean, after all, you were never going to finish falling in love with Charlotte-Fucking-Poppins."

"Don't be like that." He looked down at me, his smile not quite reaching his dark, blue eyes. "I think she realised that she was never going to replace you. I missed you."

I snorted, then hiccuped. Stupid Henry.

"Come on Gin." He leaned in and drunkenly whispered in my ear. "There's no one like you."

"Gross." I slipped out of his arms. "Why are you here Henry? Are you stalking me?"

"No, of course not. I saw you from across the room." Henry pointed over at a table where his friends Ben and Julia were sitting. "Come over and say hi."

"Nope."

"Please."

"Why?"

"They were your friends too."

My shoulders shook as I bent over in a belly laugh. "They actually weren't but sure, okay, I'll come to say hi to them, but first you come and say hi to my friends."

One of his cheeks twitched and his face contorted into a look between embarrassment and regret. I grabbed his hand and dragged him behind me to my table. "You guys! You aren't going to believe who this is!" I pointed at Henry like he was a show pony. "Henry! It's fucking Henry! I mean, could my life get any better than right this very second?"

The table was momentarily silent as they all looked at Henry with wide eyes. Courtney was the first to come to her senses and glowered at him. "So this is Henry, eh? Who said he looked like Chris Hemsworth, I'd say he looked more like Chris O'Dowd. Definitely nothing but scraps here."

Always fast with a retort Henry laughed at her. "I don't think you're any prize either darling."

At that insult Nate stood up, all six foot four of him, and crossed over to Henry in two steps. "I think you need to leave, mate."

"Ginny and I are just talking, big fella."

"I'm pretty sure you're the last person Ginny would ever want to talk to."

"I hardly think you and your douche-doughnut would have a clue who Ginny wished to speak to."

The look on Nate's face was priceless. Nate grabbed Henry's

arm and twisted it behind him, ready to frog-march him out of the bar, but I put my hand out to stop him. "Nate, it's okay. I'm alright." I stood on my toes and kissed him on the cheek. "And don't listen to Henry. Your man-bun is as sexy as hell."

"Too right it is." Nate winked at me and dropped Henry's arm. "Holler if you need me. I'll be happy to throw out this particular piece of garbage."

Ignoring Nate's comment, Henry led me across the room to where Ben and Julia were watching our reunion. Julia stood up and hugged me. "Wow, Ginger. You look beautiful! That dress is fabulous."

"Thank you." I smiled at her. "How was your engagement party? Sorry I didn't make it. Would have been awkward, kinda like it is now, if you know what I mean. I do hope Henry gave you the gift that I bought."

"Err, yes he did. Thank you."

I enjoyed watching the three of them squirm. It was clear Ben wished he was somewhere else, that's for sure. "I'm going to the bar. Can I get you a drink?"

"Absolutely Ben. How about a *rakı*?"

"Huh?"

"Don't worry. A beer would be great."

I sat down in Ben's vacated seat and wondered how much more awkward this moment could be.

Julia fiddled with her straw. "So, what did you do for Christmas?"

To prove just how fabulous my life had become post-Henry, I

lifted my chin and smiled brightly back at her. "I was in Istanbul with a friend. And you?"

"We were at Ben's grandmother's house in Bath."

"In Bath? Henry and I were supposed to go to Bath back in January." I gaped in mock astonishment. "Remember Henry?"

The corner of his mouth twitched and he looked down at the table.

"We didn't go together because Henry was too busy fucking his secretary." His face burned red, either out of embarrassment or anger, I wasn't really sure, and I patted him on the shoulder and flashed a phony grin. "But that's in the past isn't it Henry? I really shouldn't dredge up such nastiness when we're with friends."

I knew I was behaving like a total bitch, but I just didn't care. Henry had hurt me — a lot. And as for Julia? Well, I thought she was my friend as well, but I never heard from her after the breakup, not even once.

Ben returned with the beers. I chugged mine down. "Excellent. Thanks for the beer, sweetie."

Henry grabbed me by the arm. "Time to talk."

I ignored his caveman grasp and feigned shock. "Aren't we talking now?"

Henry stood up and his blue eyes flashed at me with an intensity that I found disconcerting. Ugh. He looked so sincere, so apologetic, so Thor-esque but I knew it was all bullshit. I just wish I knew it was bullshit three years ago. "Walk with me."

I didn't need to be reminded of what happened between Henry and me, thank you very much, but due to the excessive number of tequilas, curiosity definitely got the better of me, well, that and the memories of good times that we had once had together.

Don't judge me because we've all been there — all of us. Looking back on our past with fecking great big rose coloured glasses on.

So yes, I did want to walk with Henry. In fact, I had consumed enough tequila to make walking with Henry seem like a grand plan.

I stood up, teetering in my heels. "Sure. I feel like I should probably eat something before I barf anyway."

"You always did think with your stomach, didn't you?" Henry grinned at me. "Actually, I know just what you need."

"Oh yeah?" I wiggled my boobs at him. "And you're going to give it to me?"

I was *very* drunk.

"There's a great kebab place — and you look like you could use a beef kebab."

"I would lurve a beef kebab."

I giggled at my very dirty in-joke, but I stopped myself when I caught Henry studying me. In his line of work, it was often necessary to be ruthless when researching the next takeover. I mean, they make deals worth millions or even billions of dollars, so it is vital that he knows as much as he can about each adversary, both in their business and personal life. There was an excellent chance that Henry had done a little sleuthing before he "bumped" into me tonight. Was I his next takeover? He was going to be very disappointed if he thought I was.

Despite my apprehension that I was about to get Gordon Gecko'd, I laughed loudly before I blew half-assed kisses to Ben and Julia. I knew any time spent with Henry wasn't the smartest idea, but it was New Year's Eve, and I'd really had the shittiest of weeks. I just didn't care.

"We met three years ago tonight, you know."

"It's already New Year's Day in Sydney."

"True."

He tried to take my hand as we left the club, but I pulled away. We walked down to the Thames in silence. I scowled as I waited for his apology or explanation as to why he did what he did, but he said nothing.

Finally, I broke the silence. "Why did you do it?"

"It was an accident."

He looked so guilty. I couldn't help myself and I laughed at him. "Falling off a bike is an accident."

"Don't be like that, Gin." His face was a mix of guilt and smugness. "Alright, alright. I really don't know why I did what I did."

I knew I would never be able to forgive him but I also wasn't going to make this easy for him either. "Oh, don't give me that. You do know."

"Honestly? I think I was scared."

"Of what?"

"Growing up. Marriage. Commitment. All of it."

"The Great Henry Hennessey scared?" I snorted. "Never!"

He shrugged. "Charlotte was a fantasy, and I guess I got to live out the fantasy."

"And destroy our relationship in the process."

"Yeah, I did. I'm sorry about that."

We walked along in silence until my stomach started to growl.

It was beginning to feel a lot like *déjà vu*.

Henry led me down a small alley and we came to a kebab shop. "Do you remember on that first New Year's Eve? Kebabs at sunrise? You always needed a kebab after a big night. This place looks alright, well not too dodgy anyway."

Was he thoughtful? Or was I about to get played bigtime?

We entered the shop and the smell of the cooking meat together with the sound of Turkish music did me in. "Oh, God!"

"Are you feeling okay?"

I turned away so Henry couldn't see the tears in my eyes. "Just a bit queasy, I think."

"So, the usual then? With barbeque sauce?"

I smiled. The idea of barbeque sauce on a kebab would horrify Aydin. "Actually, I'd like it with the yoghurt sauce."

"Really? How strange."

"I guess I've changed since I saw you last."

He looked me up and down. "I'll have to get to know you all

over again, won't I?"

I snorted again at Henry as he ordered our kebabs (mine with yoghurt sauce) and we sat against the wall staring blankly at the television overhead. Turkish commercials played and then the program came on. I found myself staring at a close-up of Simge's perfect face. It was a re-run of One Life.

Could this night seriously have gotten any worse?

I watched Simge as she argued with an older man sporting a very dashing moustache before he threw some papers at her and stormed out.

He should've slapped her! I bet he would have enjoyed it if he had.

The scene changed. Suddenly it was Aydin's face on the screen. He whispered in Simge's ear and they gazed lovingly into each other's eyes. He then leaned her back and kissed her. So that's where he learned that move; the same one he used on me. My stomach churned and growled at the same time.

Faarrrkkkkkk! I was going to be sick. That, or I needed food. Badly.

I stood up abruptly, knocking my plastic chair over. "Turn this off!"

The Turk behind the counter stared at me. "*Ne?*"

"Turn this shit off!"

"This is not shit. This is Simge Kaya. She is very famous."

"Let me tell you something about the very famous Simge Kaya. She's a fucking bitch." I rose my voice until I was shouting. "A fucking bitch!"

The poor guy behind the counter gaped at me as he handed our kebabs to Henry. "You are crazy, lady."

"*Teşekküler, eşek.*" Spittle flew out of my mouth as I insulted him.

He stared at me with angry, squinty eyes, but then his face changed as realisation washed over him. He clicked his fingers in my direction. "Wait! I know you!"

"Fucking bitch," I mumbled as Henry dragged me toward the door.

"It's you. You're the girl from the wedding," he shouted, as we left his shop.

"What wedding?" Henry asked.

I shrugged and stomped off down the street. "I just really hate Turkish TV."

"So it seems." Henry laughed and handed me my kebab. "Lots of yoghurt sauce, that should cheer you up."

We found a seat and huddled together beside the Thames and ate our kebabs in silence as we watched New Year's stragglers pass by on their way home.

I snuck a glance at Henry. His Thor-like features looked incredibly sure of himself as he finished off his kebab. How our lives had changed in the past twelve months. This time last year we were newly engaged, happy and in love (what I thought was love, anyway). We did the countdown to midnight snuggled in each other's arms not too far from here in fact, and we cheered when the fireworks rained down on the city, both of us excited about our future together. And now we were strangers.

Jane Gundogan

"So, thanks for the kebab."

"No worries." Henry collected our rubbish and deposited it in a nearby bin. "Probably a good enough time to get you home. You're just over the bridge, right?"

It didn't even occur to me to wonder how he knew where I lived. I nodded. "Pimlico."

He put his arm around my shoulders, and I let him. Hindsight being 20:20 and all that, I probably shouldn't have encouraged him, but I blamed the alcohol.

By the time we got back to my building, I was pretty knackered. I waved goodbye as I climbed the stairs. "Wait! Ginger!"

I turned around and teetered. My woozy head and high heels had made me more than a little unsteady.

"Woah!" Henry took the stairs two at a time to catch me before I fell. "Let me help you."

I mumbled, mostly to myself, but shook my head. "I'm good."

"Don't be ridiculous. Let me help you."

I mumbled again but didn't push him away as he walked inside and to my door. I pulled my keys from my handbag and promptly dropped them on the ground. Henry retrieved them for me and unlocked my door.

"Thanks for walking me home."

"Thanks for forgiving me."

Forgive you? I didn't do that, did I?

I turned to shut the door, but Henry darted through the threshold before I could stop him. "You look beautiful tonight, Ginny."

I ignored his compliment and pulled him back toward the door. "Okay, time to leave. Bye, Henry."

"Can't I stay for a bit?"

"No."

"But I'm here."

"So what? I'm tired and I want you to leave."

"No you don't, not really."

Henry advanced towards me. He reminded me of an animal stalking its prey. Surprised by the aggression in his eyes, I sidestepped him, but he grabbed my wrist and pulled me into his body, knocking the wind out of me before he smashed his mouth down onto mine. I gulped down air as he slid his tongue into my open mouth. The taste of stale alcohol made me gag, and I tried to pull myself away, but he was much stronger and pushed me back against the wall.

"I've missed you, Ginny." Henry slammed the door shut. Suddenly, I was petrified.

"And now I can show you just how much."

CHAPTER 24

My Super Power? I Can Turn Alcohol Into Regret

My heart pounded in my chest as I tried to pull away from Henry's embrace. "Damn it, Henry, Let me go!"

It was as though he couldn't hear me and he grabbed hold of my face to kiss me again. I squeezed my mouth tight so he bit my lip which drew blood and forced me to open my mouth in pain. I turned my head away in an attempt to deter him, but Henry was too far gone to care and licked my neck. "I can't believe I was stupid enough to let you leave me."

I reefed myself free from his grasp. "You really didn't have much of a choice in the matter."

"Maybe but I've been keeping a close eye on you, Ginger Knox, don't you worry."

The way he said my name sent a chill down my spine. There was an unease in the tone of his voice and it made me turn and really look at him. Henry's Thor-like features were still there but they were twisted, a pale knockoff of his former glorious self. His eyes glared at me with such hostility that I couldn't breath. What had happened to him? This was not the Henry that I once knew. This man looked dangerous.

"You walked right past me when you left your office a few weeks ago. I wanted to speak to you but I knew that you still needed time."

I was a little freaked out at that point. While I didn't think he would actually harm me I didn't want to test that theory. I also knew I would never be able to overpower him. He was way too strong. I had to talk him down. I had to stall him until I could figure out how to get the hell away from him. "How do you know where I work?"

"I made it my business to find out." His bloodshot eyes narrowed as he spoke. "I know you leave for work at 7.15 every morning. You really hate your boss. Your closest friends are Courtney Ryan and Margaret Martin. You shop at the Sainsbury's on Wilton and you go to bed at 10.30 each night. You really are very regimented. I applaud that."

I nodded but remained silent. Again my dependence on CSI reruns came in handy because it taught me that I had to stay calm and rational. I had to continue to engage him in conversation without arousing his anger.

"I wanted to wait until you were ready, really ready, but then I saw you had pissed off to Turkey with that towelhead and I knew I couldn't wait any longer. I had to tell you that I missed you, Gin." His hands hadn't left my breasts since the moment he came through the door, and he squeezed them roughly. "And I've missed your tits as well. They were always the best part about you."

Any chance of me staying calm dissolved in that comment. Henry was clearly unhinged. "Let me go, Henry, or I'll scream."

"Seriously? You used to be more fun." He shook his head and

smiled, but his smile didn't reach his eyes. "Fine. I'm sorry, I misread your signals but I'm not leaving until we talk."

"I've got nothing more to say to you." I snapped at him. "Except that you should fuck off!"

I started shifting towards the door, but Henry took a step forward, blocking my way. "Gin, don't you see? It was destiny that brought us back together, tonight of all nights."

"No, it wasn't. It was alcohol and the fact that you're a fucking stalker." I glanced at the bathroom door. It had a lock. If I could just get to it, I could lock myself in.

"I just want you to know that things will be different this time around. I know how much you still love me."

Unbelievable. Henry was seriously deluded if he thought I would have anything to do with him after what he did to me.

I opened my mouth to reply, but Henry held up his hand, so full of himself that he misread the look on my face. "Gin, I know that the past few months have been a little rough on you, but now that we're back together, you can get your life on track."

"My life has never been better, but whatever." I side-stepped around Henry, still trying to keep him engaged but slowly moved towards the door. "So to recap, your secretary has dumped you, you're lonely and you thought your pathetic ex-fiancé would be up for it? Yeah?"

"Ginny, Ginny, Ginny. Don't overthink it. The only thing that matters right now is that... you complete me —"

Oh. My. God. He just used Jerry Maguire on me.

"— and I've missed you."

His lips curled into a smirk. It was the smirk of a man who knew me well enough to know that I lived my life vicariously through romantic comedies. The smirk of an egotistical asshole who truly believed that I was so pathetically self-lacking in confidence that I would accept his non-apology like a lap dog and nod and smile, happy for his attention.

I muttered under my breath. "Right."

"We belong together. Me, you, and that chair." His words dripped with sarcasm as he pointed at my beloved wicker chair. "I know how much you love that ratty, old thing."

I did love my wicker chair — and it wasn't ratty at all! It was a pivotal part of my life in London. It might have been a little banged up and a little broken (kind of like me) but it had been given a second chance to be loved (also like me) here in my teeny, tiny apartment. Holy shit! My wicker chair WAS ME (great analogy, Ginger), and there was no way I or my awesome, phenomenal, capable and independent wicker chair (all me! Finally!) would go anywhere near Henry or that apartment in Notting Hill (adjacent) ever again!

Heat rushed to my face. All my anger and hurt that I didn't know was still in my heart channelled itself into my brain ready to wash over me like a tsunami. I took a deep breath in an attempt to keep hold of myself but it was pointless, it all came flooding out. "I don't think you understand, Henry. I'd never move back in with you, and I wouldn't get back with you even if you were the last man on earth! I deserve a lot more than a man who cheated on me!"

"Don't be so over dramatic, Ginger."

This was never about making me happy, it was about him not wanting to be alone. My feelings and happiness were never a part of our relationship. Even after all he had put me through, nothing had changed, which just made me even angrier. "You made it very clear to me back in February that I was the last person that you really cared about, so let me just save both of us some time and say this... I can promise you that any infatuation that I once had for you is long gone and I'm certainly not in love with you. There will be no more calls from me, no more messages, no more tears, because what I have finally realised is," I took a breath and swallowed hard, "I hate you. I really fucking hate you."

"No, you don't."

"Oh my God, Henry! I bloody well do! I hate you for what you did! I hate you for hurting me, for screwing Charlotte, for making me cry. You were cruel and manipulative and there is nothing that you could ever offer me, no apology that you could ever make that would allow me see you any differently." I laughed in spite of myself. "I know how strong I am and I also know what I want and it's not you. I've finally got someone in my life who loves me and I love him. It's real."

Take a bow, Ginger.

He shook his head in contempt. "Sorry, *darling,* you can think whatever you want but I can promise you it's not bloody real, that's for sure."

"You know nothing about Aydin and me."

"He's so wonderful, is he?" he scoffed. "You think I don't know about you running around Istanbul with him? Did you think putting that photo on your social media was going to make me jealous or something? That I would come running back to you begging for forgiveness?"

"Aren't you doing just that?"

The anger on his face had turned to hatred. "And everyone knows what he did to you as well." He pressed his lips together in a tight line. "Running off with that big titty movie star while you were sitting there like a love-struck fool."

I stared at Henry aghast. "You knew?"

"Why do you think we had kebabs?" The laugh that bubbled up from his throat was positively evil. "You think you can just flaunt yourself all over internet like a whore and I wasn't going to find out? Frankly, you should have been a little more discrete. You embarrassed me with your behaviour."

"I embarrassed you?"

"And you embarrassed yourself." He sneered. Actually sneered. "You know, Ben said I'd be wasting my time. He was right, I guess. Hell, he even suggested I upgraded to a younger model."

"Ben might be a prick, but at least he's a smarter prick than you."

"Bitch. Stupid fucking bitch!" Henry snapped. His face had turned redder than a fire truck. "You just need to shut the hell up, get on your fucking back and I'll help you forget all of this ever happened!"

Who the hell was this man? I wanted to rip his Chris Hemsworth, Thor-clone head right off his shoulders and shove it hard up his narcissistic ass!

My anger reached a level that I previously didn't know was possible. I felt my hand ball into a fist at my side. "You're deluded."

"Is that a yes?"

"Don't come any closer!" I was sure I yelled loud enough for the entire building to hear, but Henry didn't seem to be listening to me at all.

"I want you."

"Get away from me!"

He stepped forward again and — blam! — I punched him right in the face.

Henry stumbled before he righted himself and rubbed his jaw. "What the actual fuck, Gin?"

"I told you to not to come any closer!"

Henry threw me a nasty half-smile, his nostrils flared with rage. "If you wanted to play rough, all you had to do was ask!" He lunged toward me and tried to pin me against the wall, but I saw it coming. I sidestepped him and lifted my knee hard, straight at Henry's balls. It found its target and he bent over and clutched his manhood. "Arrghhhh!"

"Get out!"

He was winded, but still lashed out at me and tried to grab my leg. I ran toward the door. "You fucking bitch. You're not fucking worth it."

"Praise God! Now get the hell out of my house!" I screamed at him. "Oh, and it's Ginger. GIN-GER!"

A huge smile spread across my face as I flung the door open. "Goodbye Henry."

"Ginger?"

Oh, shit!

Aydin.

My Aydin.

Standing at my door.

"Oh my God! Aydin!"

I was so surprised to see the man that I adored standing in my hallway, looking all jetlagged and rumpled and even more devastatingly handsome, that I threw myself at him. I had forgotten entirely that behind me was my crazy ex-fiancé clutching his precious balls, while I looked like a big, old, hot mess with the added bonus of the mountain-load of guilt plastered all over my face. Aydin disentangled himself from me and stood at the door awkwardly as he tried to make sense of what he had walked into.

"Aydin?" Henry stood up straight, and a sly grin appeared on his face. "Well, how about that."

My stomach lurched as I looked from Henry to Aydin and back again. I had seen Henry get that nasty gleam in his eyes before and it never ended well for his adversary.

Aydin took a step closer and put his arm around my waist. "Ginger, are you alright?"

"Henry was just leaving." My voice croaked.

Henry heard it and smirked. He was in the power position, and I knew he was about to let loose.

"Henry?" Aydin watched as Henry stepped toward the doorway.

"Thanks, Gin. This was fun." Henry leaned forward to kiss me on the mouth, but I moved so his lips found my cheek instead. It was all I could do to not burst into tears right then and there.

Henry pulled himself up to his full height, puffed out his chest and put out his hand. Aydin shook it but then Henry jerked him in so close they were standing eye to eye, merely inches apart. "You here for some sloppy seconds, mate?"

Aydin moved fast, so fast that neither Henry nor I realised what had happened. He swung and caught Henry on the side of his head, knocking him against the wall.

Henry rubbed his cheek but rallied quickly and landed a punch that spun Aydin backward against the door across the hallway. He pulled himself upright and smirked. "Chill dude, there's more than enough for all of us."

Aydin let out a yell before throwing another punch, straight into Henry's stomach. Henry let out a great whoosh of air and bent over to absorb the blow allowing Aydin to smash his knee straight into his face with enough force to snap Henry's head back.

Across the hallway, my neighbour poked his head out the door. "What the hell is going on?" He took in the scene and looked at me. "You alright?"

I nodded.

"Darling, this just reeks of Bridget Jones. You've really got to stop watching those movies."

I moaned. Jeeze, even the neighbours knew how pathetic I had become!

Aydin landed another punch to Henry's face.

"But for God's sake keep it down! This *biatch* needs her beauty sleep." He slammed his door shut.

He was right. This had turned into a scene from Bridget Jones' Diary, and fucking Hugh Grant was trying to ruin my life yet again!

I side-stepped to get out of the way as Henry lunged again at Aydin. His fist landed yet another punch, this time to Aydin's shoulder who deflected it easily and returned the favour with a blow to Henry's gut. Henry lurched but didn't go down. Instead, he launched himself at Aydin and punched him in the face. Aydin started to fall, but not before he drove a fist into Henry's nose. The sound of bone breaking echoed throughout the hallway. Henry roared in pain as blood gushed through his hands and down his shirt.

I gagged as Henry smeared it across his face while trying to wipe it away before he picked up his jacket and stormed halfway down the hall, defeated, but not before he threw one final insult. "He fights like a girl!"

"Yeah, like a girl that just kicked your ass!"

Henry disappeared down the stairs, clutching his balls in one hand and his bloody nose in the other. I wasn't at all sorry to see him go. I slammed the door behind my ex-fiancé and took a deep, calming breath as I turned around to face Aydin. There was only one thing left to do.

It was time to get the guy.

CHAPTER 25

Will I Get My Happily Ever After?

Aydin stumbled the few steps across my apartment and collapsed onto the sofa. He put his head in his hands and groaned. "I'm not sorry."

"I know."

"But I am angry."

"You have every right to be." I nodded in agreement. "But I swear to you it's not what it looks like."

"You must think I'm a fool coming here for you. You are already with another man." His face contorted in pain. "I AM a fool."

"You're no such thing, Aydin. Please believe me. Henry's completely insane. He was stalking me. I had no idea. I went out with Nate and the girls tonight. He was there."

He stood up and paced the three steps across my room to the window where he stood and stared out into the darkness for what seemed like an eternity. When he turned back to face me, his eyes were full of tears. "But you left with him?"

"Yes."

His eyes searched the room for answers. My rumpled bed. My dishevelled dress and swollen lips. It was not a good look. "And you invited him to your home?"

"No. You need to hear what happ —"

"Did you kiss him?"

"Yes but —"

"Then there is nothing else for you to expla —"

"But there is!" I shook my head frantically and cut him off. "You need to know… I didn't want to. It made me sick. I told him to stop." I fought not to raise my voice as I pleaded with him. "I even punched him."

I lifted my hand to show him my red, swollen knuckles.

"Really?" His shook his head in surprise as he examined my hand. "How can I stay mad at you when you do such crazy things?"

My eyes filled with tears. I tried to hold them back so they wouldn't fall down my cheeks. "I'm sorry."

"You're sorry? You do not apologise for defending yourself!"

"No! I mean, I'm sorry about Henry. I am. I know I should've stayed with the others. I messed up." My stomach squeezed and twisted and threatened to toss the beef kebab all over my floor. "I did let Henry walk me home, but I didn't invite him inside. I tried to stop him. He wouldn't listen."

"What are you saying?"

"He tried to force himself on me."

Aydin's face was grim, his brows drawn together in a heavy line and his jaw clenched as he realised what had happened before he arrived at my door. "I should have killed him."

"I would've let you."

The realisation of what nearly had happened finally hit me, and I started to shake. How lucky was I that I had managed to escape his grasp? My Henry. He was once my best friend, my lover, the man I had wanted to spend the rest of my life with. Now he deserved to rot in hell. I wanted to crawl under the duvet and hide from the mess that I had found myself in. Instead, I ran to the bathroom, slammed the door and vomited out all the kebab and all the liquor until I was empty.

Aydin knocked softly on the door. "Ginger, *aşkım*, are you alright? Ginger!"

"Just a minute." I quickly scrubbed my face, brushed my teeth and pulled my hair into a top knot. After I ripped off my dress and threw it in the corner, I wrapped myself in my fluffy, pink bathrobe. It had taken longer than a minute, and I still looked like a total wreck, but I was ready to face Aydin and to face my life in general.

When I peeked out the door, he stood there waiting for me. There was a hint of a smile on his lips. For a fleeting moment, hope-filled in my heart. "Feel better?"

"A little."

"Do you need to go to the hospital? Do you need to report what happened?"

"You think I should report this to the police?"

"He assaulted you. In my country that is a crime but it is up to you." He took my hand. "I will stand by whatever decision you make."

"I can't think about it right now."

Aydin stepped back and looked down at me in concern. "What if he comes back?"

"You're here to protect me."

His gaze never left my face. "With my life."

Neither of us said anything for a long time, both lost in our own thoughts. Finally, I cleared my throat. "Where's Emine?"

Aydin smiled slightly at the sound of his daughter's name on my lips. "She is staying with Simge's parents for a few days."

I was surprised to hear this. "Is that such a good idea?"

"They love Emine, and they have at least ten cats, so Emine loves visiting them as well." He chuckled. "I'll be spending the next week washing cat hair out of everything she owns."

"And Simge?"

"Let's just say Simge is now free to follow her dreams in America." He grinned brightly as he rubbed his hands together. "She signed over full custody."

"Congratulations."

After another awkward silence, Aydin scooped me up and set me down on my bed. I raised my eyebrows and he chuckled at my reaction. "Don't get ahead of yourself, Green Eyes. We need to talk, but it's cold. Aren't you cold? Why is it so cold?"

Mentally I high-fived my hygienically-challenged scumbag of a landlord. I hope he never fixed the damn heat in this place if it meant I could hop into the sack with Aydin every time it got a little chilly. So far, I was entirely on board with our talk.

I scrambled under the duvet and scooted over, so there was space for him to slide in beside me. He shook his head and sat down beside me, above the covers which ruined any potential canoodling.

My heart pounded as I waited for Aydin to say something, but when I looked into his dark eyes, I could only see sorrow. And love. This wouldn't be Aydin's moment. This was going to be my moment, my chance to explain to him what he meant to me. It was time for me to heal, to be no longer in fear or pain. I was ready for Aydin to hear those three little words that I finally understood. I loved him. Completely. I just hoped he still wanted me.

"When Henry and I... split... I was more than a little broken inside." I croaked as the words got stuck in my throat. "I... I couldn't figure out what was so wrong with me. I mean, was it something I had done? Was I so... so... unworthy... of his love? Do you have any idea what it's like to love someone when they don't love you back? No... of course you don't... I mean, how could you being that you're all gorgeous and famous... bloody girls following you around and falling at your feet. You're too beautiful to be even human..."

I knew I was losing my credibility here, but that was because I was beyond hysterical by that point and, let's be realistic, he really was too beautiful to be even human!

"I was so hurt. I mean, it was... physical... pain and it consumed me. I wasn't heartbroken, because I realised that I had never really loved him, but what he did ... the emotional manipulation, his behaviour... well... it kind of broke me. After that, I decided that no one would have that control over me or my heart... never, ever... so... I had to... protect myself so I would never get hurt like that again."

I gasped in a gulp of air and swallowed down the lump in my throat. Tears were coming, I just wasn't sure when I wouldn't be able to hold them back any longer, and they'd make their appearance. I chanced a glance at Aydin. His eyes were full of sympathy. "I guess I did dodge a bloody big bullet after what happened tonight." I sniffled and let out one grunt of a laugh.

"Ginger?" Slowly, Aydin reached out, took my hands in his and squeezed gently. Another good sign. "Stop. Relax. Breathe. You are going to pass out if you're not careful."

I shook my head and sucked in another breath. "No... wait... I need to finish. And then I met you and... you're so nice. You're wonderful, did you know that? And you're smart and caring... and a great dad... and I thought... no, I realised, that I loved you... I mean, I *really* loved you." One sob made it's way out. "It's the purest kind of love. Soul-mate kind of love. Forever kind of love."

He chuckled. "I did warn you that I was going to love you forever."

I rolled my wet eyes at him. "Yes yes, fine. And I was scared, okay? I didn't think I was worthy of anyone's love, especially someone as amazing as you. I had to knock down that emotional wall so that I could give myself to you completely... but I wasn't ready... not really ready.... I mean we'd only known each other a few days. How could it be real? And how could I possibly trust my own feelings? So, I ran. It's much easier to run, you know, and to let Simge win... because then I wouldn't get hurt. Plus, you could be with Emine. And I adore Emine. I didn't want her to be sad. I still say it was the right decision, and maybe I did have an ulterior motive in protecting myself, but when you didn't fight for me to stay, I knew it was the right decision."

"I never wanted you to leave."

"I never wanted to leave! But you didn't stand up to Simge. You should've told her you loved me. You should've told her to go to hell... but you didn't."

"I came to the airport!"

"You said goodbye."

Aydin threw his arms up in the air in exasperation. "You had already made up your mind to leave. There was nothing that I could have said that would have made a difference. I had to let you go."

"I know that. You don't think I know that?" I wasn't making any sense. I needed him to understand. "That doesn't even matter because I know now... I understand.... I don't want to live with the regret of never truly being happy because I'm... I'm..."

Don't screw this up. Say it, Ginger!

"You're what, *aşkım*?"

"Do you remember what you said to me that night we met?"

"That I think you might be a pyromaniac?"

I pig snorted and slapped him on the arm. "Stop it!"

"I know what I said." He climbed under the duvet beside me, leaned down and pressed a light kiss on my lips. "I said I think you might be mine."

"And I am."

"You are?"

"I am yours."

I know I shouldn't get off track here, but I just wanted to say that this was the moment that I had dreamed about my whole adult life. I was the girl standing in front of the boy. I was the desperate best friend holding the signs just because it was Christmas. I was Bridget Jones standing on a snowy street in my knickers (or dare I say it, my panties). I had finally gotten my rom-com moment, but now it no longer mattered. Not anymore. The only thing that mattered was that I was Ginger Valentina Knox, and that, my friends, was my obscure, slightly hysterical, but utterly heartfelt declaration of love after my leading man saved me from, well, myself.

I held my breath and waited for Aydin's answer. When I couldn't hold my breath any longer, I took another gulp of air and waited some more. I must have looked quite ridiculous (or maybe a little manic) gulping back air like a fish out of water, but I didn't care because when he finally let out the breath he'd also been holding, and that lopsided grin pulled up the corner of his mouth revealing that sexy dimple, I knew. I knew he was still mine. "And?"

"And... I love you."

"Tell me again."

"I love you, Aydin Kaya. I love you so damn much it hurts." I pulled him into a hug. "And look, I'm not afraid to say it!"

"Really?" He shut me up by pressing another light kiss on my lips. "Well, that's good because I didn't come all this way just to beat up your fiancé."

"Ex-fiancé."

"And if he ever comes back I'll finish him off."

Could I ever be any happier than I was at that moment? I pulled away from him and gazed into his eyes. I swear to you right now that I could see straight into his soul.

"And what about you?"

"What about me?"

"Don't you have anything you want to say to me?"

"I could think of a few things."

"Anything in particular?"

Aydin tucked a loose curl behind my ear and mumbled under his breath in Turkish. "*Beni delirtiyorsun.*"

"What did you say?"

"I said 'you make me crazy'."

"I think you need a little crazy in your life."

"A little more crazy, you mean?" A long moment passed while Aydin adorably chewed on his lower lip before he pulled it into a smile. "I must admit, you do look gorgeous right now."

"It's the bathrobe, isn't it?" I couldn't help but laugh. "You've really got a thing for bathrobes!"

"It's a very nice bathrobe, but I do not think that is the only attraction." He bent his head to me. "I'm going to kiss you now, and I'm never going to stop kissing you."

Can I get a whoop-whoop!

Aydin pulled me into his arms and ravaged my mouth with his own. My heart burst with the joy of his kiss. And his love. He turned his attention to my neck and nuzzled his face into it, inhaling deeply before he kissed and nipped and licked. I closed my eyes as he bit softly into my skin. "You must know I adore you, sweet Ginger. You are so beautiful, so perfect. You were made for me."

My heart expanded inside my chest and I looked up at him expectantly. "And?"

"And I love you so much, Ginger Knox. *Seni cok seviyorum.*"

I repeated the words back to him. "*Seni cok seviyorum.* I love you too, Creeper."

He chuckled. "I really hate that nickname."

"I'll work on a new one."

Aydin put his arm around me, and I snuggled into his arms. And even though I couldn't see his face, I knew he was smiling.

I was exhausted, but I was also lost in the whirlwind of love and our future lives together. There was nothing to stop me from moving to Istanbul or even Bodrum, once I found out precisely where Bodrum was. Or maybe he could come to Australia, although probably not with Emine, and realistically, he wouldn't come without Emine. How freaking hard would it be for him to get a visa to Australia anyway? He'd probably have a higher chance of becoming the next Prime Minister.

But right then, none of that mattered, because I was exactly where I wanted to be, in my teeny-tiny flat with my white wicker chair, my parched ficus (which desperately needed some water), and wrapped in the arms of my very own, forever, leading man. My Aydin.

I was his Green Eyes, and he was my Creeper (new nickname pending), and I was ready for my happily ever after.

And as the sun rose on the start of a brand new year (and my brand new life) I closed my eyes I wondered... how *does* Aydin feel about Hugh Grant?

> FADE TO BLACK
> CREDITS ROLL
> THE END

About the Author

Jane Gündoğan grew up on the northern beaches of Sydney, Australia but gave up the bright lights and big business and now lives in a small village in Turkey. And in case you're wondering if Salep and Ginger is based on real life, the answer is gawd no, because according to Jane, her love life is about as romantic as sour milk.

As well as being a loudmouth, she is also a part-time comedian (in her own mind), self-indulgent blogger and a full-time total badass. When not running around being the entire package, Jane can usually be found relaxing on her terrace alongside her very own Turk, watching the sun go down with a glass (or bottle) of red wine. The red wine also helps her morph into a Madonna-esque power ballad diva although this has never been officially verified to date.

You can keep up with Jane's ramblings about life in Turkey as well as details on her next book (God help us!) at www.janeyinmersin.com or follow her on FB at https://www.facebook.com/janegundoganauthor/

Printed in Great Britain
by Amazon